SECONDHAND SMOKE

A Jake Brand, PI, Novel

SECONDHAND SMOKE

A Jake Brand, PI, Novel

M. LOUIS

PALISADES
PUBLISHING

Editing by Kristin Thiel
Book design by Vinnie Kinsella
Cover art by Natalie Slocum

Printed in the United States of America
ISBN: 978-0-9863196-3-1

Cheers to the team
Naomi
Kristin
Laura
Vinnie
Hallie
Heidi
Thuy
Julienne
Natalie

Contents

Friday, March 1

1:00 a.m.
"Up yours, bastard..." Tommy Felton

He thinks he's safe. But he's not. He thinks he's alone and can relax. But he's not, and he shouldn't. I'm here. I'm here for him. Though at the moment, I'm freezing my ass off. I'm lucky it isn't raining. Normally I like the rain. Everyone in Oregon likes the rain, except folks who've recently moved up from Southern California. But even they get used to it, or leave. But on a night like tonight, the rain can be miserable. No matter how waterproof you think you've dressed, it isn't enough. When you're outside on a freezing, dark night, exposed to the elements, the cold wind slices straight through to your bones. If it's raining, those icy drops pierce straight through to your soul.

I've been outside his house for three hours. I've been watching from behind a shed in his backyard for two. My legs keep cramping, so I have to switch positions every few minutes. My butt is wet and dirty because I slipped once. I quickly discovered that the soggy turf could soak my pants faster than my ex could soak a credit card.

My target, Thomas Felton, aka Tommy-on-the-lam, is holed up in there. He's hiding from the police, neighbors, and though he doesn't know it, me. Tommy skipped bail a week ago, and the bondsman who secured his release is on the hook for a chunk of change. The bondsman throws me a couple of bones every so often, and even though I'm not a big fan of this kind of work, it does pay some bills. He always emphasizes the paycheck I'll get, not the risk I'll face. "Hey, Jake, I got an easy one for you. Simple as pie, no risk, no fuss, just pick the dude up and you get a paycheck." I say yes, he sends the file, and lo and behold the "easy as pie" target is a felon with a rap sheet as long as a new roll of toilet paper. Oh well, just another day at the office.

3

The bondsman provided me with a set of pictures, primarily mug shots, and details of Tommy's habits, aliases, haunts, friends, and family. He's a big man at six feet three inches, 250, with a full head of hair, busted nose, acne scars, and lots of muscle. His crimes and reputation peg him as very dangerous, with a short fuse. Plus, being on the run for a few days has a way of amping up the anxiety and fear levels. I know Tommy is going to defend his freedom with the zeal of a door-to-door salesman trying to make quota at the end of the quarter. And not a pie salesman, but a mean, ugly, and probably smelly salesman.

The house is a single-story ranch far out on the east side of town in an area of redevelopment. It seems old and lonely, like a forgotten man who has watched all of his buddies die off and is waiting for his turn.

I followed Tommy here from a bar that he is known to frequent. Why he would be at a bar that he is known to frequent is beyond me; yeah, I know, big and dumb. After I tailed him here, I parked on the street and waited in my car, a fourteen-year-old Jeep. We've traveled 125,000 miles together, and not always on nice flat highways. Its beat-up exterior makes it nearly invisible to most people. Its rebuilt motor eliminates any concerns about it stalling out. And if Tommy makes a run for it, I won't be worried about damaging the car. If I feel like running over Tommy instead of running after him, that option is on the table.

After about an hour of sitting in my Jeep and watching Tommy's dark house, the neighboring houses, and the traffic flow, I felt I had the rhythm of the area down cold. When it was time, I exited my vehicle and nonchalantly crossed the street to a thicket of rhododendrons located in front of and to the left of Tommy's abode. Clearly not having seen a pair of pruning shears in years, the plants stand six feet high and about the same width and provide lots of cover. From there I moved into Tommy's yard, shielded from the streetlights. As I circled around to the back of the house, I discovered the shed. Three of the four windows along the back of the house had been dark ever since I sat my ass in the soggy grass. The last window darkened about an hour ago.

I decide that I am going to enter the house through the front door. It seems to be the farthest entry point from the back room, where I surmise Tommy lies dreaming of sugar plums, or maybe fairies.

It's time. I advance as quietly as possible. I work my way back around to the front edge of the house. My shoes don't sink into the mud, but my socks are soaked, and I know I'll have to peel them from my feet later. Before I step out into the pool of light cast by the streetlamp, I check the area one last time for insomniacs and late partiers.

When I am pretty sure no one is watching, I move quickly to the front porch. I carefully open the screen door and lean it gently against my back. The lock on the front door is easy to pick. When I feel the tumblers click into place, I draw my weapon in my right hand and open the door enough to search for threats inside the house. Not seeing a mirror image of my gun pointed back at me, I decide it is safe enough to step inside. I enter the house and carefully, softly, slowly, close both doors. I squat just inside the front door. I keep low and still for a few moments to gain control of my breathing. I listen for indications of Tommy moving around and let my eyes adjust to the dark interior. The only light in the room is from the street and is filtered through partially closed blinds along the front room window. I keep my .38 pointed forward, still in my right hand and braced by my left, safety off, as I examine the room.

I am in a living room. I know from examining the exterior of the house that the garage is to my left. I can see a dining area directly in front of me. In between the dining area and the living room, a hallway heads to the right. Right to where I figure Tommy is zonked out. The living room has a couch and a TV but no tables or chairs.

The floor looks perfectly clear of debris, trip wires, and empty beer cans. The house smells like burnt meat and old garbage. Tommy's not much of a housekeeper.

Slowly, continuing to stay low, I move toward the hallway and shift the gun to my left hand so that I have a clear shot around the corner. Not my most accurate hand to shoot with, but good enough up close. Hopefully the gun won't be necessary. Hopefully Tommy is a deep sleeper and not lying in wait for me. I stop at the edge of the wall that separates the living room from the hallway, listening for sounds. I try to sense any presence waiting around the corner intent on bonking me on the head. Hearing and otherwise sensing no one, I quickly glance around the corner down the hall to my right while pointing my gun in the same direction. Instantly I see the dark shape of Tommy's bulk, and a millisecond later I feel an object smash into my gun and graze my hand. The blow knocks the gun out of my grasp. It skitters across the dining room as my hand erupts in pain.

It appears that Tommy actually is smarter than the average bear, or at least a lighter sleeper. I don't have time to whine about my hand. I see Tommy repositioning himself to swing what appears to be a bat at me a second time. I can tell he is feeling like Babe Ruth and means to go yard on my head with his next swing. But I'm lucky: while he is big, strong, and armed, he is also slow. Instead of moving back and out of the way, which would only expose me to the most dangerous part of the bat, I jump forward. Now my body is inside the arc of his swing. I grab at his shirt, pulling him toward me. As I look up into his ugly mug, I smell meat venting out of his mouth and stale beer hanging on him like cheap aftershave. For the instant that we are frozen in this discomfiting embrace, I feel him switch his grip on the Louisville slugger. I sense that he intends to pound down on my head with the butt of the bat. But before he can, I pull him even closer.

His expression switches from expectant to surprised, and on to confused. I imagine that he can't understand why I would get closer to him, given that he greatly outweighs me and would easily beat me in a wrestling match. So in his surprise, his first reaction is to try to pull away from me. As he does, I swing my right leg around his right leg and push hard with my hands against his chest. Tommy is no longer in control of his body. Now both of our bodies are headed in the same direction, and my right leg is preventing him from moving his feet backward. He is helpless to stop his fall toward the floor. As he falls, I position my body on top of his. With my right hand, I push hard on his face just to make sure that his head doesn't miss the cheap linoleum. It doesn't. He hits hard, grunts, and goes limp.

I take a very short moment to catch my breath. Tommy scared me with that first swing of his bat, and adrenaline is coursing through my veins. Eventually I stand up, flop Tommy over, and bind his hands and feet with zip ties I have stored in my pocket. Once he is secure, I find my gun, turn on the lights, and examine my hand. It's sore from the bat's grazing, and will bruise, but doesn't seem to be broken.

I find a chair and sit down, pull out my cell phone, and dial 911. "Operator assistance—what is your emergency?"

"My name is Jake Brand. I'm a private detective. I've apprehended a wanted fugitive, a Mr. Thomas Louis Felton. There's a warrant out for his arrest. I need you to send a squad car over to pick him up."

"Just a moment, Mr. Brand." I hear her talking to someone and the rat-a-tat-tat of a keyboard. "Where are you located?" I give her the address plus a few other tidbits, and she assures me that a car is on its way.

Next I call my employer. "Hey, it's Jake. I've got Felton and the paddy wagon is on its way. I hope your check-writing hand is warmed up."

"That's terrific; you've saved me a bundle." The bondsman waits a beat. "Is he alive?"

"Of course he's alive. What do you think—I'm a cop?"

"Tell me he's at least in tears or pain."

"Don't worry—he will be when he wakes up. He's beddy-bye at the moment. I'll check in with you this afternoon."

"Perfect. Thanks again, Jake."

I put my phone away and decide it's time for a cocktail just as I hear Tommy waking. I start opening cabinets as I ask, "Hey, Tommy, got any liquor, preferably scotch? Hey, Tommy, you need to pay attention to me." When he still doesn't respond, I kneel down and smack his cheek a couple of times. "Scotch? Bourbon?"

"Up yours, bastard."

Tommy's such a poet.

He makes an oomph sound as the toe of my size twelve makes solid contact with his belly. "I've never heard of Up Yours, Bastard bourbon before. But what the hell, Tommy, I'm adventurous; I'm a connoisseur of finer beverages. Where is this nectar you speak of?"

Tommy just stares at me with that "I'd kill you if I wasn't stupid and cuffed" look. As I pull my leg back for another "accidental" kick, Tommy decides to cooperate and shakes his head in the direction of one of the cupboards. I open it and see a couple of bottles. I pull out the brownest of them, along with a highball glass, and pour myself a couple fingers. I put the bottle back in the cupboard; don't want to be a pig about Tommy's stash. I find a cereal bowl, light up a cigarette, and place it in the bowl. The fumes billow softly up into the room, and the aroma calms me. The sound of approaching sirens means I can totally kick back and relax.

"Hey, Tommy, hear that? That's your transportation. I called them because I was afraid you weren't safe to drive, you being woozy and all."

10:00 a.m.
"I suppose that's good news..." Mrs. Pearcy

I'm up later that morning at the crack of ten. I pet Tammy, my temporary step-cat, and stretch. I look out at the gray skies and mist as I sip my first cup of joe. The thin clouds lying low over the hills shrink the world down to just this little valley. People are different here: they're used to gray and wet. Everybody goes about his or her business as if it's a sunny day. In keeping with the Portland "I believe it's summer, ergo it is summer" mentality, runners and bikers are often clad in just shorts and a T-shirt. I have to admit I love the weather. I find the cool days invigorating. The rain creates a sense of separation from the other three million–plus souls in the state. At times I feel like I'm the only person in the world. And sometimes that's what I need.

I shower, dress, and quickly consume a piece of toast. I microwave my lukewarm coffee and read the *Oregonian* for the day's news. I feel I'm missing a piece of my day on the days that it isn't delivered, and I dread the not-so-distant end of any delivery. I know that it's just a matter of time before I'll be reading the news on a cold, hard screen the size of my watch. When there isn't any paper left in the news, will they still be called newspapers or will they be called newsdigitals? I grab my coat and head out to my car. I merge into the day's traffic and drive off to the office.

The drive is easy this time of day, as I'm headed against traffic. Except for construction, I-5 is clear and quickly navigated. Just a fifteen-minute zip from Northwest Portland.

For the past couple of weeks, business has been slow. I hate slow. I hate slow more than fast. The free time plays games with my brain. I start to convince myself that nobody likes me. I start to believe everyone has figured out that they don't need me. So I do my time sitting in an office looking out at the gray and wait.

I watch the phone, hoping it will ring and bring a call to action, which will result in cash to pay some bills. Just when I think it's time to move up in the world and become a janitor, everything gets crazy. Clients call, money starts to flow, and I scramble to keep the balls in the air. I hate not having work, and I'm anxious when there's too much. But those are the only two possibilities. It never seems to be just right.

My office is in a small building in Tigard, Oregon, a suburb south of Portland. Tigard has an image issue with itself, so my mailing address says Portland. I hear the city allows that so that all of the multinational businesses and international jet-setters who need the unique and specialized skills of its citizens (who are there for cheaper rent and lower taxes) will think we're in a moderately sized city instead of a Winnie the Pooh novel.

The building housing my office is a woody walk-up made of wood (I am nothing if not the master of the obvious). It isn't a class A or B structure, and it barely stretches to class C. We're located on the second floor sans an elevator, so I get to climb up and down the stairs several times every day to tone and shape my calf muscles. In my office, my windows face Highway 217 and the building parking lot. I can watch all of the commuters heading to where they're going and back home again. At rush hour the traffic is bumper to bumper. Seems that rush hour starts at 7:00 a.m. and goes to 6:00 p.m. anymore.

I have a suite of four rooms: my office, Sarah's office, a reception area, and a small storage closet. Sarah has added human warmth to the office, tchotchkes, fresh flowers, and a smile that makes me feel (platonically) special all day long. But outside of that, the decor is circa 1996, a very unremarkable year.

The waiting area contains a desk, a bluish-gray couch, a couple of matching easy chairs, and an assortment of end tables that hold old magazines and spilt coffee. The prior inhabitant of the space left behind the artwork. It's the kind of art that is intended to take up space. It's leave-behind art; nothing about it holds your attention for long. I'm fine with it and don't have to worry about anyone trying to steal it—let them take it. My office contains my desk, my chair, and two guest chairs. No filing cabinets, no conference table; simple, tasteful, and easy to clean. The second private office is attired similarly to mine and is occupied by Sarah.

Sarah Genton is my investigator, researcher, therapist, and roommate (at home too). Though I've never said it out loud, I consider her my best friend. She's stood by me during some tough times: the end of my marriage, a fateful relationship with an old flame, and gun-toting thugs. She's also a badass at jujitsu and assorted other ways in which she can hurt the biggest, meanest human. Tall, athletic, and smart, she keeps the office and me on track, and handles cases. Every now and then, I get a feeling in the pit of my stomach that makes me uncomfortable. Like when we cross paths at home and she's in her robe or when I see her dressed up and about to go out for a night on the town. Sometimes I picture her with my arm around her. Sometimes, I picture more than that. ("Bad, Jake, very, very bad, Jake," says my little angel).

I met Sarah about three years ago. She moved to Portland from LA, where she had been a cop for a couple years. Portland became her home because the love of her life, Bobby, relocated here for business reasons. She followed him to Portland, was referred to me by a common acquaintance, and has been a true asset to the business and a friend to me ever since.

Over two years ago, Bobby decided he was the love of some other woman's life. I walked into the office not knowing they had broken up the night before and made the mistake of criticizing the coffee she had just made.

"If you don't like the damn coffee, make it yourself," Sarah barked back at me.

"Easy now—no one needs to get hurt. I'm happy to make the coffee, and you can critique my work. But I find it hard to believe that my simple observation regarding the quality of the coffee, not you, is the cause of this exaggerated emotional response." Big mistake. Before I had opened my mouth, she had started moving away from me, back to business as usual. But as a result of my repartee, she rolled her shoulders back in my direction, then her head, and then her eyes—like a tsunami gathering force to form a supersized Jake smasher.

"Oh, aren't you a sweetheart. You weren't criticizing me? No, you were just bitching about my work product. That doesn't have anything to do with me. Huh, how did I miss that subtlety? And I love, just love that 'exaggerated emotional response' bullshit. Who the hell do you think you are? Dr. Phil? You need to hang your psychology degree right next to your 'don't know crap' degree."

I was instantly reminded of a wise friend who asked me in the midst of one of my previous relationship struggles with a female, "If a man is in the woods by himself, is he still wrong?" A smart man always answers emphatically yes.

"I'm sorry, Sarah, that was insensitive of me. Truly, the coffee is fine."

I expected her to either say okay and walk away or reject my apology like it had hit bulletproof glass. Instead I got completely unexpected response number three; she started crying.

"Hey, hey, hey, what's wrong? If this is about the coffee, I really don't care and am sorry about what I said. If it's something else I did, let me know. I'll fix it."

"Oh, you can't fix this. Last night I left Bobby and moved into a hotel room. You just became part of my therapeutic release." She sniffled, and I grabbed a tissue and handed it to her. She dabbed at her nose as her mascara ran. My little angel smacked me for thinking of how pretty she looked.

I walked over and put my arm around her, hoping she wouldn't switch back to Mrs. Jekyll. She moved into the hug and wept softly onto my shoulder.

"If you want to talk, I'm here and ready to listen. Or if you just want to continue spritzing my shirt, that's okay too. It's your call."

She looked at me with questioning eyes. I wasn't sure what I was reading in those sad eyes. But I sensed that she wasn't up to being let down by two men in twenty-four hours. She turned slightly, wiped the tears away, and pulled her hair back from her face.

She turned back to me and leaped off the cliff. "Well, I need to tell someone. Last night I discovered that Bobby, the man I had expected to spend eternity with, was cheating on me. In fact, he's been cheating on me for months. Oh my God, I'm so pathetic. I'm a detective, and I never suspected. How could you possibly trust me to work for you?"

"Damn, Sarah, I'm so sorry. You don't deserve that at all. And I trust you completely. We all have blind spots in our personal lives; look how I missed what's going on with you. We trust: in stability, in comfort, and in others. It's that vulnerability that people like Bobby exploit."

She eventually relaxed, and we talked for several hours. I asked why she didn't move in with her sister until she could find a place to rent, and she explained that her sister's boyfriend had just moved in, so quarters were cramped—and all lovey-dovey-yucky. So I offered her my spare bedroom. After some arm twisting, she moved in—and then she stayed.

As I walk in to the office now, I find Sarah sitting at the desk in the reception area rather than in her office. Today, as always, she's very professional looking in her black jeans, moderately high heels, and white blouse. Her medium-length, dark-brown hair is pulled back into a ponytail, which highlights the oval shape of her face and her big blue eyes, eyes that can swallow a man whole.

I can see by the cold glare that greets me that something is wrong. "Where's James?" I ask. James has been our secretary/receptionist for the past couple of months.

"He quit. You want to know why he quit? I know you're itching to ask. It was because of you. It only took you two months to run him out."

"Me? What did I do?"

"Really, Mr. PI? What did you do? You were you. You treated him coldly. You pushed him around, and you were never pleased with his work. That's the third secretary in seven months. How many does that make in three years working here? Seven, Eight? The body count is abhorrent. How is it at all possible that you can solve people issues for people yet not understand how to treat your own staff? "

"Whoa, whoa, whoa, you can't blame them all on me. Like Francine. I didn't get her pregnant. And what's-her-face, the one before James. She was so ornery I was afraid to come into the office. And I gave James all of the respect that he deserved. I think it would've been disrespectful not to provide honest feedback to him."

"Well your 'honesty' just earned you filing and mail-sorting responsibilities. I've got the answering service set up, and I'll begin interviewing for a replacement. But you chased him, you replace him, mister. Oh, and by the way, I will be sure to be 'respectful' of your filing skills."

Sarah is comfortable enough to act as if she owns the firm. Most days that makes me happy. Some days, like today, I try to remember how I managed to let my authority slip away.

I slump into my office chair and glaze over when I see the scattered mail adorning my desk, waiting to be sorted. Give people an inch, and they take your desk. But before I poke the secretarial quill in my cap, I have to do what I get paid the real big bucks for.

Today I'm meeting with Mrs. Gretchen Pearcy. Mrs. Pearcy has been a client of ours for just over two weeks. I've invited her into the office to discuss the fruits of my labor and her cash. She suspects that her husband has been cheating on her, and she wants proof. I have some—sort of. She told me about the twenty years of devotion and the few months of happiness that she's shared with him. I sense that a part of her is hoping that he is cheating. I think she thinks she'll be happier single than married. But I'm still concerned about how this meeting will go. The information I'm going to share with Mrs. Pearcy is not necessarily a marriage ender, but it does reveal a big, and unusual, secret her husband has been keeping from her. And secrets mean trust issues.

I slide the mail off of my desk and into a drawer and observe that Sarah hasn't totally abandoned me to my own devices. Having experienced amazing tantrums with prior clients, sometimes over seemingly innocuous crumbs of information, Sarah has heartbreak-proofed my office. She's placed tissues within easy reach of the client's chair and cleared all heavy objects in the grab-and-throw zone. Most important of all, she's made sure nothing is on the floor near my chair. I may need to move quickly. My uncanny ability to sense emotional swings in others (excluding James), combined with my catlike reflexes (excluding Tommy and his bat), are critical when attempting to escape distraught clients.

I hear Mrs. Pearcy checking in with Sarah, who offers her coffee and sends her on into my office. Mrs. Pearcy walks in, fashionably dressed. She's in her early sixties but looks fifteen years younger. Her short, graying hair is stylishly coifed; her bright-blue eyes project confidence. And it's obvious that Mrs. Pearcy has been working hard to stay in shape—she's slender but not anorexic. Maybe she's already begun preparing to be a free agent?

I stand up and move around my desk, shake her hand, and wave her to a chair. "Hello, Mrs. Pearcy, it's so good to see you again." Then I resume my safe-zone position, with two and a half feet of solid mahogany veneer protecting me from a direct assault. "As

I mentioned on the phone, we've been observing your husband for a fair number of hours the past few weeks. I'd like to share the results of our surveillance."

"Well, Jake, I can't wait to hear what you've found out about my insignificant other. Do you have bad news or have you caught my husband being despicable?" Mrs. Pearcy asks. She smiles at her own joke.

"Mr. Pearcy has been meeting with a young woman by the name of Cecilia Gibson. Ms. Gibson is twenty-five and employed as a salesperson for a small boutique in Northwest Portland."

"I knew it. I knew he was despicable. Damn, damn, damn, I've become a cliché. I'm the older woman who lost her man to a younger woman. Oh, I can't handle this right now..."

"Wait, Mrs. Pearcy, there's more that you need to hear."

"Dear God, I don't think I can take more. What more can there be?"

"Mr. Pearcy isn't sleeping with Ms. Gibson."

"No?"

"No, he's reuniting. Ms. Gibson is Mr. Pearcy's daughter." I watch as my words flow over Mrs. Pearcy, pushing and pulling at her like a changing tide.

"His daughter. Kent has a daughter."

"Yes, a twenty-five-year-old daughter."

Mrs. Pearcy begins to cry, and I offer her a tissue. She takes it and gently blows her nose. She's hurt and confused, and I want to walk around and comfort her, but that's not my place. I'm the professional, the unemotional transmitter of cold, hard facts.

She looks up at me and smiles sadly. Her blue eyes have lost much of their intensity. She came in here expecting to hear that her husband was a philanderer only to find out he's a parent.

"Kent and I tried to have kids. For many years." She pauses as she reflects on the past. "But it didn't work out for us. I've always regretted that, that void. No one to love and to be loved back by. I've felt so lonely at times. Kent has been a good husband, but sometimes he can be cold, and sometimes he's just a bastard. That's when I really feel the ache. I feel like a stranger in the middle of a crowd. And he's had a child—a daughter?"

"Yes, a daughter."

"A daughter. A little girl to call his own. And he never told me. For our entire marriage, he's had his own family...and me."

She begins to cry in earnest. I can't help myself—I walk around my desk and sit in the chair next to her. I place my hand on her shoulder, and she reaches for my hand. "Mrs. Pearcy, I don't think he's been meeting with Ms. Gibson all of these years. I can't be sure, but it's possible that he may have just discovered her."

"Why do you say that?"

"Well, it's in their body language. They look like recent acquaintances, like two people learning about each other. Plus, I've managed to sit near enough to them in a couple of restaurants to overhear bits of their conversation. And not as telling, but still supportive of the theory, she just recently moved to Portland. She's only been here for six months."

Mrs. Pearcy relaxes noticeably and nods. "I see. I hope you're right. I hope...I don't know what to hope. Twenty-five, you say?"

"Correct."

"Well, I suppose that's good news, given we've only been married twenty years. I suppose we both had people in our lives before we married. But a daughter?"

"That he might not have known about."

"Yes, that is key, isn't it. A daughter he's just discovered." She looks out my window without seeing the here and now. "Do you have a picture of her?"

I walk back around my desk, open a drawer, and retrieve a manila envelope. I return to my chair and open the envelope. The entire time this is happening, I can feel Mrs. Pearcy staring at me like a hungry child, hoping for a morsel of food. I open the envelope and pull out six eight by twelve pictures and hand them to her.

She moves through them slowly, examining each in great detail. "She's lovely."

"Yes, she is."

"Jake, I think I need to go. I think I need to think about what I do next. Thanks for your assistance. No, more than that. Thanks for your kindness. May I keep these?"

"Of course."

"Thank you. I'm sure we'll be in touch. But, well I need some time. Thanks again."

Mrs. Pearcy gives me a smile that isn't happy—it's melancholy. I can't imagine wanting kids as much as she has and all of a sudden discovering that your mate has had one for years. I wish her the best as she leaves.

3:00 p.m.
"I'm not an internet search engine…" Chucky

Sarah takes off, and I lock up the international headquarters of Brand, PI. In the parking lot, my Jeep is waiting patiently for me. Soon we're headed to the Driftwood Room in Southwest Portland. I find street parking and plug the meter with my credit card. I miss the loose-coin days, all that jingling in my pockets.

The hotel that houses the bar is midcentury elegance: forty-foot ceilings, massive pillars, elegant moldings and furnishings. At one end of the lobby is a set of twenty-foot monitors rotating black-and-white photos of famous actors and actresses such as Clark Gable, Vivien Leigh, and Kirk Douglas. Nearby is the entrance to the bar. The bar itself is small and dark, like a cave—a very comfortable cave with beige leather benches and chairs. The walls are finished with dark wood paneling. The room has just enough light that by the time you finish your first drink, you can read the menu. Some Sammy Davis tunes softly complete the ensemble. It used to be that bad guys like Chucky hid out in dank hole-in-the-wall dungeons where they had an advantage with their lizard night vision. But crime pays too well these days. Now the crooks show up at the nicest establishments in town in their brand-new Lexus sedans that they entrust to a valet. No hole-in-the-wall, Driftwood is a great place to see and not be seen. I order a coffee from the solo bartender and survey the clientele. In the darkest reaches of the space is my buddy Chucky. He knows more about this city than any of those self-promoting politicians downtown. His people run the streets, manage the trash, and distribute the nickels and dimes.

Chucky Gerber doesn't look like a bad guy, but he is. His clothes are always wrinkled, though clean. He wears sandals, even in winter. And there's always a bulge under his left lapel; he's packing, or he's forgotten to remove the store security tag.

I met Chucky about four years ago when I brought down a bad guy who was trying to bring Chucky down. He's owed me ever since, though he's careful not to share that info with anyone. It would be career ending in his circles, and in his circles, careers only end one way. Chucky is nothing if not real smart. People don't get to his age doing what he does without being smart.

This seat taken?" I ask him, after I've sat down.

"Unfortunately, it looks like it."

"What are you reading?"

"First off, I know you can't read; second, I know you couldn't care less about what I'm reading," he says.

"Well, you got me there," I reply.

"I thought we were clear that this is my private space. I don't want to be seen with you. You know that but don't seem to respect my boundaries."

"Chucky, I was about to buy you a Liz Taylor bubbly drink—why all of the hostility?"

"Because we both know you need something. I'm not a librarian, and I'm not an internet search engine. Whatever it is you need, you can Google it. I'm sure you've heard of Google? If you haven't, ask Sarah to explain it to you. Speaking of Sarah, when is she going to stop babysitting a diaper hugger like you?"

"First off, you truly hurt me with your words. Why are you so grouchy? And not that it's any of your business, but Sarah is quite happy working with a boss as sensitive and understanding as me. "

"Oh, you're still her boss? Word on the street is that you work for her."

"Lies and damned lies, Chucky."

"Keep telling yourself that, Jake. Maybe you'll start to believe it. Just don't expect anyone else to."

"As much fun as this banter is, I need to change the topic. You're right—I need some help. I know, I know, you're not a search engine. But this request pays."

"Don't mistake my remaining here as any sort of binding agreement or interest in what you're about to ask."

"I have a client who was arrested by Detective Smith for holding some blow. I'm sure you remember Smith? Mr. Personality, likes to hit first and ask second? The client's attorney thinks the bust is bad, that Smith framed my client. I think the attorney is right. He and I think that maybe Smith has started a new side business, one that could affect you. We think he's cleaning out the city's unwashed for personal gain. What do you hear?" I ask.

Chucky tilts his wiry, gray left eyebrow up and smiles at me. "Funny you should ask. Just yesterday I saw Smith in a brief but energized conversation with some representatives of Southside. I figured Smith was just harassing them, but maybe there's more to it."

Everyone in town is starting to hear about Southside. It's rumored to be a group of dangerous businessmen who move whatever pays. They like profit margins and have concluded that any competition is bad competition. Their MO seems to be to send a few guys out to do business in a sector: prostitution, drugs, whatever. These first guys set up shop to see who complains. They finger the complainers, and the weight of Southside comes down hard on the whiners. Southside either absorbs the competition or crushes them. They aren't a democracy, and the only rule they have is that only they rule.

"And if I'm not mistaken, your client must be the honorable Mr. J.," Chucky finishes.

"You see, Chucky, that's why I'm here. You know everything about everyone. However, I can't confirm nor deny who my client is, but his last name does start with a J. I need to get those Southside names. I need something to move on. I need some leverage to shift the burden of proof, in a manner of speaking." Chucky stares blankly at me as he considers my request. I add, "And you know as well as I do that if it's Mr. J. this week, next week it will be Mr. G. It's in both our interests to blow this unholy partnership up."

Chucky works it out, out loud. "I hate Smith; he's stupid, mean, and stupid. But he can be forgetful and blind when the right amount of cash finds its way into his hands. I'm not anxious to see him replaced by somebody competent. But I know I owe you, and I know you're about to remind me that I owe you. Plus, I don't have a beef with Mr. J., and I do worry about Southside greed. So I'll help you, but it'll cost you real cash, not the weak stuff you normally have in your bank account. These Southside guys don't appreciate nosey Parkers. People become de-nosed for messing in their business."

"Thanks, Chucky. Give me a call when you're ready to chat."

"Sure. Now, on your way out, I need you to cause a scene for whatever wrong eyes are in the room. Spill my coffee like the prick you are and yell at me, make me cry," he says.

"You got it," I say softly. "Damn you, Chucky," I say loudly, "I'm not a patient man." As I stand, I spill his coffee, making sure most of it ends up in his lap. Then I turn and leave, listening to Chucky cuss at me all the way out the door and practically to the office.

3:40 p.m.
"Don't you get tired of stealing from her..." Sarah

Since there isn't enough time to head back into the office and try to accomplish some revenue-generating task before yoga, I head to my condo. I own the condo. Well, actually, the bank owns the condo and lets me use it for a modest fee equal to about 50 percent of my take-home pay. I've met a lot of bankers and not one has understood my pain. Bankers used to say, "Debt payments greater than 50 percent of earnings? We can get you deeper in debt." Now they say, "Debt payments greater than 30 percent of earnings? You need to learn to manage money better."

The building containing my condo is located in Northwest Portland, in the Pearl District. Built in the 1950s, it was originally used as office space for an insurance company. The exterior is glass and metal. A developer bought it in 2007, spent megabucks splitting the spaces into units of fifteen hundred to twenty-five hundred square feet, and sold them at exorbitant prices. I bought mine from a couple who bought from the developer. My price was probably less than the actual cost to the developer and at a substantial discount to what the seller paid. Even so, it was still the biggest expenditure I've ever made.

The interior of my home is contemporary. Sheetrock walls, wide-plank hardwood floors, twenty-foot ceilings with exposed heat ducting and crisscrossing pipes. The kitchen and bathrooms are warm white, gray, and blue, plastic, metal, and glass. But the feature that I fell in love with is the massive array of windows along the west side of the condo. The unit is on the fourth floor and allows me an unobstructed view of the West Hills and the north end of downtown. The hills reflect the seasons like an ever-changing oil painting. At night, the lights of the homes on the hill join the lights of downtown to form a galaxy of low stars, even in cloudy weather.

As I walk into the condo, Sarah greets me. "Hey, what are you doing here?"

"Last time I checked, my name is on the title. I'm just burning time before I head over to yoga. You know, you should try it. If only so you can watch me impress the masses with my strength, balance, and ability to sweat. I'm also excellent at falling down while never losing my pose. For some reason no one else finds it as entertaining as I do."

"No, thanks, I'm headed out with friends."

"Okay, your loss. Did you find a replacement for James?"

"Not yet, but I've found a couple of possibilities. Also, we got a call from the security people about your gig with Mrs. Hennessy. Don't you get tired of stealing from her? I mean, all you do is ride around in a limo, carry her shopping bags, and blow on her espressos. Does that really seem like a fair exchange in value?"

"You know, you're right. I'll reduce my fee. Of course, that means I may need to cut costs. Since you're so generous, can I take it out of your compensation? Didn't think so. Plus, you're ignoring the risk. What if I take a bullet to keep her alive? Are you ready to take a bullet for a client? Are you ready to battle evil forces to protect the rights of the wealthy to spend wantonly?"

"Damn, okay, bump the rate and add the increase to my pay. I bought some steaks that I'll barbecue tonight. You're responsible for starch and veggies. I'm dreaming of a wilted butter lettuce salad, the one with avocado and roasted tomatoes. Ahh, man, I'm drooling already. Got to run, but I'll be back by seven, dinner at eight?"

"That should work. See ya, wouldn't want to be ya."

"Ciao."

Sarah leaves, and the condo seems to empty of its warmth. It's as if someone turned everything off. For as much time as Sarah and I spend together, sometimes it doesn't seem to be enough.

4:42 p.m.
"Brandy, you're late. Strip down and suit up..." Sarge

At 4:42, I grab my workout bag and head out the door. It takes about five minutes to walk the several blocks to the renovated warehouse where the yoga class is conducted. The building used to house paper-product inventory, so there are lots of large spaces on two floors. Tonight, the class is being held in the largest room, with high ceilings, huge old-growth beams, and brick walls. It's used for all kinds of classes; I come here for yoga and jujitsu. Like many old buildings, this one has been renovated just enough to perform its function. One of the sacrifices that has been made is that there isn't any air-conditioning. In the winter, with thirty hot bodies straining, it's uncomfortably hot. In the summer, it's suffocating.

On a platform, a stout lady I know and love to hate, is stretching in ways I would not have considered humanly possible. Arrayed before the platform, twenty-five people in various colors of tights, black being the most common, casually stretch or lounge on yoga mats, conversing with each other, with towels and water bottles within easy reach.

I have a love/hate relationship with yoga. It's hard, but it helps so many different elements of my mind and body. Exercise has always helped my mental state—even if I haven't always remembered that. A couple of years ago, I felt lost and alone and tried to find answers in a bottle. With the help of my friends and exercise, I realized I was asking the wrong questions in the wrong places. Yoga helps me stay balanced. Plus, you just never know when you'll need to freeze in reverse warrior position for an extended period to hide from a bad guy. What I don't like are the walls of mirrors that seem to be in every yoga studio. No matter what direction I look, I see my ungainly reflection.

"Brandy, you're late. Strip down and suit up," the squatty body on the platform yells.

"Hey, Sarge, quit busting my privates. I'm not in the army anymore. And quit calling me Brandy," I shout back.

"I'll shout whatever I want at you, you lazy bag of old rusted pipes. If you paid more attention in class, you might be supple and bendable like your classmates. And you quit calling me Sarge and start arriving on time," she continues.

"Yeah, like that's going to happen,"

"Well, there you go…Brandy," she sneers.

Sarge, otherwise known as Sally Jean, has been teaching yoga forever. I've been taking classes from her for about six years. She might be squatty, but she's as hard as a rock. She's also the most flexible person I've ever met in my life. Kind of like a fire hydrant meets Gumby. She's amazing at yoga and knows every move and position that is certain to cause me to collapse in pain. I've come to believe that in English *yoga* means "humiliation."

I exit the dressing room in an old gray T-shirt and shorts. Sarge has already moved everyone into mountain pose. I unfurl my mat and work to match the calmness of my classmates.

I feel myself begin to relax as the soft music takes my mind away. The tranquility frees my brain to think bigger than this single moment of reality. But try as I might, I can't stop business from seeping in. Chucky saw Smith with guys from Southside. That can't be good for Mr. J. I know that my client is a dealer, but that's beside the point. The point is that when he gets busted, it should be because he was stupid, not because he was set up. It's up to his lawyer and ~~ to keep him from spending time in the big house, at least fo~~ hile.

"Okay, chaturanga to upper dog," Sarge says. "Brandy, get your knees off the ground."

I respond in the only way that will end the suffering. "Yes, ma'am."

"Now, downward dog. Lift your right leg to the sky and swing it through to runner's pose. Slowly rise up to crescent…"

Saturday, March 2

8:05 p.m.
"Hi, Jake..." Heather

Another weekend night on my own. Sarah's off with what's-his-name, some guy in that "more than a date, less than a boyfriend" limbo world, so I decide to grab a beer and some unhealthy food and watch whatever sport happens to be on the television at the Blitz Sports Pub, a dark loud place where it's easy to disappear. I'm lucky, the Blazers are playing the Jazz, and it's a close game. As I sit at the bar, sipping, munching and half watching the game, I feel a hand on my right shoulder. I turn to see whose hand it is, just as I feel a body bump me on the left. I turn to my left and go into my infamous deer-in-headlight face. It's none other than Heather, a childhood friend, my first true love, and the recipient of two, not one, but two, "I broke Jake's heart" trophies. The first time she broke my heart was when we were in high school when I discovered that she was sleeping with me and our other best friend Tony. The second time was after Tony, who had become her husband, was murdered. I helped her handle the thugs who killed him, we reunited, and she re-cheated on me. Well, she called it being successful at an open relationship.

"Hi, Jake." Heather smiles and leans in for a hug.

My little angel begins screaming, "Runnnnn!" My little devil says, "Oooh-la-la."

I say, "Errr, Heather, how are you?" I return the hug; big mistake. I feel the hurt and anger when she earned her first trophy. We were in high school, and she invited me over to her place after her parents fell asleep. I can still see her in her bedroom, shedding a soft cotton nightgown, spotlighted in the moonlight. It was my first time. What I didn't realize for several days was that she had been sleeping with our shared best friend, Tony, and she was okay continuing to sleep with both of us. I wasn't interested in sharing and pulled away from both of them.

Nonetheless, whenever I think of the most romantic moment in my life, I see her in the moonlight, I feel her soft body, and I smell her sweet smell. A smell that is filling my nostrils right now. Oh my God, I can't do this again.

"I've missed you, Jake. What has it been, a year? No, it's been more like two years." She looks at me anxiously, maybe hopefully.

"Two years, two months, and three days," says my little angel. I say, "I think you're right—it has been closer to two years. What have you been up to?" "Stop talking to her," says my little angel.

"Not much," Heather answers me. "I got a job at a public relations firm. I handle social media campaigns and strategies. Say, I could do that for you. Imagine all the important clients who would roll in with a targeted blitz. We'll start with LinkedIn...Do you have a Twitter account? Just kidding, Jake. I don't like mixing business and pleasure."

"You're still talking to her," says my little angel. "Oh really? I didn't realize this was pleasure."

"You're not still upset, are you? Jake, you've known me for too many years to count. You know who I am. I don't mean to hurt anyone's feelings..."

"OMG, stop talking to her," says my little angel. "Ask her out," says my little devil. "You don't have to explain..."

"But I want to. I love you, Jake. I miss you, and it hurts when you're mad at me."

"I'm not mad. Truly. I'm afraid of you, Heather." "That's my man," says my little angel.

She begins laughing as the bartender comes over and asks if she'd like a drink.

"Yes, a beer, something hoppy." He turns and begins walking away as she adds, "Oh, and put it on my date's tab." The bartender looks at me with an "is that okay?" face, and I look back with a "do I look like I have a choice?" face.

"So, fill me in, Jake. Tell me about your life. Are you happy? Dating? Married with two point five kids?"

We talk for about an hour; slowly the empty beers build up, and I relax. We fall into a comfortable patter, reminiscing, laughing, and hugging.

"I so miss you, Jake. I'm thinking we should head over to your place, I know you live nearby. We could have a bottle of wine, maybe cuddle..."

"Bingo," says my little devil. "Heather, I..."

She looks down at her hands as they fuss with each other and says, "I understand, you're busy..."

"Heather, I miss you too. But it seems that every time..."

"You don't have to say it, Jake. I know I've hurt you, and I don't want to do that again. Think about it, about us. I'd really like to see you again, soon. Will you call me? You know if you don't I'll stalk you, right?"

I look at her with a longing for lost love and a hope for rekindling an old friendship. In spite of the past pain, the good times were among the best. The beer has faded the past and softened my hurt. But not enough. "I'll definitely give you a call."

"Good." She leans over and gives me a long "we're more than friends" kiss. I almost forget to open my eyes as she pulls away.

"Bye," she says.

"Bye," I say.

"Moron," my little angel says.

Monday, March 4

7:00 a.m.
"This little piggy went to the market..." The Kidnapper

The next week starts with my occasional bodyguard gig. Mrs. Hennessy is a very wealthy seventy-plus-year-old. She was the controlling shareholder of a large local company that had deforested half of Oregon. About ten years ago, her grandson was kidnapped and held hostage for ransom. The kidnappers knew enough about the company that they didn't bother contacting the kid's parents. They went straight to the power and money, Mrs. H. The kidnappers gave her the instructions: amount of money, where to drop, no police—the usual. Mrs. Hennessy had never broken a law in her life and trusted the police implicitly. As a result, she ignored the gang's instructions and notified the police.

The gang discovered that she had deviated from the instructions, and sent her grandson back to her. More precisely, they sent her a piece of her grandson. She received a package containing one of his little toes. In the box with the toe was a note composed of cutout newspaper letters: *This little piggy went to the market...* It still cracks me up.

Needless to say, the piggies in blue were terribly agitated. But they weren't nearly as pissed off and frightened as Mrs. H.; she was a lethal blend of fear and wealth. She contacted the mayor of our fine city and told him to "clear the blue dunderheads"—her description of the police—"out of my life." Given his upcoming reelection cycle, which in his mind started the day after he was elected, the mayor had no choice but to call off the hounds. But on their way out, a cop buddy of mine named Milt, since retired, gave Mrs. H. my name. She called me up and asked me to meet her.

Ten Years Ago

Noon
"Do I sound like Bob Barker?"—The Kidnapper

"Mr. Brand, I'm Mrs. Hennessy."

We shake hands. "Mrs. Hennessy, pleasure to meet you. Will the parents be here soon?"

"No, they've given me full authority to act. I'll be your sole point of contact. My daughter, whom I love dearly, is a complete and utter emotional mess and incapable of handling the circumstance."

"That's fine, but I would like to talk to them…"

"Of course, of course. But that will have to be later. Right now, I need to know more about you. All I know about you is the reference provided by Detective Stanton. Why should I entrust my grandson's safety to your hands?"

"I spent twenty years in the army, most of that in Special Forces, including five years in a unit that doesn't officially exist. For much of that time, I was in charge of planning operations that included hostage rescues, personal protection, and any other act of force that our government assigned to us. I've led twenty hostage rescues, and all of them successfully."

"I'm not entirely sure how to judge that. I do think twenty sounds a bit limited compared to the thousands of hostage situations that are handled by the police and FBI."

"It's not the number that should matter; it's the circumstances. All of my rescues were on foreign soil with no safety nets. We had to succeed or we would be captured and probably killed. I take kidnappings very personally."

"Plus," my little devil said, "who else you got, lady?"

I watched as Mrs. Hennessy battled her demons. She seemed to be someone who was used to being in control and calling the shots. Letting go might have been one of the most difficult things she'd ever tried to do.

"Okay, Mr. Brand, I'll try to trust you. What do we do?"

"Mrs. Hennessy, you have two choices," I started. "Your first choice is to do exactly as the kidnappers say and lose your money and your grandson. Your second choice is to pretend to do exactly as the kidnappers say and save your money and maybe save your grandson. My advice is to go with choice two. Choice one is going to reward the kidnappers' behavior and encourage them and others to do something like this again. I hate to say it, but this isn't just about your grandson. It's about you and the rest of your family. If you cave this time, every two-bit punk in the Pacific Northwest will be visiting you for a payday."

She cried, and I held her, no extra charge. After a few minutes, she broke free and composed herself. "You come highly recommended by Detective Stanton. I've gained a level of trust for Stanton; he's been the most rational and understanding of the police. Plus, at the moment, I don't have many choices. So, I guess, Mr. Brand, it's up to you. I'll do whatever you say."

I called Milt and told him that Mrs. H. was bringing dishonor to his name, that she had actually called him competent. He agreed to debrief me and act as my backup when he was off duty. The next time the kidnappers called, Mrs. Hennessy told them that she had chased away the police. They thought that was just dandy until she told them that from now on they would have to deal with me.

"Lady, you're not giving us orders. Or do you want another piece of your grandson? Maybe I'll send you his cock this time?"

"I'm afraid you're not speaking to Mrs. Hennessy anymore; you're talking to her representative. My name is Jake—what do I call you?"

"Put the lady back on the phone or the kid dies, asshole."

"You can keep the kid, or you can work with me on a trade for cash. Those are the only two options. I've got time. Think it over and call us back." And I hung up.

"What did you just do?" Mrs. Hennessy shouted.

"I'm establishing ground rules and value. If they think they can get what they want by going around me to you, that's what they'll do. What do you think lowlife scum like these guys will do if you show up with a satchel full of cash? They'll take you, the cash, and your grandson and go to the next bidder on the list. And if they think we'll do absolutely anything to save your grandson, that's what they'll demand. We have to take control."

"And what if they don't call back? What then?"

"Milt has the police files, and there are clues as to where the kidnappers are located and their identities. Besides handling the calls and setting up a swap, he and I are investigating other angles. We'll get them eventually. Mrs. Hennessy, you have to trust me. I know it's hard to trust when a loved one's life is on the line. But there is no other viable option."

As if on cue, the phone rang. "Let me answer it this time." I walked over to the phone, but I let it keep ringing a bit longer before I picked up. "This is Jake. How may I assist you?"

"Hang up on me again and you'll regret it."

"Call me asshole again and I'll hang up."

"Who are you? Don't you understand that you're messing with the life of a kid?"

"Listen, mister, as far as I'm concerned, he's already dead. I'm only dealing with you because of the old lady." I looked over at Mrs. Hennessy and put my hand on the mouthpiece and whispered, "You're not old. I just said that to mess with him."

Mrs. Hennessy's eyes shot mind bullets at me.

"Okay, Jake, let's play it your way. I want $2 million in small bills, and I want it in twenty-four hours."

"I need two weeks for that kind of money. Or you can have $250,000 in twenty-four hours."

"Do I sound like Bob Barker? This isn't the *Price Is Right*. I said two mil."

"And I said no. Two fifty in twenty-four hours. Take it or keep the kid." I heard mumbled speech over the phone. It sounded as if a couple of guys were arguing. The fact that they called us and were still on the line demonstrated that they were amateurs. That could be good or bad. It was good if they weren't mean-stupid amateurs.

"Five hundred thousand in twenty-four hours. You're going to put the money in a suitcase and be ready for my call with instructions."

"Okay, call me at this number. I'll be waiting." I hung up and looked at Mrs. Hennessy, and I thought I saw a bit of respect creep into her expression.

"I'll have my banker pull the money together in the next few hours. Then what? We just sit?"

"No, right now the money is plan B. Plan A is to check in with Milt." While she looked at me with questions on her lips, I called Milt on my cell.

"Did you get it?" I asked.

"Yes, they didn't even try to bounce the signal. I've got the location of the building. It's an apartment complex on Southeast Foster. It has seventy-five units, low income."

"Okay, pick me up. We'll ride over there together."

"Roger." And he hung up.

"I want to know the plan," Mrs. Hennessy said.

"First, we're going to set up your phone to forward calls to my cell. Next time the kidnappers call, they'll ring through to me. Second, Milt and I are going to scout out the apartment complex to try to locate them and your grandson. When they call again, we'll have the equipment to locate the call to within ten feet. Then we pounce on them. If all goes well, we'll be back here with your grandson in less than twenty-four hours."

"And if it doesn't go well?"

"We'll be back to pick up the cash and move to plan B." I smiled at her. "Mrs. H., you can trust us. Milt and I do this for a living. You can trust that we'll get the best result possible. We will get your grandson back. One way or another."

She stared back at me, knowing I'd overpromised but wouldn't underperform.

10:00 p.m.
"Are you always a smart-ass..." The Kidnapper

Milt and I sat in his Taurus across the street from the apartment complex on Foster for what seemed like forever. The area was a lower-income residential neighborhood, with Foster Boulevard, a major thoroughfare, being the neighborhood's commercial spine. The street had scattered traffic at this time of night and only a few cars parked along the curb.

It used to be that when you looked at Milt, you saw a frumpy short guy who didn't comb his hair. I figured that it was just his professional attire. He was always volunteering to do undercover assignments, most of which were better suited to disheveled-looking people. On closer examination, anyone who was paying attention could see that he was sinewy. He was lean muscle disguised by wrinkled-baggy clothes. I never worried about my back with Milt riding along. Today, he's still short, he's still wearing the same clothes, but he's no longer sinewy, and he keeps what little hair he has trimmed military short.

The apartment building was a two-story structure shaped like a *U*, with parking in the middle. At that moment, the parking was about two-thirds full. It appeared that all of the units faced the parking. An exposed walkway ran in front of the units, with exposed stairways for accessing the second level. The building appeared to be in such a state of disrepair that it wouldn't have surprised me if it collapsed in front of us.

Milt and I each walked through the complex a couple of times to see if there were any indicators of where our party might be. About half the units seemed empty; a few emitted sounds, like children playing or couples arguing. We decided that it was unlikely they held our kidnappers. Eventually, we narrowed the list of possible units to five, but that was just a guess. The plan was that as soon as my phone rang, Milt would wander over and pinpoint the source of the call. Once I was off the phone, we would crash the party.

While we waited, we took turns watching the complex. While I watched, Milt shuffled through papers.

"What's that, police homework?" I asked.

"No, these are my brokerage statements. My broker is under-performing the market, and I'm getting a little ticked." Every time Milt spoke, I thought of a deep-bass country singer. I kept expecting him to sing his responses.

"You have a broker?"

"Of course. Don't you?"

"Do you have to have money to have a broker?"

"Yes."

"Well, there you go."

"Someday you're going to wish you had started saving sooner."

"Sure, someday; just not today."

"Which reminds me, how much are you paying me for this?" Milt asked.

"I'm not paying you anything, and if you keep whining, neither is Mrs. H. Don't forget that she's the one person in the world who thinks you're competent. She's the wrong person to let down."

"You're such a tough guy." Milt paused midthought and then continued. "Changing the subject, I haven't told anybody else, but I'm thinking of retiring. I'm getting to that point where I don't want to ask perps questions or arrest them. I just want to punish them on the spot and let them go. You know, like shoot them in the foot for stealing or cut a finger off for flipping me the bird. I've lost all patience for the system."

"I feel your pain. But, Milt, you're necessary. I agree that the system can be frustrating, but it does slow these guys down for a while." And then my phone rang.

"Showtime. Give me a couple of rings to get into position." Milt jumped out of the car and ran over to the structure.

I waited four rings and then answered. "Jake's Diner, come check out our specials. Would you like to book a reservation?" I heard silence on the other end. Finally I heard a voice.

"I'm looking for the Jake that works for Hennessy."

"That's me, buddy. I've got the money. What now?"

"Are you always a smart-ass? Do you have any compassion for this kid?"

"Yes and yes. Speaking of the kid, before we move any further, I need to speak to him."

"Whoa, whoa, whoa, you don't seem to understand that I'm telling and you're doing. Not the other way around."

"That's true on most of this, but I'm not paying hard cash for a dead boy. I talk to him or I hang up."

I heard muffled voices on the other end. A new voice came on the line. "This is Mark. They're telling me what to say. Please help me. I'm afraid."

"One question, Mark. What's your mom's maiden name?"

"Jackson."

"Okay, put your roomie on the phone."

"Satisfied?" the kidnapper asked.

"I am. How do you want to make the exchange?"

"I want you to take the cash to JT's Junkyard on Foster. Be there at 3:00 a.m. sharp. You'll drop the bag just inside of the gate and then step back onto the sidewalk. You'll wait there while we check the bag. If the money's right, we'll toss you a key to a car and tell you where it's parked. The kid will be in the trunk. We see anybody else, and I mean anybody, the deal is off and the kid is dead. Got it?"

"Got it," I said as I saw Milt give me a thumbs-up from across the street. "See you at three." And I hung up. Milt jogged back across the street and hopped into the car.

"They're on the second floor on the end nearest the stairwell, so we can come at them directly from below rather than having to pass any other second-floor rooms. Curtains are drawn. I can't tell how many are in the apartment, but there can't be more than three or four plus the kid. The stairs are solid, no squeaks and, as far as I can tell, no alarms. I think we head up and scout. Wait a bit and one of them will come out. We grab him, and use him as a human shield to go back in. Or we could call the police. But I think the kid has a better shot with us."

"I agree. I like your plan. Let's get going."

We were both dressed in black clothes with black stocking caps. We wouldn't be invisible but damn close. A soft breeze and light rain would cover most any sound that we made. We navigated our way to the base of the stairs without any effort. I signaled Milt to step out from under the upper walkway and keep an eye trained on the target while I made my way to the upper level. Once I was at the top, I positioned myself around the corner from the doorway to the unit and waited for Milt to soundlessly make his way to me.

I could tell that the walls were paper thin, as I heard distorted voices emanating from within the unit. I decided to risk moving around the corner and pressing my ear against the windowpane. I heard a TV: some inane situation comedy was playing, one of those programs that recycles the jokes every three weeks. During about two minutes of window pressing, I heard two voices and the name Paulie. I also heard talk of offing the kid. He'd seen too much.

I moved back around the corner and whispered to Milt. "We were right—these guys have no intention of going through with the exchange. I think they plan on killing me and the kid after they have the money. We need some way to either break in or lure them out. I'm not excited about sitting out here forever. Eventually someone will see us and ask questions."

"I agree. It would be nice to have a diversion. If you were a good-looking chick, we'd be ready to go. But you're not even a good-looking guy." Milt's eyes flicked down to the parking lot. He nodded, beckoning my eyes to follow his gaze. I turned and saw a car with a lit-up pizza company sign on top pulling in. "How about I divert that pizza to these bozos? Maybe they'll be stupid enough to open the door."

"I don't have any better idea."

Milt moved quickly and silently down the stairs to the parking lot.

As I waited, I fretted about the situation. It was always unnerving to be going into armed conflict with limited info. We thought there were only two, but we weren't sure. We thought the kid was with them, but we weren't sure. We didn't know the layout of the room, and we didn't know what kind of weapons they were carrying. We knew they were amateurs, which could be good or bad. But hey, that's why I got paid the big bucks.

I heard a conversation in hushed tones below me. After a couple of minutes, I saw Milt on the steps walking toward the apartment. He was wearing a red-and-white pizza uniform shirt that barely fit, a baseball hat with a crazy animal logo on it, and a goofy grin. He held a pizza box up above his shoulder on one palm. I signaled him to pause at the top of the stairs, and I moved back around the corner and pressed my ear against the window. It was the same TV show, but the boys seemed to be quiet. I moved back and signaled Milt to move forward. He knocked on the door with his free hand. I stayed out of sight of the window.

From behind the closed door came a voice. "Who is it?"

"Pizza delivery."

"We didn't order no pizza. You got the wrong place."

"Hey, man, the receipt says number 215, Foster Boulevard Apartments. Must be you guys."

"Get out of here, dude. We didn't order it."

"Hang on while I check with my dispatcher." Milt made noises like he was talking on the phone. I saw a change in the light cast from the apartment window. They were checking him out. He finished pretending and put his phone back in his pocket.

"Look, man, my dispatch messed up. He sent me to the wrong place. But he's already sent a replacement pie out to the right location, and he said I could keep this pizza. I'll sell it to you cheap. I'm done with my shift and just want to get home. You sure you don't want it?"

"How cheap is cheap?"

"Ten bucks. It's a $17 pie. Come on, man, do us both a favor."

"Seven bucks and you got a deal."

"Done."

I risked a peek, and Milt nodded at me. I moved to Milt, staying as low as I could. I heard the door being unlatched as I reached Milt and tapped him on the back to confirm that I was ready to go. An instant later, the door opened, and Milt slammed the pizza box into kidnapper number one's face, shoving him backward into the room while pulling his gun from his waistband. I jumped into the doorway and drew down on kidnapper number two, who was reaching for a gun on the table. Milt and I both yelled at the two punks as loud as possible to get on the ground. But number two didn't take us seriously. He reached his gun just as I completely cleared the doorway. Milt concentrated on number one, who was on the ground with his hands up and the barrel of a pistol bending his nose sideways.

"Get down," I yelled again. "There's a sniper. Get down before he blows your brains out." This caught number two by surprise, and for a moment his gaze shifted toward the window for the mythical sniper. I was hoping he'd give up, but the look in his eyes was that of a fighter. Before he could decide his next move, I reached him. With my left hand, I grabbed his right, which was holding the gun, and simultaneously smashed my gun squarely into his face. I heard the snaps of teeth and maybe his nose. As he reached for his face with his left hand, I slammed his right hand as hard as I could on a table corner. The gun fell to the floor as he gurgled out a scream. I looked up to see blood gushing from between number two's fingers. Then I twisted him so that he was off-balance and fell backward to the floor with my knee squarely planted on top of his belly. There was a whooshing sound as number two's lungs expelled all of his air. My little devil was on a thrill ride. Even my little angel said, "Ahh, he had it coming."

I pressed my gun as hard as I could against number two's left eyelid without punching through to his pea brain and yelled, "Where's the kid? Tell me now, or I'll blow away your eye. I'll probably miss your brain, given how small it is."

He hesitated for an instant until he recognized the conviction in my voice. With one of his raised hands he pointed at the bathroom door.

"Is there anyone else in here besides you two and the kid?"

"No."

"Turn over on your stomach and keep your hands above your head."

He did as he was told, and I zip-tied his hands and his feet. I looked over at Milt, who'd done the same with number one. I signaled Milt to cover me while I advanced on the bathroom door. I turned the knob and pushed the door open, while standing to the side of the opening and pointing my gun inward. A quick glance confirmed there was only one occupant in the room, and he was duct taped and lying in the tub in his underwear. But the real shock of the moment was the smell. The kid had to be dead to smell this bad. The combination of body odor and human waste was nauseating.

I walked over to the occupant of the tub and pulled the tape off of his mouth. "Who are you?"

"I'm Mark Hennessy. Are you Jake?"

"Yes, I'm Jake." The kid was shivering, with fear or fever or because he was freezing, I wasn't sure which—probably all three. I saw a bloody towel wrapped around his left foot and waste sitting in the bottom of the tub.

I finished removing the tape just as the first squad cars raced into the parking lot.

I helped him out of the tub and half carried him into the bedroom. I laid him on one of the beds and covered him with a blanket. "Want me to kick them for you?" I asked him.

"No, just make sure they get ugly-mean bunkmates in prison."

I nodded with a smile on my lips. I liked the kid. He was about getting ahead, not even.

Monday, March 4

8:00 a.m.
"Lie if you have to—I need you to charge my juices..."
Mrs. Hennessy

Mark recovered nicely, and now he's a VP at the family corporation and never lets me buy a drink when we get together. He's barely legal to drink, but he sends me a bottle of eighteen-year-old single-malt scotch on several holidays each year.

Since then, the company's corporate security coordinates personal security for key personnel, including Mrs. H. She will allow only me to fill that role. For the next few days, I'm on duty, and first up are a few hours of shopping.

The perimeter of her estate is fenced with a twelve-foot iron-and-cement wall. I drive up to the gate and press a buzzer to announce my arrival. The gates open, and I'm admitted into the compound. Mrs. H.'s car is waiting, along with her driver, William. As I get out of my car, Mrs. H. steps out of her house and comes down the steps to give me a hug. Of course, calling the structure a house is like calling the White House a cottage. Mrs. H.'s house is in the hills near the Pittock Mansion, an old newspaper baron's home that has been turned into a museum. (He "dabbled" in other business deals too—I guess even in the 1800s newspapers didn't buy mansion luxury.) I've been on the tour, and that house is a scaled-down version of Mrs. H.'s place.

"Mrs. H., it's so great to see you."

Mrs. H. is looking dapper as always. She dresses in more elegant fabrics and fancier brands for a day of shopping than most people I know do for their wedding. Today she's wearing stylish pants, riding boots, and a warm coat, faux fur, of course. It's never any fun wearing red paint.

"It's good to see you too. Now, let's get started. William has beverages and snacks in the limo, and I want to hear about all of the girls you've been dating. And if you tell me you're still pining for your ex-wife, there will be no tip. Lie to me if you have to—I need you to charge my juices."

I hear William smile (he has noisy lips). He's truly devoted to her, and he and I have become friends. He can be trusted, something rare in my line of work.

The next few days are pretty full. We visit shopping meccas and top-notch restaurants. Mrs. H. insists that I eat with her, just in case someone tries to poison her. We visit many of her close friends, some of them in assisted living and a couple in hospice. At night, I stay in a guest room in the mansion that's about the size of my condo. The place is big enough that I wouldn't have been surprised if it had its own post office for inter-room message deliveries. I dine with the family, which is a tremendous treat. Mrs. H. and her cook and I work together to prepare and serve each other. We also clean together. Mrs. H. is a true believer in staying connected with real life—if you can call having a driver, a cook, and a bodyguard while living in a mega-million-dollar mansion "real life."

But it isn't all fun and games. Mrs. H. has a compassionate side. She's not one of those wealthy people who is trying to constantly increase her net worth. Mrs. H. told me once that she believes that if she doesn't spend every last dime by the time she dies, she has failed as a human being. We visit hospitals and homeless shelters and other social welfare organizations. At each she gives generously of her time and leaves behind unbelievable sums of money. One guy running a temporary shelter for homeless moms with kids breaks down and cries. I turned away to clear some dust from my eye.

Sometimes my little angel makes me feel guilty about charging for spending comfortable time with her. But my little devil always smiles when I get the check in the mail. One time I spoke to Mrs. H. about discounting my fees, and she raised them. I've thought about bringing her into the office to work that magic with some of my other clients.

Thursday, March 7

8:00 p.m.
"Alvin never keeps product around the house..." Pete

After several days of nearly around-the-clock service for Mrs. H., I need a break. Don't get me wrong—Mrs. H. is charming and enjoyable. But when your job is to take the bullet headed at your client's vital organs, you remain alert so that the shot can be stopped or averted before it hits you in the chest. The stress is subtle but real, even when it's masked by a visit to the mall or a fine meal.

At the end of a stressful period, I like to spend a couple of days at the coast. I have a place in Seaside. It and my condo (along with the mortgage) are all I have left from my failed marriage. Well, that's not entirely true. I did get a bill from my attorney for his time spent joking around with her attorney. But I can't complain. He also sent me a bottle of wine for the holidays; it's always nice to be remembered.

The drive to the coast is as relaxing as being at the coast, a straight-shot hour and a half from doorstep to doorstep. The first thirty minutes is in city traffic, and the final sixty minutes is in primal forest. The forest is home to amazing old-growth trees, trees that reach one thousand years in age, ten feet in diameter, and hundreds of feet in height. Being in a stand of these sentinels is like standing in nature's New York City. I sense God's presence in moments like that.

Seaside is the best of ocean relaxation. It's most famous for being the end of the Lewis and Clark trail. Meriwether and William, along with their band of merry men, established a fort fifteen miles north of the current city and eventually set up a salt extraction plant (five kettles, salt water, and fire) in what is now Seaside. Today, the city has a very touristy side for parts of the year and the feel of a forgotten toolbox collecting dust and rust in a shed for other parts of the year. There are plenty of places serving casual food, and even more casual and friendly residents. My house is fifteen hundred square feet of ocean blues and greens with a little bright-red and yellow mixed in. It isn't on the beach, so I have a fifty-fifty chance of surviving the always-imminent tsunami that is certain to happen within the next fifty years—but most likely tomorrow, not today.

The residents are worried enough about a tidal wave that the city has an alarm siren. When you hear it, you're supposed to run up a hill and chug a bottle of Jack Daniels. I heard the siren once. I ran startled to the street, frantically looking for an escape route and a liquor store, not in that order. But I noticed some locals casually walking around. After two minutes (which is an eternity when you know you have less than fifteen minutes to get to safety), I asked one person why people weren't running around frantically. Hadn't they heard the alarm? I was informed that it was in fact the alarm, but it was a test of the alarm. In order to keep all of the locals on their toes, the city tested the alarm at five o'clock every Wednesday. I asked the local, "What happens if the tidal wave comes at five on a Wednesday?" He wasn't amused.

When I'm there, I'm a bum, no cooking and no cleaning. I have a lady who comes in after I've left, to sweep away the crumbs and carry out the garbage. I have wood delivered for the wood-stove. Every meal is at the same slate of restaurants. Friday nights I walk four blocks to the U Street Pub; on Saturdays I head over to Dundee's to watch sports and sip a beer. I know I can make it home on foot, so I don't have to worry about my consumption level of either.

At night I light a fire in the woodstove and read. I like historical fiction—that's the way history should be taught in school. I also read case files, office paperwork, or other items that are always sadly staring at me from my desk as I'm about to leave the office. I believe that if I bring them to my restful place, they'll get done and I'll be rested. Something is wrong with this picture.

Tonight I need to complete my final reports on the Pearcys. It seems my educated guess was right. Mr. Pearcy didn't know about Ms. Gibson until she recently moved to Portland. Mrs. Pearcy has been overjoyed with meeting and getting to know Ms. Gibson. As she puts it, it's probably how a grandparent feels. And as a side benefit, she's been as happy as ever with the mister.

Next on the list is bill-payment approval. That's easy enough: make them all wait.

Finally it's time to review the file on Jankowitz, the client who was framed. I spend most of the next couple of hours reading about my falsely accused, but truly criminal, client. Alvin Jankowitz has been a lower-tier bad guy for most of his thirty-five years of life. He started with jacking cars and then moved on to drugs, almost exclusively marijuana. I once asked him what legalization meant to his business. He said he loved the idea. He is happy to take lower margins in exchange for keeping the police and gun-toting thugs out of his life. He is setting up a chain of legal distribution sites in Washington where usage is legalized and is supporting legalization in Oregon.

At the moment, the Oregon operation is small, fueled by product exported out of the great state of California. The pot is loaded into tractor trailers and driven up I-5 into the waiting lungs of its adoring fans in Oregon. He hires young gentlemen to meet the mule who has brought the drug to town. The gents and mule complete the purchase, and the young men split the load into smaller containers and redistribute it through an established marketing channel—Alvin's words, not mine. Alvin never comes into direct contact with the product, and he isn't a user.

On the night of the bust, Alvin had been with a lady friend at a concert. They returned to his place and had just settled down with a nice bottle of wine and some soft R & B when his front door blew inward. The door was followed by Copper Smith's ugly little shoe, which thankfully covered his ugly little foot. Smith and his goons grabbed Alvin and the girl, cuffed them, and made them sit while they executed a search warrant.

The cops only checked one location in the entire condo. They walked directly to a desk, opened a drawer and, what a surprise, there was a package of blow inside. Now, what are the odds that a search hits pay dirt on the first shovel? Zero. It was a plant, a bad plant, not even the right plant. But now it's a cop's word against an Alvin's word. I finish my review of the case and decide to go for a walk.

It takes about two minutes to casually walk the five blocks from my place to the beach. Tonight it's cool and misty. But above the mist is a large moon that lights everything up. The world looks like an old movie from the era when they filmed nighttime scenes during the day and used a filter to create the appearance of darkness. Stars are actually visible. I wind around until I find my favorite log at Surfer's Cove. It's called Surfer's Cove because dudes in wetsuits ride two-foot waves there during the day. But at night, it's just me, the waves, and the stars. The waves luminesce as they break in the soft beacon of light cast by the moon. They rumble and roll forward, shifting sand, rocks, sea life, and what's left of what was sea life.

It's tranquil here, and I can clear my thoughts. I try not to think of anything but the view, smells, wind, and rumbling waves. But my best ideas and insights travel along this road. I miss married life; I'm a married kind of guy. Even though I've learned my lesson: you have to be picky and careful. A mistake means lawyers, shouting, lawyers, bills, and did I mention lawyers? I'm convinced that lawyers invented divorce as a blood sport, and the lawyers end up the only winners. Enough, I finally tell myself—it's time to head back, time to read some Patrick O'Brien. I love that manly British naval war story stuff. Imagine a bunch of little boys with weapons of war, out to sea for months on end and no moms. What could be more fun?

Monday, March 11

9:00 a.m.
"Find some sweaty fifty-five-year-old smoker..."
Sarah

When I get back to Portland, I head to the office. Once there, I toss my paperwork file onto the receptionist's desk and walk into my office. I go through my mail and see a couple of job possibilities that I'll try to tee up later today. It's nice and sunny. Early March is the tease of the year. You start to see flowers and hear lawn mowers, and there are days when a coat seems out of place. Then the next day is back to frostbite and rain, and of course you've forgotten your coat.

I shuffle through the case files sitting on my desk. The only thing I hate more than sitting in a car for hours on a stakeout is sitting at my desk doing paperwork. It feels like prison. But I know that it will pay dividends down the road. I finish my notes on Mrs. H. and prepare my billing summary to send to the security company. I check my email but find nothing worth noting. Since I started using an all-in-one Swiss Army smartphone, I rarely need to actually use an outdated object like a real desktop computer. I fire up the coffeemaker and am reading the paper and taking my first sip of dark hot coffee as Sarah enters.

"Hey, Jake, how was the beach?"

"Natty: free of other people and other people's problems. I was able to completely fixate on my own issues and shortcomings. As it turns out, I rediscovered that I'm a pretty well-adjusted guy. Plus, I wasted my time and money on cheap booze and silly carnival games. How was your time with what's-his-name?"

"Tyson, his name is Tyson, and you know it. We had fun, lots of fun. I need you to take more vacations. Did you have any questions on the bills?"

"Sis, I hope you and Tyson were safe. I don't want you running home in tears because of some accident. Go ahead and pay all of the bills."

The look on Sarah's face moves from nonchalant to "how dumb are you?" "Don't call me sis. I'm not your sister, never been your sister. When the hell are you going to get that through your primitive cranium? And what I do on my dates is none of your business. Just because you've become a eunuch doesn't mean I will as well. You need to get out and find some sweaty fifty-five-year-old smoker with a scratchy voice and overgrown toenails."

"Are you hinting about something? Are you suggesting that I should go out and find some sort of quick sex fix? When did you become so liberal?"

"You find the right girl, and we'll talk about liberal."

"Good point. What's on the calendar?"

"In fact, you should look up that attorney, Sally what's-her-name. She'll beat the ornery out of you."

"You mean the Sal-inator?" Sally was my wife's attorney during our divorce. After Sally sliced me to ribbons in depositions, and sucked all of my wealth out of my bank account, she seduced me, using cocktails to wash away my inhibitions. I felt so cheap. "You've got to be kidding. I feel like carrion around her. She practically bites me on the neck to keep me from jumping out of bed."

"So what? You need to get over this "woe is me—I don't have a girlfriend" mentality. Just live. The right woman will come along if you aren't so depressing all the time."

"Can we change the subject? Calendar?"

"I'm just saying…"

"Calendar. Please."

"All I see is Chucky at the Driftwood at eleven."

"Oh yeah, Chucky is always so entertaining. What news is there on Jankowitz? Did you hear anything from his Peter? When does James the Receptionist Part II start?"

"Peter's getting very anxious. The court is rejecting his motions because they think he's just delaying, which he is. We've got two weeks tops to find an out or Jankowitz gets locked up. He's waiting patiently, ha, for the magic bullet you've been promising him. I have meetings with two finalists for the reception job this afternoon. They want to meet you. I'll set it up, and you better be on your best behavior."

"Got it. I'm already tired of filing. As for Mr. J., right now, Chucky's the key. I'll give Pete an update after I meet with Chucky."

Before I head out, Sarah catches me up on all the phone traffic that went through the office while I was drifting in peaceful limbo at the seaside. I store the info in my brain, no need to take notes. Notes can be used against you in a court of law. All in all, it was nice and quiet while I was away.

11:00 a.m.
"Ram the bastard..." Little Devil

After our last meeting, Chucky called the office to arrange this tête-à-tête. I glance around the Driftwood for him, but he's not in sight. I grab a coffee (or, teeth-yellowing elixir) and settle into a chair at a table at the back of the room. I blow across the top of the coffee to cool it, with no apparent effect. As I flinch from my first sip, a young man enters the bar and nervously surveys the room. He's college age and dressed like he comes from money. He's wearing a golf shirt, ironed Dockers, and nice slip-on shoes—no socks, of course. His hair is a styled mess, and he wears old-school dark-rimmed glasses like he's Clark Kent. He sees me and smiles like he's caught a mouse. He saunters over and slides into the empty chair at my table.

As he settles in, he eyes me like I'm a curiosity in a museum. He's both uneasy and seemingly confident at the same time. He's making me anxious, particularly since I don't who he is or why he is sitting at my table.

"That chair is reserved," I explain to him.

He looks at me with a smirk; his glasses slide slightly down his nose so that he is looking down at me. He projects a "you're not very cool" vibe at me, and he's pretty convincing.

"Yes, I know," he whispers. "For Charles, if I'm not mistaken? He sent me here to exchange packages with you. You do have Charles's package?"

"I see," I whisper back, no longer wondering if I should be impressed. "This must be your first undercover assignment. Did you double back to make sure you weren't followed? Wait, don't move, don't look around, there's a suspicious eighty-year-old Caucasian female ordering a mocha, no whip. Could be a signal...no, don't worry, she hasn't gone for her gun, and she's exiting the premises. Whew, that was a close one."

"Very funny. Charles mentioned you were quite crass," he says with a sneer. "You know why I'm here. Charles couldn't make it, and I owed him a favor. I'm a little behind in my financial commitment to him. So let's just get down to business."

With that said, the punk reaches into his backpack and pulls out an envelope. He darts looks around the room as he passes an envelope to me under the table.

I look at him like the moron he is and say, "You must be Bond, James Bond. You think evil forces are watching our every move. You think that acting covert is less noticeable then acting natural. Well, all you're doing is drawing attention to us. Here." I toss my envelope at him. His surprise is comically written all over his face. He fumbles and flails before the envelope skitters off the table and onto the floor.

"That is for Chucky, as agreed. Let him know you need to work on your double-blind fake-a-rooski handoff skills," I say with a chuckle.

He's clearly pissed off by my uncultured demeanor. But he's too flustered to respond. Instead he picks up the envelope and inserts it into his backpack. He glares at me as he slowly pushes his glasses up his nose and back to standard position, stands, pivots, and exits the bar.

I shake my head. A punk kid who thinks he's learned how to be a spy by watching TV. I'm sure he also believes he's a fierce commando because of his hours playing Master Chief in *Halo*. Oooooooh boy.

I open the envelope and pull out a single sheet of paper. On the page are three typed names under the heading *Smith's Entourage*, but I don't recognize any of them.

I put the sheet in my jacket pocket and head out into the sunlight. It's still crisp outside but not winter crisp. It's more like "spring is close enough that you might risk shorts while golfing" crisp.

I hop into my Jeep and head back out to the office. Traffic is light this time of day, and I can feel the heat of the sun warming my mood, so I'm not in a hurry. Mount Hood is standing tall under lots of snow overlooking the eastern side of the city. The Willamette River is glistening in the sunlight. As I move with traffic, I notice a newer SUV a dozen cars behind me knifing through traffic like he's Mario Andretti, forcing everybody else to break for his anxiety-driven childishness, ruining dozens of fine citizens' days as he makes his convenience their inconvenience.

"Stay in your warm comfort zone, your safe place. You can't change him," my little angel implores.

"Ram the bastard," my little devil screams. "Or at least trap him, so he has to slow for a while."

I must be getting old because I listen to my angel (who flips off my devil). The SUV passes me, and I stare at the driver, memorizing his face so I can return the favor if I run into him on the street or in a grocery store someday. "Let it go, Jake, let it go," my angel says. "Oh, aren't you the mature one, Mr. Middle Finger," my devil says. But my angel is right: back to my warm place.

When I arrive at the office, I find Sarah entertaining a lovely young woman in our reception area. Her blond hair and fair skin are perfectly contrasted by her blue blouse and a skirt that reaches just above her knees. But it's her long, shapely legs that capture my attention. I glance at them only briefly. *I'm a pro,* I think as my little angel screams, "Eyes up, you filthy bugger." Even though the woman is dressed in a professional manner, she seems hard somehow, like she would be comfortable in a dark-and-dirty booze joint. She watches me like one cat eyes another that has just entered her territory. She must be okay with me, as she attempts a smile with puffy eyes that betray her having cried recently.

Sarah introduces us. "Jake Brand, meet Jan Center; Jan, meet Jake."

Jan stands, and even her sad smile flashes at a thousand megawatts; she extends her right hand. "My pleasure."

"Jake," Sarah interrupts, "could I have a minute of your time before you meet with Jan?"

"Of course," I say. "I'll be with you in a minute, Jan." I follow Sarah into my office and close the door.

"Is she the sex surrogate you were asking me to find? If so, I completely approve," I say.

"Ha-ha, she's a new client—her live-in boyfriend is missing. I noticed how hard you were working not to leer at her," she says.

"First off, how can I be in trouble for working hard *not* to leer? And second, my line of sight remained above her neckline at all times."

"Yes, but your damn jaw was on the floor. Men are so obvious. I thought you were supposed to have some semblance of professionalism. Plus any normal person could see she's upset."

All I can do is surrender. "Well, at least today I'm a *man* rather than a lecher or beast or cretin or fill-in-the-blank."

"Ahh, Jake, honey, don't you know by now that those are all synonymous?" If she weren't so lovely, correct, and able to kick my ass, I'd give her a piece of my mind.

Instead I decide to be mature and respond with my quick wit and sly intellect. "Oh, aren't you Ms. Funny Pants. Send her in. But before you go, I need you to do a background workup on these names and cross-check them with Copper Smith. Charge your time to Jankowitz." I hand her the sheet of paper that I got from Chucky via Magnum, PI.

"Will do," she replies. She opens the door and whispers to me, "Be nice to her." To Jan, she says, "Come on in."

As Jan walks in, I get motion sickness from her swaying hips. Did I mention she's attractive?

"I need help," she says bluntly.

"You just became my favorite kind of person: a client. Smoke?" I offer her.

"No, but go ahead if you'd like," she replies.

I light up a Pall Mall and set it in the ashtray, perfectly positioned to take advantage of the natural airflow in the office. "How can I help?"

"My boyfriend has been missing for a couple of days. I'm afraid he's in trouble, and I'd like your assistance in finding him."

"Why do you think he's in trouble? Why not in Vegas or shacked up with your former best friend?" I ask as I lean over the ashtray and sniff a small whiff of the smoldering cigarette. "Have you contacted the police?"

"No, I haven't contacted the police. I've been told they won't do anything for seventy-two hours. Plus, I don't want his employer to find out that something might be wrong. May I?" She reaches for a tissue. "Of course." She takes one and looks at me, obviously trying hard not to break down.

"Pardon me for being blunt, but usually when someone doesn't want to go to the police and is worried about an employer more than a loved one's safety, they know something that they aren't sharing. Or at least have a suspicion," I state. "What aren't you telling me?"

"I do care about his safety. It's tearing me up inside." She begins to sniffle, and I begin to feel like a heel (says my little angel) or manipulated (says my little devil). I hand her another tissue.

"I'm sorry for being rough, but I'm trying to understand what's happened and how you fit in."

"No, you're being fair. But you need to believe I do care about him. I haven't contacted the police because of a note he left me. It says that he has a plan to make a large sum of money, and I'm not to trust the police. He didn't tell me anything about what his plan was or why I couldn't trust the police. So I'm here, asking you for help. Can you help me?" she asks.

"Maybe, but before we move forward, I need to know how you chose me. How did you pick my name? Dart board? Palm reader?" I have found in the past that who refers a client to me is important.

"I got your name from an attorney who Tim, my boyfriend, had recently been in contact with. Do you know Peter Jennings? He speaks very highly of you." I nod yes. Do I ever. Pete is an attorney and a friend. I know it sounds impossible that he could be a friend, given that he's an attorney, but Pete's one of the good guys. I'm presently working with him on the Jankowitz case.

"Mr. Jennings didn't have much to say about his conversations with Tim, but he recommended you under the circumstances. I wish I could tell you more, but I don't know any more than that. I don't know where else to turn."

I take another whiff of the cigarette and get an odd "what are you doing?" look from Jan.

"My doctor told me to quit smoking, but he didn't say anything about secondhand smoke. So if a client won't light up, I light one up for the room," I explain.

"I thought it was illegal to smoke in a public building."

"Ahh, but I'm not smoking."

From the look on her face, Jan is clearly second-guessing her decision to choose me for help. But that's fine, since I don't trust her—only a chump trusts a client. But I am a sucker for a pretty-pouty mouth attached to a lovely face, attached to a, well, you get the picture. What's an honorable man to do?

"Okay, Jan, I'm in. I charge $150 per hour plus out-of-pocket expenses against a prepaid retainer of five grand. Once your check clears, we'll meet and start getting background info," I say.

"No need to wait," she replies as she pulls a wad of cash out of her purse. She counts out a cool five g's and hands it to me. "Now, what would you like to know?" she asks.

I look at the cash on the table and the bigger wad she shoves back into her purse. I don't know if I should ask for more or call the cops. The cash makes me nervous, but checks bounce and cash doesn't. I decide there's more upside potential than downside risk. I agree to take the job and have her sign an engagement letter. We spend most of the next three hours discussing her and Tim's lives.

Tim Larson is originally from Minnesota, went to school in the Midwest, and has been in Portland for four years. He's a loan officer at the Tualatin branch of First Century Bank. He's five feet eleven and 185 pounds; he has brown hair and blue eyes; he's thirty-two years old, and he's a runner. She gives me a recent photo.

Jan is from SoCal, no college, just lots of odd jobs while she tried to find success in front of a camera. She moved to Portland a year ago to escape the LA world of make-believe. She met Tim shortly after she moved here, and they've been living together for six months. She's currently unemployed, and they've been talking about marriage.

She's brought Tim's banking records with her. She says that they've begun to merge finances but still maintain some separation. We also cover info like email addresses, past home addresses, and professional and personal affiliations. I try to get a broad picture of their finances, their personal lives, and their secret lives. When asked about the cash, she tells me it's from their rainy-day fund. Right, like everyone has that much cash lying around the house, rainy or dry.

I stand and walk around the table to shake her hand. She moves past my hand and hugs me. Her curves press against me, and her forehead brushes my neck. I look down at her, and she looks up at me. "What is happening here?" My little angel is running around, hands in the air.

"Please, Jake, please find Tim."

She keeps holding on.

"I'll do my best, Jan."

She smiles, a very enticing smile. "I know you will. Thank you so much."

Tuesday, March 12

"If she had wads of cash, you must have a client..."
Pete

Pete Jennings's office is in a multistory, red-brick class A building, just across I-5 from my office, in the Kruse Woods area. People who hire Pete know they're going to pay a premium for his services. But they're happy to write the check. Most of the time, he saves them from prison, bankruptcy, and other assorted dark sides of life. Like, for example, divorce. At the time of my brokenhearted pleasantries, I resented his cheery disposition and mind-numbing invoices. But he was there for me not only during our appointments with my ex and her attorney but also as I worked my way through the emotional jungle of splitting.

Pete is always busy representing high-profile crooks and, according to Pete, once he even represented an innocent man. (I'm not sure that was me.) In his midforties, he still has a slender build, dresses very snappily, and is incredibly smart about the law. His thinning hair betrays his age in contrast to his baby face.

His office has space for about fifteen people, and he employs only eleven, six attorneys and five assistants. He's offered me the use of some of the space, but he's not the only attorney I represent, so I've declined his fine offer. I don't want the others lawyers getting jealous.

As I walk in to the reception area, Pete's secretary, JJ, smiles. "Hey, Jake, it's good to see you. Can I get you something to drink?"

"Hi, JJ, how goes the business of meeting and greeting the guilty and the really guilty? Thanks, but no, I'm good. I really just need to chat with Pete for a minute—Mr. Jennings done with his makeup for tonight's show?" I ask.

JJ chuckles and replies, "No show today. Pete's been suffering through several days of bad ratings. The network wants to go with Connie Chung, a real newsperson..."

"Give it a rest. Do I make fun of your names?" Pete asks as he walks out of his office.

"You would if you could. You just don't have JJ's or my quick wit," I reply. "He's relied on teleprompters too much, me thinks," I half whisper to JJ, who snickers in a conspiratorial manner.

"If you two cards had fifty of your friends here, you still wouldn't have a full deck. But you'd be funnier." Pete turns to me. "I think I know why you're here—come on in."

"Bye, JJ. Try to keep the paparazzi at bay. I don't want to see my ugly mug in the tabloids." She laughs, and I follow Pete into his office. He closes the door, moves around his massive desk, and sits in his stately chair.

I sit in a seemingly expensive but terribly comfortable client chair.

"When did you get to meet Arnold Palmer?" I ask as I see a picture new to Pete's collection of his celebrity meet-and-greets.

"That was at the charity golf tournament last summer. The one I invited you to that you blew off because of some crazy lady you were working for. But focus. I assume you're here because of the lovely Ms. Center."

"That's right. She said you sent her to me, just before she flashed a wad of cash in front of me," I say. "Do you know anything about Tim that you can share?"

"Tim talked to me about seven months ago at a chamber lunch. When Tim apparently disappeared, Jan found my card and came in to see if Tim had hired me or if I knew where he was. I said no on both accounts and sent her to you. If she had wads of cash, you must have a client," he says.

"I do have a client. Can you tell me what you discussed with Tim at the lunch?"

"Yes, since he's not my client. Tim was asking about whistle-blower statutes. He asked if I had ever been involved in one or helped someone through the process. I said I was familiar with the statutes but hadn't actually been involved in a case. I laid out the basic structure, gave him my card, and never heard back from him. And no, he didn't give me any details. Oh, and FYI, Jan didn't feel right to me, so I didn't tell her about the whistle-blower piece," he tells me.

All of a sudden I'm thinking I undercharged Ms. Center. I'm also thinking she has good reason to be worried. If Tim is blowing a whistle, then someone is going to be angry, and Jan and Tim could be in for some trouble. Blowees don't take too kindly to blowers.

"That's all I have on Tim" he says. "Have you made any progress on Jankowitz?"

"Actually, yes, I got some names of Southside guys who've been seen jawboning with Smith. We're checking it out. I'll let you know when I have usable intel."

"Okay. Are you going to make it to poker tonight?"

"I thought I'd give it a go. How about you?"

"Of course. I can't afford not to be there. You guys are funding my kids' college funds."

"Well, after tonight's game, your kids better be happy with a community college. I have a feeling there's going to be a big sucking sound caused by all of the moola moving in my direction."

11:30 a.m.
"Right away with the smart mouth..." Detective Smith

I leave the building and head to my car. Even though his office is less than half a mile from mine as the crow flies, I-5 separates us and makes walking a blood sport. My Jeep is parked at the back of several rows of business-type cars looking all shiny and new. Even though every third car is a four-wheel drive, I know that the only four-wheeling most of them ever do is accidentally running over a curb. I can see the hulk of my car standing out in the distance. Its finish has dulled, and it looks uncomfortably out of place.

As I meander back through the lot, I discover the infamous and previously mentioned Copper Smith in his car. He's decided to park in a manner that blocks my car's exit. As he is sitting in the driver's seat of his car, I can't see all 240-plus pounds of his squatty frame. But I can sense his sweaty pits through his suit coat. And I can see the disgusting thirty-five strands of hair wound around his head to hide 30 percent of his oily pate. As always, he has his badge hanging from his outside suit jacket pocket and his gun in a shoulder holster, causing his left teat to look twice as big as his right.

Smith and I have had run-ins in the past. He even arrested me once. I've always found him to be stupid and lazy. He's drunk on power and seemingly more concerned about his pocketbook then the safety of our fellow citizens. And I've told him all of that before. Maybe that's why he's always trying to bust my chops.

"Well, well, if it isn't the famous Jake Brand, hero to the criminal element of our fair city. I hear you're helping Jennings on the Jankowitz bust. Anything for a buck, sounds like to me." Which is his way of saying hello.

"You have a reason for blocking my car, detective? I think you're committing a crime—either you're holding me prisoner or you're assaulting my eyeballs with that hairdo. That's a very nice car you're in, a brand-new Caddy? Have a rich uncle who died or just sticky fingers?" Which is my way of saying "you're ugly and stupid."

"Of course, right away with the smart mouth. I get it—you feel safe because you think we live in a civilized society," he says. "But you are sorely mistaken, Brand. Bad things happen to people who wander down dark alleys. Do not mess with my investigation or you'll be rooming with Jankowitz in county, or worse. Do not doubt me." He glares at me.

"I have no doubts about what you're capable of. And by the time I'm through, neither will the district attorney." I glare right back at him. "Sometimes the bad guys do end up in jail, you know. I have a sneaking hunch that this will be one of those times. Have you ever spent time with your kind behind bars? I hear it can be uncomfortable."

"You're such a funny guy. I'd caution you too about prison violence, but I don't think you'll make it that far. It's a nice day, Brand. You better get home before it gets dark." Smith's eyes project anger, and his smile projects bad dental care as he slowly drives away.

1:00 p.m.
"Well, that's a mare of a different shade..." Sarah

After lunch at Stanford's, I head back to the office, and I hear Sarah in her office abusing her keyboard. Her fingernails sound like a couple of Dungeness crabs tap dancing. I lean in to say hi; she pauses to respond in kind, types a few more words, and then follows me into my office. She brings with her some material she's pulled together on the Jankowitz and Larson cases for us to review. We start with Jankowitz.

"I ran the three names Chucky gave you through Google and the public records site," she starts. "All three have extensive criminal records, no known employment, and no known assets. They're definitely connected to Southside and, surprisingly, all were busted in the past fifteen months. And here is where it really gets interesting. All three of them had their charges dropped because of technical failures in the investigation or their cases or problems with evidence disappearing. I made some calls, and my contacts say that none of the failures tie directly to Smith," she says.

"How do you know they're linked to Southside?"

"Tats. I found copies of their mug shots, and they all have an *S* tattooed on the right side of their necks. Those are Southside muscle badges."

"Okay. I'll check with Milt to see if he's heard anything. What about Larson?" I ask.

"Tim seems to be exactly what Jan said he is: average and boring, everything you want in a banker. He's respected by his company, he's had regular promotions, and he's a member of all the right business organizations. He's average financially: decent savings, a mortgage and a car loan, and he pays off his credit card balances each month. The most interesting thing I've found is a checking account that he set up eight months ago. It's not on the list that Jan gave us, so I don't know if she knows about it or simply selectively edited the list she gave me. I've been going through the transactions in that account. There aren't many, but I've found a series of payments to a small IT company called Byte Me Support. It's owned by Finn Hankins. Finn is well-known to law enforcement. It seems he has a history of crossing electronic lines, if you get my drift," she says.

"Print out what you have on Hankins for me. What about Jan?"

"Well, that's a mare of a different shade. It appears that Jan Center didn't exist before she arrived in Portland. But being the creative that I am, I took her prints off the water glass she used."

"Damn, Sarah, did you get any DNA?"

"Wouldn't have helped—it would have been polluted by your damn eyeball ooze. The way they popped out and soiled her, nothing was recoverable," she retorts.

"I'll shut up. Please continue, ma'am."

"It appears that her prints are those of a somewhat successful and highly priced escort by the name of Jamie Sinclair. She's been incarcerated three times—the last time was two years ago. She served thirty days in a county jail down around LA for solicitation. She was part of an international escort site called Honey Bunnies. Very exclusive, very beautiful, very willing, you might say," she says.

"Well, that was unexpected. What have you got on Honey Bunnies?"

"I'm still working on it. I should have something tomorrow."

"Print out the computer-guy stuff, and I'll check him out," I reply. "What else do you have?"

"I've hired the James replacement. Our new receptionist starts Monday next week."

"I thought I was going to get a chance to interview a couple of candidates?"

"That was the original plan, but after I interviewed them, I decided you didn't have a vote. Jessica is a former army reserve lieutenant. I told her the problems that you've created in the past, and she smiled." Sarah chuckles at the dismay that paints my face. "I decided right then and there that she was perfect. She can type, she's great on the phone, and I think she is more than equal to the task of dealing with your crap. "

All I can do is stare at my too-honest associate. My little angel is laughing hysterically; my little devil is yelling, "Bring it on." I choose to ignore both of them in favor of asking the most obvious and necessary next question.

"What does she look like?"

"Oh my God. Is that really your first question? What the hell do her looks have to do with anything? Why not just ask how big her boobs are? Don't you care about getting some work done? That's why you're no longer allowed to make personnel decisions. I'm not sure I should allow you to even interact with staff. I'm officially taking over. I'll field all of the complaints about you, and I'll make sure we aren't sued for harassment. You damn well better shape up, mister."

"You're right, you're right. I was insensitive and need to be more respectful of people in the work environment. I promise to be especially careful and professional around the office." Someday I know I'll figure out this whole inside-voice/outside-voice thing. In the meantime, I have Sarah to train me.

"Don't think you're fooling me. I know you're just pretending to understand, but this is serious stuff."

"Sarah, I do get it. I know what it's like to feel cheap because the opposite sex just wants you for your body."

"Don't confuse your mom wanting you to take the garbage out with what we're talking about. By the way, I'm out with Tyson tonight—can you feed Tammy?" she asks. "I won't have a chance to go home before I'm supposed to meet him."

I used to call Sarah's cat my roommate cat, but she upgraded her to step-cat when these kinds of favors started being requested more and more. "Can do, but I want you home by ten, and I'm dusting you for prints," I say.

"Ha-ha," she says. "Don't wait up for me."

"Actually, as you know, I have poker tonight. The boys are awfully upset that you aren't going to make it, by the way. But I will visit Tammy and try to convince her that Mommy still loves her."

6:00 p.m.
"I'd launch a scud at one of them..." Carl

After I've settled Tammy for the night, I head out for my evening with the boys. Poker is at Milt's house, a comfortable ranch in Beaverton. His father passed away a few years back, and he inherited a couple of cash-cow Laundromats and dry cleaners. With no one pointing guns at him and all the cash a single letch can spend, he decided to retire from the force. Not a bad soft landing. I pull up in front of his place and see Pete Jennings's and Carl Wayne's cars already parked. Normally Johnson Thibodaux and Sarah are part of the game, plus subs who rotate in and out.

As I walk in, Milt points me toward the makeshift bar. Tonight I decide to start with a Domaine Drouhin Pinot Noir, bold and flavorful, very European in style and made from Oregon grapes. Carl's opening a can of IPA. Carl is chiseled from stone, tall, lean, and lethal. Former Special Forces, he hires out these days. Mostly he works kidnapping rescues, personal protection, that kind of thing. We've known each other for fifteen years, having served together in the army and on a few classified missions. We've bonded for life. Even though he hasn't lived there in years, he's still Texas to the core. And when he's had a few cocktails, the accent thickens and you'd think he rode a horse over.

"Hey, Carl, how's the secret-assassin biz?" I ask.

"Good. Ya'll got a job for me?"

"Yeah, a new-model SUV I encountered on I-5 today. He treated the freeway like it was his own personal speedway. I need you to apprehend and punish him. But your method of retribution needs to be slow and excruciating," I reply.

"Oh, I know that type of fella'. Been seein' him and his like a lot lately," Carl says. "I'd launch a scud at one of them, but I can't do the jail time. Can't help you, son; wish I could."

"That's unfortunate. I guess that proves that all of those legends about you are just that, legends and old wives' tales. Excuse me." I turn away before his attempt to outwit me. "Milt, can I talk to you for a second?"

"Sure, what's up?" he asks.

I describe what's happening in the Jankowitz case and ask him if he's heard anything about Smith. I'm hoping that even if he hasn't, he can make some calls about the Southside cases that have been thrown out. Milt has stayed very connected with his blue brothers. He regularly plays basketball with a group of them and is actively involved in a charity associated with the police union.

"No, I haven't heard anything, but I'll check it out and get back to you," he says.

"Appreciate it."

As we turn, Johnson and one of the subs walk in.

Johnson is your normal bureaucrat, overworked and underpaid. But he has a passion for his job as an assistant DA. Things can be pretty intense when he's trying to imprison one of Pete's clients. They've worked out their own social interaction code. It's called strict silence when it comes to business. Fortunately, he's not involved in the Jankowitz case.

The sub looks like red meat. Hopefully he'll just roll over and play dead as we drain him of his lifeblood of cash.

It's time to play.

Everyone grabs a cocktail and finds a seat. Milt and Pete fire up cigars. The table is set and ready to go. Buy in is $200. One rebuy is allowed, and no one gets hurt.

"Here we go, children. High card gets first deal," says Milt as he tosses a card faceup in front of each of us. "And that is me. Seven card stud, nothing wild."

Cards flash around, two down and one up. I have high card up, a king of spades.

"King bets $1," I say as I throw a white chip into the middle of the table.

Carl calls, Pete folds, Milt raises $2. Milt's neighbor folds, Johnson folds, Pete and I call. Milt deals the second upcard to all of us, and I get a second king. A jack is dealt to Carl's ten and a queen to Milt's jack. I throw three whites into the pot, and everyone folds.

"I quit," I announce as I rake in my winnings. "My sole goal was to take some money off of Milt. Mission accomplished—boo-yah!"

"That's why you'll never retire," says Milt. "Your financial goals are as high as mine were when I had a paper route in junior high. You need to connect with my financial planner—"

"Don't go there again. Just blow some smoke over here and pass the deck, loser," I say.

"You and your secondhand smoke," says Milt as he blows a puff at the ceiling. "You know you can get secondhand bad breath if you aren't careful."

"He's right, you know," says Carl. "You probably should meet up with a financial planner."

"You don't have a financial planner?" Pete joins in.

"Damn, have you all become wives?"

"No, we just don't want to pay for your retirement home. We know you're going to end up on the street the way you're going. My financial guy says—" Milt says.

"Milt, I love you like a brother. Don't become my dad."

"Just saying…"

"Shh."

11:55 p.m.
"Anything for my polite prince…" Sarah

I get home a bit before midnight. I haven't had a cocktail for a couple of hours. There's no way I'm going to spend the night splattered on the road—or in the drunk tank; been there, done that.

As I walk through the front door, I hear a sad Roberta Flack song playing. I guess that's redundant. I see Sarah sitting on the couch facing outside with the room lights low and the night lights of the West Hills glowing through the window. The music has the scratchy clear sound of a turntable. Life should be one LP at a time.

"I thought you were going to be out doing nasty unspeakables with Tyson tonight," I say as I take my coat off and toss it on a chair. I pour myself a generous two fingers of fifteen-year-old single malt and add one small ice cube. There's a part of me that wants to add a finger or two. But I've been down that road, and it doesn't lead to anywhere healthy.

I see her shoulders lower slightly as she tells me, "Tyson said he needs to move on. He doesn't see us at the next level, and he's moving out of town for a new job." She hesitates for a moment before she says, "Hell, I thought we were already at the next level."

I sit down and wrap my arm around her shoulders. Sarah's told me about past romances that didn't pan out and the anxiety she experienced at each ending. She believed that the relationship with Tyson was going to be real and long-term. I can feel despair seeping through her skin, wrapping her mind in confusion and self-doubt. I know she's thinking, *Why me? What's wrong with me?*

"Nothing is wrong with you," I answer her unspoken question. "Shall I hunt him down? I can add some character to his pretty-boy face."

"Sure. Can I watch?"

"Oh, you really know how to turn me on. You know we'll be dressed the whole time, right?"

"Well, then, don't waste your energy, if you're going to be a granny about it," she says. We sit quietly for a moment and look out the window. "I know how much you hurt after you and Sue divorced. I see how you're still, I don't know, *afraid* isn't the right word. I guess you're hesitant about a new relationship. I don't think being single is working for you, and I don't want that for me."

Sue was my wife of seven years. Two years ago she said, "Later, big guy," and ran off with the milkman. Literally, the dude owned a dairy. "I'm not avoiding commitment; I'm avoiding the breakup that happens after commitment."

"So you've given up?"

"No, I want someone in my life badly. It helps having you, and Tammy," I say, as the cat launches herself onto my lap, "but I know I want more. I just don't want to mess up again. I don't want to kiss someone goodbye in the morning and come home to a kiss-off note in the evening: *It's not you—it's me. Well, it's sort of mostly you, but me too a little...if that makes you feel better.* Too many people get hurt."

"How do you find the right person if you're closed off?"

I see Sarah studying me intensely. Somehow, the conversation has swung from her to me. Sue hurt me deeply. I spent months recovering from Sue's departure, relying on alcohol to salve the pain. Then it took months to recover from my recovery.

"You're right—I've been hiding, and it isn't working. I know there's more to life. So, bottom line, use me as an example of what not to do. Don't run to a bottle or away from risk. At best, those are just delaying tactics." I hug her closer. "You'll find him. I know you will. Now, I said don't lean on the bottle, but you are allowed a glass or two, especially tonight. Need a refill on that wine?".

"No, I just need a shoulder. A warm shoulder," she says.

"Absolutely, Sarah, absolutely."

I flip the record over and sit back down next to her. She snuggles closer, and I place my arm across her shoulders. I feel her relax and settle into a comfortable sleep. I look at her and have a moment of clarity. I know just how beautiful she is on the outside and, even more so, on the inside. We've been friends for so long, I'm afraid I've started taking her for granted. My hand gently moves a wisp of hair off of her face. A small thing, but it has a comforting effect on me, one that I want to hold on to. After about twenty minutes, Roberta calls it a night. Not long after that, so do I.

Wednesday, March 13

9:00 a.m.

"Has Ms. Center been paying you in singles…" Finn

I'm burning up. Someone is trying to cook me. I attempt to open my eyes, but my eyelids refuse to comply because of the brightness of the sunny day beaming into the condo. I move my left hand to block the light, convince my eyes it's okay, and gingerly glance around the room. I'm still on the couch from the night before. My right shoulder has twisted and frozen into an embrace of the space once occupied by Sarah. But it doesn't hurt since it's sound asleep. The rest of my body feels stiff and angry. But the pain of the moment is chased away by the smell and sound of breakfast in the making. I grunt and hear Sarah laugh at my obvious discomfort.

"You're getting old, Jake? I would have thought you could sleep anywhere and bounce up in the morning refreshed and energized," she says.

"Mock me all you want. Just promise me that a sliver, a crumb, a slurp of what you're making is for me," I plead.

"Anything for my polite prince."

"Polite Prince? Don't you mean Prince Charming?"

"I suppose to some desperate creature you might be considered charming. But like you said last night, I'm special, and we both know that you don't measure up."

But she's laughing with compassion as she walks over and hands me a steaming mug of coffee, which I grasp with my one working hand. Ahhh, the smell alone is invigorating. I let the warm fluid flow down into my body, slowly masking my discomfort.

I get off the couch, and my numb right arm swings uncontrollably at my side as it regains feeling. I stagger to the table and stare at the food with puppy-dog eyes. I know it's going to taste better than it looks, and it looks, and smells, awesome. I can't wait to dig in, and I promise myself I'm going to take my time and savor every morsel.

When Sarah hands me a full plate, the first bite erases all memory of my promise, and I scarf down the food. Man, that is good stuff.

After breakfast, I do the dishes while Sarah gets ready for her day. Then I shower and dress and exit for my first meeting. It's a new day in the City of Roses. Sounds quaint, but roses are a serious business here. Portland is home to the International Rose Test Garden, which contains nearly seven thousand plants and hundreds of varietals. Portland also hosts the annual Rose Festival, which features the second-largest all-floral parade in the country. Rosebushes are in practically every yard, right next to marijuana plants (but never more than an ounce). Okay, so maybe I exaggerate—on some of that. Anyway, it's time to meet Finn, the IT guru.

The drive from Northwest Portland to the Hawthorne District is relaxed side-street driving. Except for the pedestrians who are intent on forcing their right of way by crossing the street in front of me; and except for the bikers who believe they can beat me in a game of chicken; and except for the other drivers who don't seem to understand that they aren't as important as me.

I pull up outside of Finn's office on Southeast Hawthorne Boulevard. It's a gentrified area of town with lots of quaint shops, restaurants, and small, neighborhood-friendly businesses. I'm able to parallel park right in front of Byte Me Support, an old one-story space carved out of a block-long building with an aged red-brown-and-gray-mottled brick facade.

I enter through the front door into what feels like a dark cavern. Behind me, facing the street, a line of filthy windows absorbs most of the sunlight before it can enter the room. My eyes slowly adjust to the darkness, and my nose attempts to filter out the musty odor that permeates the air. I begin to recognize the dark shapes around me. I'm in a seedy sitting area of tattered and worn chairs, end tables stacked with old magazines, and fake ferns gathering dust in cheap plastic pots. In front of me and to the left is a hallway leading deeper into the building; to the right is a reception desk.

Seated at the reception desk is a woman seemingly undisturbed by my entry, pecking away at a keyboard. I look to her for assistance, thinking she's paid to help visitors. My mistake—my entrance hasn't slowed her fifteen-words-per-minute single-finger pace. She looks to be in her sixties and is wearing a flower-patterned dress that's fastened up to her neck. Her hair looks like a dirty cotton ball, but it matches her more-gray-than-blue eyes.

"Excuse me, ma'am," I start.

"I see you there. Hold your pants up. I'm not a multitasker," she responds without looking up at me. She moves her glasses up onto her forehead and leans in to squint at her computer screen. Apparently satisfied with her pecking, she turns and addresses me. "Okay, what can I do for you?"

"I'm interested in hiring someone to maintain my office computers. I have a small business that's growing. Do you handle that type of thing?"

"No, I don't, but Finn might be interested." I smile at her earnest comment that I might have assumed she'd be able to take my case. "I'll check with him. Wait here," she says as she rises from her chair. Before she starts down the hall, she glances back at me and pulls her cardigan closed across her chest. She makes me feel as if I'm a frigid wind blowing up against her.

She walks deeper into the darkness, and I hear voices. She emerges from the back and waves me through. "Finn will see you."

I walk back into the only office past the reception area. The space is lit primarily by the glow from various computer screens and a single desk lamp, whose light is cast downward. As my eyes adjust to a new level of darkness, I see a smorgasbord of techno gizmos. Most of them look dead or broken. On the whole, the place has the appearance of a technology graveyard. But on the back wall, behind a desk and the back of a creature that I assume is Finn Hankins is an impressive array of wide-awake screens. Finn remains seated facing the screens, beating on a keyboard. The undertaker himself seems the typical geek: tattered polo shirt, long and ratty hair, a Beavers baseball cap turned backward, and an aroma of stale sweat.

From over his shoulder, he says, "Have a seat Mr.…I'm afraid Delores didn't give me your name."

"Jake Brand. I have a small business in Tigard."

"Great. Why are you here?"

"I have a detective business, private investigations and such. I think we need assistance with keeping the system running. Plus, I'd like to have offsite access to our server, and occasionally we have specialized needs for cases."

At this, he turns and faces me for the first time. He has the pale-white skin of one not often exposed to the sun. An expression of curiosity fills his face, but then I realize it's actually the beginning of a sneer. "What kind of specialized needs? Are you asking me to do something illegal? You must be a cop," he says.

"A cop? That's funny. You must not spend much time with cops if you think I'm one. Here's my PI license; check me out—I can wait." I pull my wallet out of my back pocket, open it, slide my license out, and set it on his desk.

As he stares at me, he picks up my license. He lowers his gaze to the card, looks back at me, and nods. "Okay, buddy, I will."

Then it begins. He starts typing, and the screens start flashing like a pyrotechnic show. Slowly I start to recognize images: my skimpy bank statements, military record, past cases, pictures of me posted on other peoples websites. He's prematurely eulogizing my life's highs and lows. All of a sudden, I'm feeling old and exposed by the vast chasm in my technology skills. Damn, I need to hire this guy.

He reaches the end of memory lane; the typing slows and then stops, and Finn turns to me. "Wow, what a mess. The PI business must be your passion. Based upon your bank records, it's definitely not a profession," he says.

"Actually, the investigative side is just a way of getting into show-biz. See how much I've entertained you?"

"Nothing personal, buddy, but I can definitely help you."

"And how can you help me? I need someone to do more than just make sure all the cords are plugged in."

"First, I can clean up some of this clutter about you on the net. I won't make you disappear entirely, but I can give you some dignity," he begins.

Ouch, that's going to leave a mark. "Easy, Finn, I have feelings," I say.

"Second, I can protect your information from creeps like me. Third, I can expand, speed up, and organize your search queries. Someone in your office has decent skills, but he or she is leaving fingerprints all over the place.

"But most important, before we move forward, I need to know why you're interested in Tim Larson. And don't tell me it's a coincidence that you're here," he says.

He's caught me flatfooted, and by his smirk, I can see he sees it on my face. "Well, Finn, it's funny you should ask. Tim's girlfriend, Ms. Center, hired us to find Tim. Seems he's missing. I found some payments he made to you and thought maybe you might know something that would help us locate him. I wanted to meet with you before I went to the police. I'm sure they'd want to spend time reviewing your work product to try and find the missing Tim."

"Really, and has Ms. Center been paying you in singles? I assume that your hacker is good enough to have tripped over her background. I find it hard to believe that Bambi is going to want cops involved."

"Bambi?"

"That was one of her stage names in LA. I even have pictures of her, if you're interested." He turns, hits a few keys and, voila, Ms. Center, aka Bambi, aka Jamie Sinclair. Same eyes, more of the same body, and it appears that she's staring right at me. Little devil, be quiet.

"How did you get these?" I ask.

"The details are a trade secret. But in general, I take a snapshot of the web every so often, started about ten years ago. I archive each shot and can search it, using my own algorithm. Let's see, I'll do a search on you on my oldest archive and strip out all images that have repeated since then. That should leave only items that have been deleted since then."

As he works, I become anxious, even though I don't have any interesting secrets to be discovered. What secrets I have are my secrets, and nobody has a right to them but me.

"Ahhh, here is a nice mug shot of you, buddy. Did you happen to have a run-in with the police about ten years ago?"

And there on the screen is a younger, grizzled, greasy, unwashed me; me from my drunk-and-disorderly days. I had accepted a jerk's invitation to meet him outside a bar, kicked his ass, and got mine rolled into the drunk tank. I'm older and more mature now. Well, I'm at least quicker at leaving the scene and avoiding the police.

"Finn, you've got my attention."

"Why stop now? While you were in ogling Delo—"

"Now you're just being sick."

"Save it. While you were in my *reception area*—"

"You mean that dark and filthy exaggerated hallway?"

"—I took a picture of you and ran it through facial-recognition software. I knew your name and some of the stuff I've shared before you ever came back here. Here's your investigator's license from 2005. Do you ever wash your hair?"

At this point in an interview, I'm typically staring down a confused and frightened dishonest person who is trapped in a lie. I then use my powerful analytic brain to project knowledge of his deceit through my eyes and directly into his brain. This causes him to squirm, cave, and confess all. As I sit opposite Finn, I can feel him trying to emit powerful contempt into my brain. It's causing me to face myself, and it makes me uncomfortable.

"I have a grand that says you can be bought," I say.

"If he brings his twin sister, you've got a deal," he replies.

Well, it is Bambi's money. "Okay, two grand. I need to know everything that you and Tim did together."

Finn begins repopulating the screens with financial records. "Tim asked me to help him hack company financial records. About fifty companies and twenty banks in the western US. Don't worry—we didn't touch the money. That would be suicide. The feds would have been all over us in hours. But we were able to print off a bunch of financials. I put them on a flash drive and gave them to Tim."

"Did he say why he wanted them?"

"No, he never did, and I tried to dig it out of him. But he was very nervous and secretive. He could never relax when he was here."

"Can you give me a copy of all the data you pulled?"

"Sure."

What do these banks and businesses have to do with whistle-blowing? What did Tim do with his copy of the information? And where is Tim now? Finn hands me a flash drive, and I place it in my pocket.

"Finn, I want you to go through these financial records and look for patterns or unusual activities. I want you to look for the kinds of things that embarrass people when they become public knowledge."

"Got it, buddy; I'll get back to you in the next forty-eight hours."

I leave Finn's office, concentrating on all that I have heard. As I cross the sidewalk to my Jeep, I see an older, dark-blue Buick parked thirty feet ahead of mine, with someone in the driver's seat. I notice that the side and rearview mirrors appear to be tilted to allow the driver to view the front of Finn's office. Before I have a chance to introduce myself to my admirer, his engine begins to sing, and he drives off. I move quickly to my car to try and follow him. But he makes the light and disappears into traffic.

Thursday, March 14

9:00 a.m.

"No police, not yet; I know you'll find him…" Jan

I arrive at Tim Larson's house, a two-story split-level in a bedroom community southwest of the city. It's one of those places where the builder lost creative interest after the fourth house and just kept repeating the same four floor plans over and over. But he wasn't a stupid builder: he had four different paint combinations, so he really had sixteen different house choices. The houses look subtly different from the outside, but mostly the exteriors just confuse the buyers into thinking their special home is special. That builder is such a sneaky wabbit.

Sarah called Jan yesterday to request an opportunity for me to meet with her at Tim's house so I could give and get updates. But the real reason I'm here is to search for clues—kind of like a real detective. I park in the driveway next to a compact Mazda. The property looks like it takes time and money to maintain, with mature bushes and an edged yard—one of the reasons I'm in a condo. Almost immediately after ringing the bell, I hear Jan's footsteps, and the door opens.

"Come on in, Jake. Is Sarah with you?" Jan is dressed very stylishly: designer pants, heels, silk blouse, and an assortment of moderately priced baubles. Not that I spend a lot of time pricing baubles. Her makeup and hair are perfect, and her smile is radiant. I must be very special to her to have earned such a warm greeting.

"No Sarah today—she's off stalking bad guys. How are you holding up?" I ask.

"I'm not going to lie—it's a struggle. I just can't imagine what's happened to Tim. I keep going over the last few days before he disappeared, hoping I recognize a clue, questioning everything I did and said."

"So you haven't heard or learned anything new since we last met?" I ask.

"No, I was hoping you were coming over to give me some good news, or any news."

"I wish I was, but I don't have any new information either. But it's early," I say. "Don't forget that we can go to the police anytime you want."

"No police, not yet; I know you'll find him. Would you like something to drink? I have coffee made."

I say yes to coffee. The entry opens up to a living room with average furniture and mass-produced art and tchotchkes. From the living room, we enter a great room that includes the kitchen and TV room. Jan pours two cups of coffee and offers cream and sugar.

"So, if I remember correctly, you met Tim about eight months ago and moved in with him about six months ago? How did you meet?" I ask.

"Yes, about eight months ago we met at a Rotary meeting. A friend of mine said that might be a good way to make contacts in a new city. We sat at the same table. Went on a date a few days later and, well, we really hit it off. I told him I was in a month-to-month rental, and he invited me to be his roommate. We agreed I'd pay my way."

"But things became more serious pretty quickly, and it felt good." She looks at me with a smile as she remembers better times. "I haven't always been lucky with men, but Tim seemed good for me. And now I just don't know what I'm going to do."

"Give us some time, we'll figure it out." I say as I put my hand on top of hers. She gently grips my fingers, squeezing twice before she lets go.

"I have a question, Jake."

"Shoot."

"Have you spoken to the attorney, Mr. Jennings? When I met with him, I was certain he knew something he wouldn't tell me."

I smile and say, "I have spoken to him. He says his interaction with Tim was strictly introductory. No business was discussed."

"And you believe him? I got the sense that he knew more. It might make sense to ask him again."

I examine Jan's face. Her expression leads me to believe that she expects to get her way. I'll let her this time, so I can get mine. "I'll double back to Peter." Her face softens a bit. "Jan, do you mind if I look around?" I ask.

"Oh well, I suppose not. What are you looking for? Maybe I can help?"

"Well, that's the fun part of searching for clues—I won't know what I'm looking for until I see it. Bedrooms are back this way?"

"Yes, I'll show you..."

"That won't be necessary. I'll stumble around and be back in just a few minutes. I get antsy with someone looking over my shoulder."

"Oh, sure. I'll be here if you need anything."

I smile at her, turn, and start down the hallway. The first door is on the left, and I enter what appears to be a spare bedroom containing a dresser, bed, and nightstand. I pull out all of the drawers and find nothing. I check the back of the drawers for taped items or other hidden gems; nada. Next I check out the closet and find a few sets of spare linens with nothing hidden in the folds. I check heat registers, windowsills, and around doorframes, all with no luck.

I head back out to the hallway and on to the next door. This one is on my right and is a guest bath. I proceed with the same kind of search as in the previous room with the same result.

The last room is the master bedroom-and-bath combo. I start with the bathroom. I find all of the things I'd expect to find for a bachelor: shaving supplies, grooming supplies, and cleansing supplies. What I don't find are the types of products that Jan would want around. I move into the bedroom and find more of the same masculine decor, with minimal female clothing, and one picture of the happy couple. I repeat the search of drawers and vents. I carefully look between mattresses and bed sheets. But I can't find anything out of the ordinary.

As I look around the room trying to decide what to do next, I reflect on when my wife first moved in with me. We practically broke up the first week because I wanted my velvet Elvis picture on full display in the living room while she wanted a portrait of her parents in our bedroom. We were both disturbed decorators. Elvis ended up leaning against a wall in the garage and my in-laws haunted me for years each time I traversed the hallway. I swear their eyes followed me and changed expressions based upon how intimate their daughter and I had been.

Sue's possessions invaded my house quickly and completely. It didn't take long before I started tripping over them. She had pictures of friends, family, and the sky at the coast. Our decor was early thrift shop and hand-me-downs. The little things that took up space on counters and tables were memories without intrinsic value, not store-bought stuff without emotional value. This place looks like Tim lives alone and has no history. I expected to see two distinct decorating styles in armed conflict. Where are all of Jan's overflow boxes? It's possible that they're the tidiest couple I've ever met, or maybe they even have a storage shed somewhere. But it doesn't feel right to me.

I finish my search and turn to head back to Jan. As I turn, I see Jan watching me from the doorway.

"Oh, you surprised me. I was just finishing and heading back to talk."

"Did you find anything?" Her eyes look flat with intensity.

"No, nothing to speak of."

"He's gone isn't he? We'll never find him."

Her volume is so low, I step closer. As I do, she moves toward me and presses her lips to mine. Her hands caress my face as her tongue caresses my lips. I move my hands to her shoulders and gently move her back away from me.

"Jan, I don't—no, can't; I can't do this. You're a client."

"Jake, I'm so sorry. You must think I'm a terrible person. But I'm not, Jake; I'm afraid and alone. I need someone, and with Tim missing, I don't have anyone else. Just you. You see that, don't you?"

She tries to move closer, to kiss me again. My little devil is breathing hard. My little angel is screaming, "Mayday, iceberg dead ahead." It takes all my willpower not to lose myself. I mean, let's face it. The Jake charm can be difficult to control. But this is kind of crazy; I barely know her, she's a client, and I'm being paid to find her significant other? This is not right on so many levels, even my little devil decides I should back away. Back away fast.

I hold her out at arm's length and say, "I'm sorry, Jan, but you're paying me to find Tim. Remember Tim? The love of your life?"

She bursts into tears and moves into the bathroom and closes the door. I could swear that a moment ago I had the moral high ground—how did she flip the table so fast? How could I go from feeling good about a really good decision, to feeling like a heel? "It's all about the waterworks, my friend," says my little devil. I look at the door and try to understand the creature behind it. I move back to the kitchen and wait for the grieving live-in, seemingly open-relationship girlfriend to return. When she does, she's composed and firm. She avoids my eyes at first, as if embarrassed. But within a few seconds, she's looking directly at me. With a simple change in her lips, her face seems to move from curious to inviting.

"I'm sorry, Jake. I'm just confused by all of the emotions I'm experiencing. I'm sure you understand."

"I do."

"What's important now is finding Tim," she says. But her eyes seem to imply that Tim may not be the only man on her mind.

11:00 a.m.
"I'd love to play poker with Tim..." Finn

I get in my Jeep and head back to the office. Sarah joins me in my office to hear my report.

"Well, what happened?" Sarah asks.

I hesitate before I reply. While I was driving, I went over the encounter in my mind, trying to make sense of it, but I'm still confused. "She didn't have anything new to share. I went through the house, and the only unusual thing I noticed is that for six months of cohabitation, there is very little Jan there. The decor seems staged, as if someone went to Pottery Barn and created memories of the mall. If she hadn't told me they were living there, I would have never guessed that they were. I would've guessed that the place was a model home used to sell others in a development."

"That's it?"

"No, not entirely." I hesitate; for some reason I'm uncomfortable telling Sarah about the kiss. I know that somehow I'll be held responsible.

"Are you going to tell me the rest?"

I look at Sarah to gauge her response. "Before I begin, I want you to know I'm just relaying facts, not wishes."

"What the hell are you talking about?"

"She came on to me."

Sarah looks at me in silence as she wraps her mind around my disclosure. "What do you mean, she came on to you?"

"She hugged me and kissed me. She didn't say it, but I got the impression that she was willing to do more."

Sarah again looks at me without saying anything. And then: "Bullshit. You're either messing with me or your little devil is messing with you."

"Leave him out of this." I made the mistake of telling Sarah about my mental buddies, and occasionally she has the bad taste of remembering the disclosure.

"Right, I'll bet your little devil told you she digs you, and you jumped all over it."

"It wasn't like that."

"Oh no? Where did she kiss you? On the cheek? And what did you do? Stand there and take it like a man?"

"On the lips...including a little tongue. I pushed her away once I figured out what was happening, but it all hit quickly."

Sarah's look moves from skeptical to disgusted. Maybe the tongue thing was more than I should have shared. "Okay, I believe you. Just no more details." She thinks for a minute and says, "I don't get it. Why is she trying to manipulate you?"

"Whoa, whoa, whoa. Why manipulate? Why can't she just dig me?"

"Jake, she hired you to find the love of her life. She doesn't want you. But it seems to fit a pattern, doesn't it?"

"I don't follow."

"Think about it. She meets Tim, and two months later she moves in with him. She has a dubious past, and now she's hitting on you of all people." She laughs as I rise to her bait. "Just picking on you—chill. But think about it, Jake. What if the Tim thing wasn't real to her? What if she was manipulating Tim, and now she's trying to manipulate you?"

"You think I have something, other than the obvious, that she wants?"

"Exactly."

I think about the timeline, money laundering, Jan and Jamie and Bambi. "I've got an idea." I dial Finn's number.

On the third ring, Delores picks up. She puts me through to Finn.

"What's up, buddy?" he asks.

"Did you ever tell Tim about Jan's Bambi days and, if so, when?"

"I did, about two weeks ago. He was pretty stunned, had no idea. I'd love to play poker with Tim: zero facial control."

"Okay. Thanks." I hang up. "He told Tim two weeks ago, just a few days before he disappeared. What would you do if you were afraid of your girlfriend and weren't ready to go to the cops?"

Sarah looks out the window and thinks for a moment. "Well, if I was really, really frightened, I'd set up a false identity and go hide somewhere. In fact, I might even have one set up before I started investigating with Finn, just in case."

"Right, me too. But that requires money and connections. Tim's an amateur, and it's unlikely he prepared for the worst. Hell, he probably couldn't imagine the worst. If he did try to set something up, there should be a paper trail. That's what I think you look for next. That, and we need to learn more about Jan."

5:58 p.m.
"No man or pets…" Abby

Later that evening I'm back at the warehouse that has been converted into a gym. Only this time I'm taking a jujitsu class, *and* I'm on time. Sarah is among the twenty-five or so people meandering and chatting. I wave at her and simultaneously note that Sarge's evil eye is trained on me.

"Hang on, Sarge—I'm on time. I expect you to act civilized and at least treat me with the respect due a prisoner of war under the Geneva Convention."

"First off, Brandy, you aren't on time until you're dressed and in place. Unless you intend to get your butt kicked in street clothes,

I suggest you change quickly. Second of all, think of this as Gitmo and I'm George W—no conventions and no hand holding."

I shake my head and quickly move to the dressing area to the background music of a group chuckle. I change into my gi and reenter the gym fifty-eight seconds late. Damn, I can feel the abuse coming.

The good news is that one of the newbies is standing next to me. She's attractive, late thirties, with brown hair and dark-brown, mischievous eyes that are looking in my direction. I try to be subtle in my reaction. I don't want the newbie to think I'm easy, and I know that on some level, Sarah is watching me. If I start flirting, I'll not hear the end of it.

"I'm tougher than she makes me seem," I say. "My name's Jake."

"I'm Abby. Nice to meet you, Jake; what's with the colorful nicknames? Are you two related?" she asks.

"Dear Lord, no. Do I look like a repressed and emasculated dwarf to you? Don't answer that."

"Brandy, stop hitting on the young lady—you're supposed to be stretching," I hear from afar. "How about you let Sarah demonstrate today's movements using you as the dummy? We all know how good you are at falling."

Class goes the way class always seems to go; I'm up, I'm down, I'm back up, I'm getting thrown back down. By the end, I feel emotionally and physically bruised, but at least I seem to have a new acquaintance from the ordeal. Sarah, Abby, and I agree to get a dehydrating adult beverage together. We walk a few blocks to Blitz Sports Pub, find seats at the bar, and place our orders.

Blitz is a great place to go when you're sweaty—you fit right in. In fact, it's almost a requirement. The bar is dark, so no one can see if your makeup is just right. Not that I'm wearing makeup, at least not tonight. The waitresses are quick, and the bartenders are generous with their pours. It doesn't always smell that great, but once you have a gin and tonic tipped toward your lips, the smell just becomes part of the charm.

"How long have you two been together?" Abby asks.

"Oh..." Sarah begins.

I jump in. "We're just really good friends.

"And colleagues," Sarah says.

"And temporary roommates," I admit.

Abby's eyes say, "Right, just friends."

Sarah's eyes ask, "Just friends?"

My little angel says, "Oops."

My little devil says, "What a moron."

I gather what wits I have and say, "We've known each other for what, about three years?"

Sarah smiles and says, "Something like that."

"Yep, Sarah moved up here for love and found me."

"You're real funny. Didn't I embarrass you enough in class?"

"Yes, you did." I return to Abby. "She's invaluable to the firm. Having been a cop helps a lot. Over the years she's learned a lot about computer investigation techniques, stalking, undercover, and office decorating. She's a great detective...and an even better friend."

"A cop?" asks Abby. "What enticed you to law enforcement?"

"Oh, I grew up in a rough-and-tumble family. My dad loved to wrestle with my brothers, and being the youngest kid, with two older brothers, I wanted to belong. So I'd jump in, thinking, 'Oh, what fun.' Then I'd get kicked in the stomach. It didn't take me long to learn how take and dish out pain."

Abby seems uncomfortable as Sarah is speaking. Must be my magnetic personality.

"How about you, Abby, who are you?" Sarah asks.

"I'm a pharmaceutical rep."

"Oh, I'd love a pen with Viagra written on it," Sarah says.

Then in a conspiratorial whisper that we can all hear, "Jake's birthday is coming up."

My foot searches for Sarah's shin. "Really, Sarah, pray tell why you would want me to have such an object?"

Before Sarah can reply, Abby jokes, "Sadly, I don't think I have any of those on me."

I can sense Sarah sticking her mental tongue out at me. Sometimes she can be such a sibling. But instead of responding to Sarah, I decide to focus on Abby. Hah, I win again. "Is it your passion, being a rep?"

"No, definitely not. But it can be trying at times. I mean, all I want to do is educate the docs on our products. But there's so many of us, the clinic administrators get tired of seeing us, even with the free pens. It's not a career, just a patch while I figure out what I want to be when I grow up."

"You are definitely not a beginner at jujitsu—did you learn your impressive skills kicking administrator ass?" I ask.

"I've participated in martial arts since I was a kid. My dad wanted a boy. When he saw me, he decided the next best thing was a girl who could punch like a boy."

"You have kids? A man? Pets?" Sarah asks.

"No, none of the above. I moved here from Seattle about three weeks ago. I'm still trying to build up my rolodex."

"Well, welcome to the Northwest chapter's weekly meeting of the Nobody Is Romancing Me Yet Club," I say. "Cheers." We all laugh and clink glasses.

We work our way through another round as the conversation moves comfortably among us. It feels like we've known each other for years as we one-up each other with bad-date stories. Eventually Sarah says goodbye and heads home. I hope I'm the only one who sees her wink at me as she leaves.

"I know what I must look and smell like at the moment, but are you interested in grabbing a bite? They have a good burger and better salads here," I say.

"I'd love to; let me go to the restroom and clean up. I'll meet you at the table."

"Perfect. I've got the tab."

While Abby is gone, I pay the bartender and carry our drinks over to a new table as directed by the server. Not long after I'm seated, Abby returns looking refreshed. She's wearing a designer baseball cap with her hair pulled through it in a thick ponytail. She's reestablished her nominal makeup, including lipstick that makes her lips shimmer. Even after sweating for the past hour, she looks fantastic. I can tell that she smiles often, and now is no exception. I'm mesmerized, which makes me anxious, which ties up my tongue, which makes me a dweeb.

After we place our orders, she asks, "So, what kind of investigations do you do?"

"Pretty standard stuff: wayward spouse, missing money, lost cat."

"Are you busy now? Like, how many cases do you work at the same time?"

"It all depends. We're working two at the moment. One is for the defense in a criminal drug case, and the other is a missing person case. But sometimes we'll have up to five cases, or we can be swamped by one case."

"How do the cases typically play out? For instance, take one of your current cases, like the missing person case. How do you get the case, where do you start, etc., etc.?"

"Cases can come from anywhere, a victim, a victim's attorney. In this case, it's a family member who hired us. We start with an interview of the client and begin searching. Lots of interviews, internet searches, bank record searches, anything that can give us an indication of where to go to next. It's really pretty boring most of the time. But eventually a pattern appears, and you discover strange conflicts, or you get a hunch that takes you in a direction, hopefully the right direction. It's very labor-intensive and, like I said, pretty dull most of the time."

My little angel begins to critique me. "You're putting me to sleep, and I'm you! Tell her about the gun fights, the car chases, all of those cool detective things she sees on TV."

My little devil is surprised. "For once, I agree!"

"So, using this missing person case as an example, what kinds of clues have you found? Where do they lead?"

The waitress delivers our food, and we decline additional drinks.

"Where were we? Oh yeah. Not many clues yet. Most clues are dead ends, but you keep on searching."

"Still, it must get exciting sometimes. You're right—this is a great salad, very fresh. Oh, and this dressing is great."

"I'm glad you like it." We spend several minutes talking about the case, strategy in general, and the boring life of a detective. The entire time I'm watching Abby, searching for flaws. I know that early in a relationship you don't notice the misplaced hair, the wrinkle below her eye or the gambling habit, but I don't care. The closer I look, the better she looks.

"I've never had someone quite so interested in what I do—are you interested in a career change?" I ask.

"No, no, I guess I'm kind of a groupie when it comes to investigation stories. Normally the closest I get to the real thing is a paperback. I like to hear the details, the facts, the deceptions, the discoveries, you name it. It's just my luck that I'm with a true-life PI. Am I bothering you?"

"It's not a bother." I can't help smiling at her. Her brown eyes sparkle and make me feel special. I want to know what she's thinking behind those eyes. Is she thinking, "What a dweeb. I can't wait to get out of here"? Probably not yet—she doesn't know me that well. My little devil nudges me. "Your turn to talk, moron."

"So, changing the subject, on Sunday Sarah and I are going to play bar trivia. It's a popular thing around here. Are you interested in joining us?"

"I'd love to."

"Super, the place is called Brix Tavern on Northwest Hoyt. Sarah and I will be there around five."

"Perfect. I'll see you there," Abby says. "Well, I should get going. Would you mind walking me to my car?"

"Not at all."

"Nice," my angel says.

Abby pays the dinner tab, though I battle valiantly for the privilege. She's parked a block away. I walk her to her bright-blue Lexus IS, we say goodbye, and she drives off.

It's been a long time since I've felt energized by a new acquaintance. I haven't dated since about the time that Sue and I broke up. Some early missteps after the divorce taught me that I was looking for love in all the wrong places. But Abby feels good to me. How do dates work these days? Hell, do they even call them dates? I guess it doesn't matter what it's called—it's all about connecting with someone, for some unidentified time frame, for some to-be-determined level of intensity.

I wander home and find Sarah on the couch showered and relaxing with a book.

"Well, how did it go with Abby?"

"We talked about absolutely nothing, and it seemed pretty entertaining. I invited her to trivia on Sunday."

"Really. Did you think maybe you should check with me before you did that?"

I realize way too late that I've probably crossed another one of those invisible lines. And I know that my next few words are going to go a long way toward determining how relaxed I'll be for the next few hours. "You're right. I should have asked you first." Nailed it!

"Well, too late now. I'm going to bed; see you in the morning."

"Night." On reflection, *nailed it* may have been premature and overconfident.

Friday, March 16

"I agree with him, Craig—I am an ugly lady..." Milt

I'm up and out of the condo early on Friday morning—it's time to make hay. Though I have to admit I've never made hay in my life, unless you count mowing the lawn when I was a kid. But I still say it like I have. I drive out to Milt's island dry cleaner, the Stay Clean. It's Milt's visible means of support, with three locations on the west side of town and its worldwide headquarters located in Beaverton. That's where Milt's office is.

The dry cleaner is a standalone structure in the middle of a parking lot (ergo island). At one end of the parking lot is a much larger building that houses a bowling alley. Milt has a 220 bowling average, which is a good indication of just how taxing the dry-cleaning business can be. Rumor has it that in addition to the dry cleaner, Milt owns the land underlying the parking lot and the bowling alley. Like I said, cash cow.

I walk inside the dry cleaner and instantly catch the aroma of recently pressed and cleaned dress shirts, skirts, trousers, blouses, jackets, and scarfs. I've always liked the soft, warm fabric feel in my nose, but I know it would drive me crazy if I experienced it every moment of every day. Pristine plastic-wrapped clothes hang by hooks from long winding tracks attached to the ceiling. A high school kid, in his Aerosmith T-shirt and faded jeans, is at the counter. His clothes are spendy reproductions of the beat-up, dirty clothes that we wore in the '70s. But to his credit, this youth is hustling to shuffle dirty clothes in and clean clothes out. He finishes with the customer in front of me and pleasantly asks me for my ticket.

"Why, is there a carnival ride in here? Actually, I came to see the bearded lady. Is Milt around?" I ask.

"Milt, you have company, and he called you an ugly lady."

Milt emerges from behind the plastic centipede and smiles. "I agree with him, Craig—I am an ugly lady. Or am I a truly handsome man? Hmmm, you may never know for sure. Come on back, Jake."

Milt is wearing one of the ugliest and dirtiest Hawaiian shirts I've ever seen. The colors look like the shirt lost a bet, and I'm sure Milt was paid by a store to take it off their hands. But even worse, the colors are hard to see under the many and varied stains. There are so many stains that he looks like a walking Picasso chessboard. His shorts are too short, but thankfully they're too baggy as well. And just to make sure no one thinks he's just having a bad style day, he completes the ensemble with an old pair of bright-orange Crocs.

"So, Milt, can't find a good dry cleaner?"

"Funny. These are my work clothes, the ones I wear when I'm servicing a machine."

For all the money that we all think he has, Milt is the fix-it man for the company. I'm sure he's chosen the role as a stress-relieving passion as opposed to a money-saving necessity. And as long as he doesn't go out in public dressed like that to meet me, I couldn't care less.

"Did you get any scoop on the infamous Detective Smith?"

"Yes, I did. You're right about those bad cases," he begins as he fiddles with a press of some sort. "All three of the arrests came in and looked good at first. But something happened inside the station house on each one. A witness's identification went south on one, some evidence walked out of the station on a second, and a confession got thrown out because of a bad Miranda on the third. In all three cases, a different detective was blamed for the mess-up, but all of the cases started with Smith. Smith had access to everything—evidence, notes, witnesses—for all three cases.

"In fact, Smith was the only person with easy access to all of the files. And all of the detectives who got caught with their pants down insist somebody buggered them. There's a suspicion, unproven, that Smith made the cases go away and diverted blame. He's never been popular, but now he's openly disliked."

"So, nothing I can use in a courtroom, but enough that everybody in the know believes it's not a rumor—they think it's the truth."

"Exactly. The word around the precinct is that Smith is getting close to retirement, and he's positioning for a little extra cash. And since he'll be gone from the force soon, he's not too concerned about hurting feelings and reputations on the way out. Stand back—I don't want your heirs suing me if this thing hiccups after I turn it on."

I step away as Milt lowers the upper part of the press and pushes a button. Instantly, I can hear steam being pushed through the apparatus, and everything seems sunny in Milt Land. But just as rapidly, hope drains from Milts face as the gizmo coughs and snaps. By the harsh criticism emitted by Milt, I deduce that it still isn't working properly.

"I can see that you're more than close to this machine—buy her something pretty sometime, would you?"

That snaps him back on track. "What are you going to do about Smith?"

"Me? Nothing, of course. I would never cross swords with a copper. Plus, I don't want you testifying against me…unless you're going to wear that outfit on the stand. Thanks for the info; I'll see you later."

I exit the building to the sound of several colorful insults, or expressions of love, directed by Milt toward his press.

Sunday, March 18

5:00 p.m.
"She probably won't show..." Sarah

Brix Tavern is a great place to meet for cocktails and old-fashioned American comfort food. It's clean, it's close to the condo, and it's filled with people who think they know you well enough to smile at you but not well enough to ask for a loan. Sarah and I have arrived and grabbed our favorite table, smack-dab in the middle of the room.

"She probably won't show. She probably recognized that you're a project. She's too cute to want to work that hard."

"You are brutal. Maybe she's just finishing a fitting for an intensely sexy outfit that she's picked just for me. Didn't think of that one, did you?"

"I've done a study on men, and I've determined that they can't go more than seven minutes without interjecting sex into the conversation." Annoyance is written all over Sarah's face.

"Well, your research is flawed. Sex is in every conversation at all times. But we may not say it out loud for as long as seven minutes. And if you weren't thinking about sex, why did you say *interjecting*? Yeah, got you there."

"Hi, Jake, Sarah—it's good to see you again."

Sarah and I exchange quick looks of differing meanings as we hear Abby's voice. Both Sarah and I get a hug from Abby, though mine lingers a bit longer.

The server arrives with our beers, and Abby orders a gin and tonic.

"Jake, you look awfully dressed up—what's the occasion?"

"It's his standard look: black shoes, dark jeans, white dress shirt, and sport coat. On St. Patrick's Day, he'll add a very old, very beat-up green tie, loosened, of course," Sarah says.

"Okay, I guess it's a '70s Tom Cruise kind of look. Though maybe he's Tom's older brother," Abby says to Sarah.

"No, I think he's more like Tom's dad, inching toward grandpa. Look at the gray on the side. He's trying to hide it, but it's there."

"Hellooo, I'm here, right in front of you. Do you want me to start critiquing your looks?"

They both stare at me. Sarah has a "try it if you think breathing is overrated" look and Abby has a "no guy is that suicidal" expression. I glance at one and then the other.

"He could use a trim. His hair is hanging a bit over the collar. Who does his hair, or does he do that to himself?" Abby asks.

"He doesn't do it himself, but I'm sure whoever he pays to do it reads Braille instructions while he's cutting," Sarah says.

"So, Abby, you look radiant tonight. I love the powder-blue blouse. Very lovely," I say.

"Why, thank you, Jake." She turns and looks at Sarah. "He knows powder-blue from blue?"

Thankfully I'm saved by the start of the trivia contest. In between questions, we get to know each other better. Abby laughs at all of my jokes, for obvious reasons, and Sarah seems relaxed and entertained, at least on the surface. As well as I know her, I recognize scrutiny when I see it. Sarah is evaluating Abby.

We share where we went to school, where we grew up. We talk about family and jobs and all the mundane stuff that takes time to share, and is important, but is actually just an easy way to coax a conversation along. Eventually we make it to the sillier stuff, like, what movie best represents who we are. I tell them that my movie is *Gladiator*. Sarah scoffs and says I'm wrong; that it's *Get Smart*.

"Does that make you Agent 99?" Abby asks Sarah.

Sarah looks at me and says, "Oh Max, you're so needy." She and Abby laugh in harmony with my little angel and devil.

The next trivia question is "According to a recent survey, the most commonly preferred sexual position in America is..."

I look at Abby, and she blushes. "Separate beds was mine and my ex-wife's," I say.

Abby laughs, and Sarah just shakes her head.

"Sorry, Jake," Abby says, "that's not an acceptable answer, but it does remind me that it's time to head home. To bed. But just to sleep. I have a big day at the office tomorrow. Sarah, it's been so good to see you." She and I stand. She hugs me and kisses me on the cheek and says goodbye softly.

I watch her walk away and smile to myself. I turn back to Sarah, who has a look of concern. I push my warm feelings about Abby away and ask Sarah, "Okay, what's wrong? I sense you don't approve of Abby."

"It isn't my place to approve or disapprove. I just know I'm going to be cleaning up the pieces in about six months."

"Pieces of what? Do you plan on breaking something?"

"I'm not breaking anything—she will. She doesn't feel right, Jake; go slow is my advice. But I can see you're already out over your ski tips. You're going to fall a long ways and land hard."

"You sound like I'm ready to marry her."

"Not marry—mate."

"Oh, please, how many guys have you been with, and I helped you through the pain."

"I'm not saying I won't help. I just want you to know how I feel now so I can rub it in later."

Monday, March 19

"I will disavow you and your team…" Pete

I call Pete and suggest that we get together to review the Jankowitz file. He tells me to come on over. He's not busy and needs somebody to bill. Traffic is light, and I have the top down and my sunglasses on. I also have the heater going full blast and a coat on, since it's forty-five degrees out. I am bound and determined to live the life of perpetual summer, even in March.

Once I'm in Pete's suite, JJ waives me to a chair in the reception area while Pete finishes up a phone call. "I hear you were the winner at poker. Peter says you cheated, that you were counting cards or had special contact lenses or some other equally absurd claim. I told him he was wrong, that even a blind PI can find a clue once in a while." JJ chortles.

"It's true I was the big winner. I was going to buy you some roses because I appreciate your warm personality. But Pete told me not to waste my time, that you don't respect men who bear gifts."

"He did, did he, that scoundrel. I think I'll have to punish him. Maybe I'll misfile a few documents, see if that gets his attention."

"You would utterly destroy him. He seems to be pretty anal about that kind of stuff," I say as Pete comes out of his office.

"What did I miss? Was she telling you about my amazing round of golf?" Peter asks.

"No, she was telling me that she's planning on hiding a few files to see how long it takes you to find them."

"JJ, whatever I did, I'm sorry. Could you hold my calls? Please."

We walk into his office. I sit as Pete moves around his desk, pulls out a file, and starts to thumb through some pages.

"So, what do you have? I hope it's good—I'm beginning to get anxious." It shows on his face. Pete really, really doesn't like to lose.

"I spoke to Milt, and it's clear that Smith is playing games. He got three Southside cases dismissed and shifted the blame for the failed police work onto three other officers. He's becoming an unwashed at the station as he's closing in on retirement. People think he's feathering his financial nest and not worried about having any friends left when he rides off into the sunset.

"We don't have anything that we can directly use, can't get IAB after him. Nobody is willing to or capable of pressing charges. But it's clear that he's tied to Southside. I think we can set him up. And the setup only need be halfway believable. He's burned so many bridges, the force probably won't work very hard to stop him from falling. We just need to give him a little push."

"Jankowitz's next hearing is in three weeks," Pete begins. "Right now I can't find any way to defeat the charges. There's been no technical violation by the police, and he's a known dealer, even if this product wasn't his normal drug of choice. We can't exactly say, 'Hey, Judge, this wasn't his blow. He doesn't deal in blow, only marijuana, and he never keeps product at his house.' And I can't slow the process. Unless you make something happen, Alvin is going away. Oh, and I don't want to know what you're going to do. What you do with your free time is up to you. If you're captured, I will disavow you and your team. I've always wanted to say that."

"I don't have it completely worked out, but I have an idea that should bounce the charges. I'll set it up and let you know after we pull the trigger. The idea is to get Smith so tarnished that all of his cases are thrown out."

"I'm sorry, what were you saying? I was focusing on my computer. What was that?"

"Exactly—we never had this conversation."

Wednesday, March 21

After another round of jujitsu, Abby and I head to the Blitz, this time without Sarah. This will be our first time that starts and ends with us alone. I hope she doesn't think I'm a hussy.

"Sally Jean worked us pretty good today," Abby says as she collapses into a chair. "But that's okay. I definitely needed to burn off some emotional energy: my parents are going to be in town in a couple of weeks. Do you have any suggestions on how I can distract them from talking grandkids and careers?" Abby asks.

"Food is always good. Takes time to get to the restaurant and eat, and old people fall asleep as soon as they're finished. There are great restaurants all over. In Northwest, my favorites are Andina, Blue Hour, and Irving Street Kitchen. In Southeast, I'd look hard at Le Pigeon. Do you need more ideas?"

"I need to write those down and check them out," Abby says.

"I could help with your research—maybe we could scout one together."

"I'd love that. You pick one, and I'll pick the night?"

"Okay, I pick Irving Street Kitchen."

"Good, I pick this Friday. Does that work for you?"

"I'll make it work. If you'd like, I'll pick you up. Never know what the weather has in store."

"Awesome. I'll get my address to you. What are your plans the next couple of days? All work or some play involved?" Abby asks.

"Just work."

"Right, I think last time we talked about work, you were looking for a lost soul."

"Still working that case; we have a few leads."

"Really, like what?"

"Well, I can't talk specifics about an open case. I could charm you with a past case or two," I say.

"Sure, pick one with lots of romance."

I proceed to share the best stories I have. They involve weapons and thieves and police and sex and fights and lawyers and jail time. Abby seems to be truly interested, and the evening moves quickly. Eventually it is time to walk her to her car.

"Goodnight, Jake. I enjoyed our time." She moves closer, and I receive a kiss on the lips. Her lips are soft and a bit salty. Our eyes remain open, each of us watching the other. Part of the ritual, I suppose. We're doing that dance of trying to figure out how far we can trust each other; how far we want to go with each other. Every day we have a vote, yes or no. Tonight, for me, it is a big hell yeah.

Friday, March 23

6:00 a.m.

"What the hell do you think you're doing, you rodent..." Smith

I'm up early Friday morning and staking out Smith's house. But not in my Jeep—he knows that vehicle. Instead, I'm in Sarah's Honda. It blends in with the inner Northeast neighborhood that Smith inhabits. He's living in a seventy-year-old bungalow that was a beautiful home in its time and will be again once Smith moves out and a young family with a soul moves in. The place is quiet, and his Caddy is in the drive. I relax in Sarah's car with my coffee, listening to Emeli Sandé on the radio and watching the early-morning stretch of the neighborhood.

I watch a pickup truck with a kid in back slinging newspapers. Joggers begin to run past; guys in pajama bottoms dressed up with tennis shoes start walking their dogs. I think you can tell a lot by the type of dog a guy is walking; a guy with a German shepherd wants people to back off, a guy with a collie has at least three kids, a guy with a tiny dog has no kids and a wife who wants kids, and a guy with a poodle should be shot.

After about four hours, at 10:00 a.m. (he's definitely a government employee), the charmer himself comes out of the house. And, lo and behold, he's accompanied by a very young, very beautiful lady. By the way he's grabbing her ass, she's not his relative, or he's sicker than I thought. I start snapping pictures for my scrapbook. She must be a pro, or she's trying to poison herself on Old Spice aftershave.

After Smith retrieves his tongue from her trachea, they break their love grip. Smith heads to his car, and she heads to a hot little Mercedes parked along the curb. She's wearing a short skirt and a tight blouse, neither of which leaves much to the imagination. Her heels are taller than some buildings, and her walk is entrancing. She has the relaxed gait of a cat that just has finished off a meal.

I decide I have more to gain by following the sweet little number than by following Smith. My little devil agrees; my little angel tsk-tsks. Smith gets into his Caddy, and luckily he's headed in the opposite direction down the street from where I'm parked. The young lass fires up the Mercedes and rolls right past me. I duck down low so she can't see me. When I come up, one of the pajama-clad zombies is on the sidewalk staring at me. His eyes are saying that he thinks I'm some sort of weirdo. My eyes tell him to buy a mirror.

Smith's sweetheart heads through Laurelhurst. I manage to stay back about fifty yards. I doubt she's worried about a tail or capable of even seeing one, but it never hurts to be careful. She gets on I-84 and heads straight downtown. After a couple of turns, she pulls into the parking garage of a newer high-rise office building. I follow her into the lot, park a few spots away, and follow her toward the elevator.

This is one of those buildings with elevators that link just the lobby and the garage, with separate elevators for service from the lobby to the upper floors. I manage to get onto the same elevator that Smith's dental hygienist is on, and we quietly share the short ride from the garage to the lobby. When we reach the lobby, we exit the elevator, and I see security. Judging by his look, the security guard is a sixty-something former cop. He warmly smiles to the young lady and nods a hello to me. She heads around a corner to the bank of elevators that rise to floors thirteen through twenty-seven. Just as I'm about to nonchalantly follow her onto the elevator, I get smacked on the back of the head and am nearly knocked to the ground.

"What the hell do you think you're doing, you rodent?" Smith asks.

"Jesus, Smith that was not very neighborly." I try to recover quickly from Smith's out-of-thin-air assault. "I'm exercising my civil liberties. You want me to bring charges?"

"Go for it, rat dung—there aren't any witnesses that are going to save your sorry ass."

Smith swings hard at my head. By going for broke, he gives me time to shift out of his target zone and nail him with a punch to the belly. My fist sinks through several layers of fat and causes him to bend at the waist and struggle for a breath. I grab him by the collar and slam his face against a wall.

"Thanks for reminding me about the no-witness thing," I say to him. "I agree that communication is a little freer flowing without pesky police authority, you piece of shit. And you can take this to the bank: you sucker punch me ever again, and you won't get up."

"That sounds like a threat. I could haul you in for that, stupid."

"If you could, you already would've. Since we're having this dance, what's up with your lady friend?"

"That's none of your business," he manages to grunt. "You better stay away from me. Next time I catch you casing my home or tracking me or my guests, you'll be running from a swat team. Let go of me." I let him shake free.

"Just remember what I told you about sucker punches, you toilet filth." I don't move out of his way so that he has to push through me to get clear. As he walks away, he's still trying to catch his breath. I put a lot of emotional energy behind that punch. After he clears the front doors, I start checking out the building company listings. Nothing interesting strikes my eye until I hit the Hs. HB & Associates is on the twenty-seventh floor. Why does that ring a bell? I finish the list but don't feel any more warm fuzzies.

I decide to pay HB & Ass a call. I get on the elevator and push the button for floor twenty-seven, but nothing happens. I try it a second time, same result. Then I notice a little slit made for a key card. It looks like they have some security concerns at HB & Ass.

I exit the elevator and wander back around to the security desk. I turn on the Brand charm. The guard adds to his multitasking, now splitting his vision between an old paperback, the camera monitors, and me. I know he must have heard the scuffle I had with Smith. "Do you know that guy I was just with?"

"Who's asking?" he asks.

"Benjamin," I say as I slide a $100 bill toward him.

"He's a regular. I don't know if he's security or a john. But he moves in and out of the twenty-seventh floor all the time."

"Why a john?" I ask.

"'Cause that's the only explanation for all the hotties who move up and down that elevator. It's got to be an escort service."

And then it hits me: HB equals Honey Bunnies. "So how do I get up there to check out their wares?"

"Beats me," he says. "You have to have special permission or a card. They don't even have a number so I can call up for drop-ins like you. They're for sure exclusively an outbound service."

"Thanks; you mind if I leave my card? I wouldn't mind knowing if that cop or john, whatever he is, comes back. Or if something unusual happens, I'd like to know." I hand him my card, and he puts it in a pocket unread. "Oh, and do you recognize this sweetheart?" I pull up a picture of Jan Center on my phone and hold it out to the old dog.

"Sure, she's been through here a couple of times. She's not one of the friendlier ones. If she sees me looking at her, she gives me a death stare. You know, like Maude from that old TV series."

"That sounds nasty. And info equals cash in my world. Don't be a stranger."

6:58 p.m.
"You are awfully kind and a bit attractive yourself..." Abby

I make it to Abby's place with two minutes to spare. My time with Copper Smith stretched my day to the last minute. I visited Pete and gave him a quick update on Jankowitz and the deformed and mental Copper Smith. From Pete's office, I headed to my own and took care of a million details, composed mostly of short phone calls and quick document reviews. I scrambled to get out, but Jessica is already having an impact. She wouldn't allow me to leave until I finished my paperwork. She reminds me of a combo drill sergeant/anally retentive accountant. She has her list of what needs to be completed and when, and noncompliance is not tolerated. And for some reason she doesn't trust me to complete the tasks she's assigned to me; she hovers over me until I'm done. It's as if she thinks I have sheets hidden away in a desk drawer that I'll tie together and use to escape through my window. "You totally would, you know," says my little angel. By the time I reached my condo, I had just enough time to shower, change, and make a quick stop at the store.

I ring the bell, and after a few seconds, the door opens, and Abby doesn't disappoint. She stands framed in the doorway in a red dress, cut low at the neck and high above the knees. It's styled to emphasize her curves, and the red draws from the brown of her eyes and hair. But her attire is lost in the radiance of her smile. "Did you just think those words?" asks my little devil. Damn, she's smoking hot when she cleans up, unlike when she's a little sweaty and in workout wear and is smoking hot. I find myself imagining when she might not look hot, and I'm coming up empty. But I know better than to let her know my feelings because it will just go to her head, and I'll have to work twice as hard to get that next kiss.

"Wow, I am going to be the envy of the city," I say as I hand her a bouquet of flowers.

"You are awfully kind and a bit attractive yourself. Do we have time for a glass of wine before we go?"

"Actually, our reservation is upon us, and the restaurant is nearby—we should probably head out."

She grabs a purse and shawl and locks the door. I hold her hand as we walk down the steps. I'd hate for her to fall off her six-inch heels. I help her into my car. My Jeep requires a big first step to get in. So I find myself trapped in a dilemma: do I push her on the derriere to help her get in, or do I let her struggle while her dress rides up her thighs? After a brief sidebar with my devil, I go with option A. I press her shapely behind ("No squeezing," says my angel) to help her up into the car while apologizing.

"I appreciate the push." She smiles back at me. "But I am glad I wore underwear—how about you?"

"Yes, I am wearing underwear, and I have mixed feelings about your wearing them."

She laughs as I walk jauntily around the front of the car.

"Did you successfully push some drugs today? I imagine you did if you wore that outfit. Who could resist?" I ask.

"If it were all about the outfit, I'd wear it every day. How about you? Take any dirty pictures of cheating spouses? Or find buried treasure?" she asks.

"Oh, in a way I suppose I did. I got to punch a cop, and I'm not in jail—can't have a much better day than that."

"How do you punch a cop and walk away?"

"You aim your fist at his fat belly. After that, he's focused on breathing rather than arresting. Here we are," I say, "Irving Street Kitchen. I love this place. Everything is awesome. Of course, I'm not doing a very good job of managing your expectations. And I'm not giving you much wiggle room if you don't like it. I'm just being honest. You can be honest with me about everything—I can handle it." I stare into her eyes, and I sense a twinkle.

"Don't worry, Jake. I'll be brutally honest about the cuisine, service, ambience, and company." Yes, there's definitely a twinkle.

We park, and I help her out of the car, averting my eyes as she grabs the hem of her dress to keep it from sliding up as she slides out. We walk into the restaurant and are instantly awash in the aromas of spices and sauces, simmering meat, sautéed onions, and garlic. We're surrounded by soft music, the clinking of plates and silverware, and the whispers of dirty nothings among the patrons.

At least that's what I smell and hear.

The interior is industrial: exposed steel girders, wood rafters, pipes, and vents left over from the building's warehouse days. The dining area is separated into two spaces by a massive bar that seats forty. I've reserved a booth with twelve-foot curtains that can be closed for greater privacy. The tables are covered in brown butcher paper and are accented with fresh flowers and mason jars containing candles. A young waiter dressed in casual but stylish clothes presents us with menus.

"Everything is on the menu, no specials. My favorite is the bourbon-soaked chinook salmon. Could I interest you in something to drink? Wine? Cocktail?" the server asks.

I look at Abby, who is pretty in any light but stunning in the warmth of the candle. "Abby, would you like some wine?" I ask.

"Why, yes, fine sir, pick whatever you like."

I glance through the list. "Could we have a bottle of the Terrasse du Diable?"

"Very nice, sir, I'll have it to you in a moment." Off he goes.

"Abby, I was recently thinking of a major oversight: I don't know your last name."

"Dicer, like someone who cuts food into tiny little pieces."

"It's a pleasure to make your acquaintance, Ms. Dicer."

"The pleasure is all mine, Mr. Brand." We shake hands, holding on to each other just a moment longer than a normal handshake.

The sommelier arrives with our wine, opens the bottle, allows me to sniff the cork and Abby to first swirl and then sip a small pour. We both approve; the woman pours and leaves.

"Cheers to you, Abby. What do you think so far? Do you approve?"

145

She looks at me with her liquid-brown eyes, and time seems to slow.

"Approve of what? The restaurant, the wine, or you?" my little angel asks. My little devil smirks. I feel myself blush as I realize the question could be misinterpreted. But I don't rush to clarify; I want to stay inside the moment.

"Hmm, very nice," she says. "And the wine is great—nice choice, Jake. Are you a wine connoisseur?"

"I could be if I had the cash. Right now I hunt for great pours under $20 per bottle. Every now and then I splurge and go for that spendy-trendy choice. There's a local grocery store that has massive sales twice a year. When they do, I stock up. I have several cases at home. But I can't hold it very long because I don't have the right temperature controls. How about you? Are you a wine aficionado?"

"I've spent enough time in Napa and Sonoma to be excited by the experience, but I'm not ready to invest heavily in a collection."

The waiter delivers bread and olive oil. We each order a meal and sip our wine.

"What do you do when you're not fighting bad guys or sniffing corks?" she asks.

"I like music, any kind of music as long as it's done well. I love going to concerts in the park. It's my kind of camping. A few friends, lawn chairs, blankets, ice chests, beautiful weather, and engaging performers. You should join me sometime. The performances begin in July."

"I'd love to. Where are they held?"

"All over, my favorites are in Lake Oswego. How about you? What do you do when time and money aren't limiters?"

"I travel a lot—mostly for business, but I always try to tack on some personal time—and I love music...Most recently I spent some time in New Orleans. There are incredible sounds all over that town. And most of the time it just seems to happen spontaneously."

"I've always wanted to go to New Orleans—it sounds exotic compared to everywhere else in the US. Did you like it?"

"I loved it, one of my favorite places in the world. Not only amazing music, the food is delicious and the people entertaining. You need to go while you can still handle the calories."

The conversation moves on. Slowly we open up our worlds, learning to trust a little bit more. But we haven't begun to share our flaws. Those can wait until later. This is the honeymoon portion of dating. If you can't be excited about someone early on, then it's time to move on. And speaking for me, I'm excited.

The food comes and is everything I thought it would be. Abby is genuinely impressed. At least she isn't a picky eater. She finishes her main course and accepts bites of mine. Dessert is amazing—we split a slice of pecan pie with ice cream and peach slices.

I pay the bill, and as we're about to walk out, an attractive couple walks in. I look at the woman and do a double take. Dressed very elegantly, with a nice hairdo and well-engineered makeup, is our very own Sarge. This is the first time that I've ever seen her dressed in anything but tights. It's also the first time I've ever seen her look relaxed or happy, let alone both at once.

As I stare in total confusion, she smiles at me and says, "Hi, Jake; hi, Abby. This is my friend Mike."

I extend my hand to Mike. Mine is an unfocused shake as I try to wrap my mind around her friendly tone. I even notice her use of my actual name. "Sar—" I start to say when I get a modest elbow in the ribs from Abby. What is it with women and elbows?

"Sally Jean, it's so good to see you," she begins. "And, Mike, it's a pleasure to meet you. We've just finished, and it was fantastic. I envy you just starting on your meal."

The whole time Abby speaks, Sarge is staring at me with a smile on her lips, but her eyes project pain, my pain.

"Yes, Sally Jean, you look lovely tonight," I say.

"Sal, excuse me for a moment. Jake and Abby, would you mind keeping Sal company while I hang up her coat?"

"No worries, Mike." After I watch him leave, I turn toward Sarge and ask, "Sal? Did he just call you Sal and live?"

"Listen to me, Brandy," she whispers up close to my ear with the intensity of a hurricane. "I'll be nice to you when there are normal people around. But if you make any smart-mouth comments in front of Mike, I'll demonstrate a new self-defense move I've perfected. You'll be flat on the floor before you know you're falling."

Before I have a chance to cower from Sarge, she switches back to Sal. My head is spinning. Then Mike is at my side; sweet Jesus, Mike, don't leave again.

"Our table is ready. So good to meet the two of you—have a great evening," Mike says.

With that, Abby and I continue out to the street. I'm trying to figure out what just happened, and Abby is laughing uncontrollably.

As we drive, Abby brings up work. "So, Jake, any luck finding your lost boyfriend?"

All of a sudden, I'm feeling uncomfortable. Something isn't right, and I can't put my finger on it. I look in my rear and side mirrors, but I don't see a tail.

"Are you okay? You look strange, like you saw a ghost."

"I'm fine, just a strange feeling. I get them from years of being chased and targeted. Sometimes the wires get crossed. Where were we? Oh yeah, the missing person case. Nothing new on that front. I'm sure something will pop up soon."

And then it dawns on me. I don't remember telling her there was a missing boyfriend. I'm pretty sure I always said missing *person*. Suppose I'm right? Maybe it's not a coincidence that she is always going back to the case.

I'm about to say something to her when my little devil pops up: "Dude, even if she's playing you, enjoy the ride for a while." I glance over at Abby. She's still stunning. My little devil's right—I need to relax and not overanalyze. I need to let my subconscious turn this one over a few times.

All of these thoughts happen in a heartbeat. I file them away to dissect in the future when she isn't watching, and probably evaluating, me. But I know that the tone of the evening has changed for me. I think it's time to pay more attention to her in a professional way.

We arrive at her place, and I help her back out of the car. As we walk to her steps, she says, "I had a fantastic evening. I hope we get to do this again, and next time it's my treat. In fact, if you're interested, how about coming to my place tomorrow night and I fix dinner for you?"

"Unfortunately, I'm busy…Oh, wait, my phone is buzzing." I pull my inert phone out of my coat pocket and mock answer it. "Hmm, it seems my date for tomorrow night just canceled; I guess I'm available after all." As I look up from replacing my phone in my coat, Abby leans into me. Her soft lips press against mine. Her warm breath and sweet aroma heats me to my core, as her hand gently holds the back of my neck. The kiss lasts for a few seconds, and I don't want it to end, but it does.

"Seven tomorrow," she says, "and don't be late. I time the food to a regimented serving pace, and if you're late, you don't get to join the party. Thank you again, Jake." A quick smile full of future promise and she disappears into the building.

I watch the door for several seconds after it closes behind her. I look at the empty space that was Abby Dicer and realize I am in trouble. I really, really like this woman, and I'm not sure I can trust her.

Saturday, March 24

The next morning my first stop is at Finn's technorama. As before, I parallel park on the street directly across the sidewalk from Byte Me. I walk into the dark interior and see Delores sleeping in her chair. I walk back to the door, open it, and close it a bit louder to wake her. She jumps, looks around, sees me, and says, "Oh, you. Finn," she shouts, "the broke PI is here again." Her stare dares me to say something, anything. But I'm not stupid—I know how calls get dropped and papers go missing when you piss off the receptionist/secretary/old bat. I smile, tip my imaginary cap, and silently walk back toward Finn's office.

Finn waves me to a chair while staring at his wall of screens. Finally, he ceases his staccato typing and turns and smiles. "Howdy, buddy, what's shaking?"

"You're awfully chirpy."

"I've found a bit of info on the companies that Tim identified. Starting at different points in the past ten years, each company's gross revenues increased, but profit margins decreased. I don't know what it means, but I can at least identify which of the companies we should be concerned about. Does that mean anything to you?"

"Actually, it does. When criminal types come into large amounts of cash, they want to clean it, or launder it. Otherwise, it's tough to spend, and they always have to worry about the cops trying to take it away. So they set up, buy, or steal a company and start flushing cash through it. For example, the bad guys transfer $100 to a company they control and make it look like a regular business transaction. Then the company pays $90 back out to the bad guys as if they were working for the company. If the cops ask the bad guys where they got the money, they point to the company and say that they were paid for performing services. It makes it way harder for the cops to prove that the money came from illegal activities.

"On the company side, it received $100 and paid out $90, leaving it with a $10 profit, which is a profit margin of 10 percent. So if the company had a gross margin of 40 percent before the laundering began, and it doubles gross revenue with dirty cash that has a gross margin of 10 percent, the gross margin shrinks to a blended 25 percent."

Finn and I work together to calculate how much money is being laundered. Eventually we agree it's a big number.

"Holy crap, potentially $400 million of bad cash that went through these companies just last year." He types away for a few more seconds. "The year before, laundered money was in the neighborhood of $200 million. Can crime be that profitable?" Finn asks.

"Oh yeah, people are willing to spend a lot on sex and drugs. But I'm amazed at how much money is going through this single setup. It's monstrous."

"That is a crazy amount of moola," Finn says.

I return to my seat and let the info percolate. Things are starting to move in my mind. It dawns on me that big money typically comes with big bad guys with big guns and even bigger personality disorders. I start to think defensively. When you stumble into this kind of mess, a mistake means a machine gun–toting masked goon appearing at your doorstep at any moment. The problem is most people react too late and leave themselves and their friends exposed too long. I'm not going to make that mistake.

"Finn, this just got very dangerous. Do you have a way of disappearing but staying in contact with me?"

"Sure," he says, as though he gets asked to do this all the time. I suspect he's just excited to live out an episode of his favorite TV

show. "I'll just fire up the private jet and fly to my condo in Hawaii."
He looks at me like he thinks I'm joking with him.

"I'm not kidding. You need to get hidden. It may be nothing, but
if I'm right, it could be dangerous."

"Jesus, buddy, you're serious. Yeah, yeah, I can get moving. I'll
set up a website for us to bounce messages through. I guess I can
head to another space that I use for storage for a while. I'll write
down the address. All my computer information gets backed up
there already. I can set up some protocols so we can stay in touch.
Should I go get stuff from my house?"

"No, stay clear of your house and don't use your phone. I'll get
in touch with you once I have a better feel for what's happening."

"When do you want me to go underground?"

"Yesterday. After you and I met the other day, I saw a suspicious
car outside your office. Either I was followed or someone was already watching you. If I were a betting man, I'd say they were feds.
Bad guys drive way nicer cars. But if feds are watching you, so are
the baddies. Get Delores out of town with enough cash to lay low
for a month. I'll front the cash."

"Okay, okay, let me think for a minute. I'll need ten minutes to
blow this place up." Finn sees the concern on my face as I visualize
the explosion. "Jesus, buddy, I'm not literally going to blow it up,
just wipe all the equipment so nobody can pull any info on us or
our actions from here."

"I have another background search I need you to do while you're
hiding out." I give Finn Abby's vitals and as much of her background as I can remember.

Once we're all ready to leave, I check the street and don't see
any strange vehicles or pedestrians. Delores makes it to her car
and drives away. To be safe, I follow Finn for a while, checking for
tails. Not seeing any, I head for a massage.

2:00 p.m.

"I don't have time to go inside, you prick…" Muscleman

With Finn out of harm's way, I figure I might as well get back on Smith's tail.

I hate surveillance. Anytime someone says they want to be a PI, I say, "Oh yeah? I got one test. You pass, and you've got a shot. You follow your best buddy around for fourteen hours per day for seven days. Take copious notes and pictures, survive on cold cuts and coffee, identify restroom strategies, don't get caught, and don't fall asleep. Then come back here and report your findings to me." To date, either no one's been stupid enough to try or they have tried and failed.

The real secret to spying is timing your efforts to the probable times that the target is misbehaving. It doesn't take long to figure out patterns. Once you know those, you can reduce your hours significantly and still get the job done.

It's a lot different when you're spying on a cop. Especially when you know he is watching for you. It helps if the cop's dumb or lazy. This is my lucky day since Smith is both. I've spent twentyish hours over the past few days keeping an eye on the pudgy goof. In addition to learning about his Honey Bunny lady friend, I've discovered that he likes to take an afternoon siesta at a downtown massage parlor.

I park outside the establishment, and I know by the presence of his Caddy that he's inside. I'm trying to decide whether or not I should go in and rub some oil on his back. Then I get lucky—incredibly lucky. Smith comes out through the front doorway just as one of the Southside musclemen Chucky fingered is walking in. Because I'm a super-lazy spy, I pull out my combo scope camera and directional mic. I train the sight on the two pals, hit record, and start snapping pics. I want to record the conversation for Smith's going-away party.

"You're late," Smith grunts.

"Easy, cowboy, I thought dirty cops had all the time in the world." Muscleman snickers.

"Watch your mouth, or maybe that evidence will resurface and you'll be doing a nickel at the fed pajama party. You tell Simpton that I'm not putting up with this shit. Let's go inside and finish this," Smith rages.

"Wrong. Here." Muscleman extends an envelope to Smith. "I don't have time to go inside, you prick."

"Put that away and get inside, whale dung."

"You have three choices: take it, pick it up off the ground, or get it surgically removed from your rectum. I don't really care." At which point the muscleman pushes the envelope and his fist into Smith's gut, causing Smith to bend over, grunt, and take the envelope. It looks like all of us tough guys see the same weak spot in Smith.

"Simpton's my next call, Borg. You want protection? You gotta treat me with respect and in private like was agreed."

By the looks on their faces, it seems to me that they've agreed to disagree. A few seconds of stares and barely audible growls and they head their separate directions, dripping trails of testosterone in their wakes.

I'm thinking I'd like to know more about the muscleman, so I let Smith scurry away, and I follow Borg. Borg pulls out of a lot in a newer black GM Denali. The muscle business must be profitable. I follow him for about fifteen minutes and pass him as he pulls into a gated yard on Council Crest. The muscle business doesn't pay this good.

I park up the street and call Sarah. I give her the address and ask for info. In ten minutes she tells me the place is owned by Russell Simpton. He paid two mil cash at the bottom of the market for the place that just accepted Borg into its kind embrace. Simpton has his fingers in a bunch of businesses, and she reads a list to me. Never been arrested, lots of cash.

"Do me a favor. Send all of this to Finn to see if he can scrounge up some more info." I give her Finn's new email account, she says okay, and I sit.

Forty-five minutes later, Finn calls me. "Bingo, buddy, you hit the mother lode. That's definitely your man."

Now I'm confused. "What do you mean? I'm not looking to get married to the dude, no matter how much cash he has."

"I mean, this has got to be the guy Tim was after."

"Tim who?" And then it dawns on me. "Tim Larson? You think this guy's tied to Tim Larson? Why do you think that?"

"He has to be. Most of the companies that Sarah named, plus a few more I matched up, are on Tim's list. I bet they all are. Jake? Jake, are you still there?"

I know Finn is out there talking to someone, probably me, but I'm frozen and in need of a reboot. Smith is tied to Southside, which is now linked to Simpton, who is tied to the companies that Tim was studying. And Smith and Jan are tied to Honey Bunnies. I'm not sure who my client is anymore. No, that's not true: I'm pretty sure I'm representing me.

After Finn finishes, I call Sarah.

"What's up, boss?"

"Plan G starts now. Notify Jessica," is all I say. G is for Go Now. She's to head to a rendezvous spot using an envelope of cash that is stored in her desk along with a burner phone.

"Really? Now? Okay," she says in an annoyed voice and hangs up.

I've tested her before. Knowing me, she assumes this is another test.

About that time, a car comes rolling out of the gate, a limo all blacked out. It heads back the way I came from. With several guards along the perimeter of the property, I decide it's not safe to flip around and follow them. So I start my car and casually head the opposite direction, toward the office.

I scramble to get to the office as quickly as possible. But it seems that the universe is testing my patience. Every driver in the country who religiously drives at or below the speed limit is in front of me as I wind around and through and over and under to the office. I park the Jeep, jump out, and rush up the stairs. I open the door to the office, and I see Sarah, along with a dapper gentleman and two obvious federal agent muscles.

"Ah, there he is. Mr. Brand, I was just chitchatting with your lovely assistant...Sarah, is it?" asks the dapper one.

Sarah nods. She's clearly uncomfortable with four armed men in the room staring at her. I thought she was mentally tougher than that. Of course, I wouldn't want to look into a mirror at the moment and see what she's seeing. Why is she still here? I don't see Jessica, though—at least she isn't on the shooting range with us.

Mr. Dapper is eyeballing me in unison with the muscle clones. All three are armed, and all three seem amused by my surprise and obvious discomfort. But the most shocking thing that I notice is that Mr. Dapper is wearing a three-piece suit with darts in the pants. "That is so '90s," says my little angel.

"I'd ask if you were looking for some investigative assistance, but it looks like you brought an entire police force with you. Are you expecting some shenanigans?" I ask.

"It's my experience that you just never know when or what trouble might pop up. Having associates who can calm the agitated among us tends to forestall problems. Wouldn't you agree? I'm sure you do. But let's jump ahead, Mr. Brand. I was wondering if you could spare a few moments of your time. I have some very important items to discuss with you. Just a few questions and we'll be on our way." Mr. Dapper's lips smile at me while his eyes chew a hole in my face.

I shift my gaze from his sly grin to clones one and two. They have yet to move any part of their bodies but their eyeballs, which roam around the room like two pairs of marbles on an uneven surface. I'm confident that they won't hesitate to bash me if I reach too quickly in the wrong direction.

"I just happen to have an opening in my calendar, Mr....I'm sorry, I didn't catch your name."

"De Cola, Agent Frank De Cola. Would you like to see my badge? I would, if I were you."

"That would be awfully kind," I say as he hands it to me. I look it over and see that it says exactly what he just said plus, in some caps, *Department of the TREASURY— US.* "Come on in, Agent De Cola. I'm afraid there isn't enough room for your associates. They'll have to wait out here."

"No problem. I'm sure they'll be happy to keep Sarah company."

"Actually, Sarah, did you get that file on Jenkins yet? You know I need it ASAP."

"I was just leaving when the gentlemen arrived. I'll go now and be back in a jiff."

"It's so nice to meet you, Sarah. You are such an obvious asset to Mr. Brand," De Cola says as he holds Sarah's hand between his two. I can tell she feels slimed, and I feel like I'm watching a really bad horror flick.

Sarah leaves, and I let out a huge but secret sigh of relief as De Cola and I walk into my office. We sit, and he smiles at me. His face never wavers; I'm sure he's waiting for my confession, any confession. He just wants justification for his contempt of me. But I've been through enough interrogations in my life to know that he's trying to intimidate me. He wants to get me talking first and hang myself. I simply stare right back into his beady eyeballs. Blink, bastard.

Finally:

"Mr. Brand"—yes, I win—"may I call you Jake?"

"Jake works, Frank. Mind if I smoke?" I don't wait for him to respond as I light up and set the cigarette in my ashtray. At the moment I desperately want to keep the cigarette between my lips and suck hard. But I'm a true believer in modern medicine. Not to mention the commercials that show people smoking out of a hole in their throat.

"You know, Jake, cigarettes can be very hazardous to your health. No less than the Surgeon General of the United States of America has said that."

"Actually, I don't smoke. My doctor cut that out a couple of years ago. I just like to get a little secondhand smoke now and then." I say this partly because it's true but also to lead him to believe he's dealing with a half-wit. I can see it's working.

"Why, that's very novel, Jake. But you're probably wondering why I'm here." At which point he pulls out a set of papers that looks like a warrant or subpoena or some other nastygram. He hands it to me. It's a search warrant demanding all info related to Jan Center and Tim Larson.

"So, Frank, what do you want with a couple of everyday folk? Did they fail to yield at a flashing red light?"

"You know, Jake, that's an interesting question. But I'm afraid it's classified at the moment. Let's just say they are persons of interest, not criminals. We just need to talk to them, and we understand that you've been in contact with them."

I'm about to respond, but his cell phone rings, and he grabs it with one hand and holds his other hand, one finger raised, out toward me to keep me from interrupting. He doesn't say a word into the phone, just listens, nods, and grimaces while glancing my way a couple times and then hangs up.

He looks at me as he decides where we were and how he wants to proceed. "I need to find them, Jake. One of my men is pulling a copy of all of your computer files as we speak. Yes, yes, I know, that's more info then we're authorized to take. But I've discovered it takes too much time to take just the authorized info and then realize that's not enough and then get another warrant and then come back here, yada yada, you know how it goes. No kiddy porn, I hope. Just kidding, Jake, just kidding. You need to relax. This shouldn't take all that long."

While I'd like to deny him everything, the warrant trumps my emotion. So I tell him everything I've learned about Jan and Tim. Well, nearly everything. It seems a few things slip my mind. Like Jan's secret identity, and Tim's secret bank account, and Finn, and the car in front of Finn's, and I guess a couple of other things. Frank smiles and nods but doesn't take any notes. Eventually one of his grunts comes into my office and starts sorting and searching for hard copies of anything that looks related.

"Jake, Jake, Jake, I thought I was very clear and polite. I said everything. If you don't cooperate fully, this search warrant can easily become an arrest warrant. I know you've met with a Mr. Finn Hankins. In fact, that call I just took was from an associate of mine. It seems my associate went to visit Mr. Hankins's place of employment. What's that place called?"

"Byte Me Support."

"Oh yes"—he laughs—"very creative. Anyway, it seems that Mr. Hankins isn't at his office or his home. Even more interesting is that all of his computers have been wiped clean. We were thinking maybe you might know something about that."

"Well, I do know Finn. But my conversations with him haven't had anything to do with Jan or Tim. And I have no idea where he might be or why his computers are messed up. I was thinking of using him for some of my computer work, but he's too expensive. Doesn't sound like he does a very good job of taking care of his own stuff, does it?"

"Jake, that's very interesting, but I'm confused by what seems to be the oddest coincidence. It's my understanding that Mr. Hankins has had conversations with both you and Tim. What is the likelihood of that happening? I personally believe it nearly impossible to be a coincidence." He stares at me in silence for a moment. "When I find him, I'll have to ask Mr. Hankins if he remembers more of your conversations than you do. I do hope your stories match up. Do you think they will, Jake?"

"If he tells the truth, they will." I smile back at him.

"Of course they will. Well, it seems that my associates are through here. We'll be leaving. Oh, by the by, you are not to leave town without my permission. Here's my card in case you remember anything else about the lovely couple. I find it's always more comfortable for someone to tell me something they may have forgotten before I hear from someone else that they were not totally forthcoming. If you get my drift, Jake, and I truly hope you get my drift." And there it is, the tough federal agent "I'm going to crush your windpipe with my irises" stare. Been there, done that.

"I do, Frank, I do get your drift. Now, I'm afraid I need to excuse myself. I have receipts to file and a few items that have somehow been shuffled about." I say this with my best "eat shit and die" stare. Based on his smile, this sounds appealing to him.

"Well, Jake," he says as he stands, "I'm sure we'll be speaking again…soon."

I move to my office door and watch as Frank saunters through the rest of the office. He's followed by the sauntering clones. All three of them take the opportunity to cast an evil eye back at me as they exit.

5:00 p.m.
"I want a pay increase…" Sarah

I watch out the window as the three amigos clear the building. They pile into an all-black, brand-new BMW 7 series with tinted windows. Slowly they move through the parking lot and out onto the street. No turn signal—I should call the cops.

My mind starts to scramble. First I was worried about Mob money launderers. Now I've got feds to worry about. It's obvious that home isn't safe and the office isn't safe. It's time to meet up with Sarah at the rendezvous.

A couple of years back, I stumbled into a nest of bikers while I was tracking a dad who was delinquent on his child support payments. The club didn't respond well to my sleuthing and tried to strike back. I was on the run for several days before everything calmed down. Turns out the club thought I was a fed. When they discovered I was chasing a deadbeat dad to collect back child support, they relaxed. In fact, they actually paid off the wayward dad's debt to his family. Turns out they liked the wife more than they did their member. Last I heard, the dad was about to reenter "initiation."

Anyway, the whole time I was running, I was worried about Sarah. I was afraid the bikers might grab her and use her as leverage. I tried desperately to warn her. But I couldn't get in touch with her. It turned out that she had the audacity to be out of town with friends the whole time I was freaking out. She can be so insensitive. That was when I set up protocols for us to follow in an emergency. Step one: grab cash and burner phone. Step two: dump car and regular cell phone and credit cards in a parking garage. Step three: walk at least a mile away from the parking garage and grab a cab. Step four: head to the designated burger joint off of Stark. Step five: wait. Step six: wait some more. Yeah, I know, not a great plan, but better than nothing.

Sarah has a fifteen-minute head start on me and should be waiting at the restaurant, ready to chew me out once I arrive. My list is the same as hers except for one additional step. I use my smartphone to send out a drafted email. The email is set up to go to several hundred people. But only one recipient knows what it means:

Carl Wayne, my former–Special Forces poker-playing pal. When Carl gets the email, he's to head to the same rendezvous location.

If all goes well, Sarah and Carl will be waiting for me at the restaurant, drinking coffee and arguing over which of them is my best friend.

I grab my burner phone and cash and dash out through the doorway. I leap down the stairs and rush out to the parking lot. As I'm about to get into my car, I notice a couple of thugs rolling out of a vehicle behind me. I turn and give them my best "gosh, can I help you?" smile. They respond with their best "your ass is grass" smile as they walk up to me.

I learned in the army that there is no such thing as a fair fight. There are only winners and the deceased. No points are awarded for best form or most congenial or second place. Usually, you want to outgun the enemy five to one. When that isn't possible, you want to sucker punch them. The army calls it an ambush. I may be wrong, but I think these two gents mean to harm me; they look like they could be Southside soldiers. I decide I'm not going to wait to find out.

As big guy number one moves toward me, big guy number two makes a mistake: he follows his buddy single file. Because of the cramped space between the parked cars, they can't both engage me at the same time. When big guy one gets two feet away, I shoot my palm straight up into his chin. I make sure to rotate my hips into the punch to obtain maximum force. I hear his teeth crack together. As he slumps toward the ground, moaning, I bring my right knee up into his face as hard as I possibly can. The force flips him backward into the arms of the advancing big guy, who tries to catch his buddy instead of shooting me.

As I advance on him, he drops his friend to the ground and throws a jab at my nose. I manage to move my head to the left. His fist grazes my temple. Damn if it doesn't hurt—a square shot would've ended the fight. Before he can reload, I punch him in the gut. Then I give him a tight hook to the ribs and, the pièce de résistance, I slam my right foot into his right knee. The knee buckles, and he joins his buddy on the ground. I see his gun holstered under his left arm, so I stomp on his right hand. Just in case he had hopes of drawing on me.

Big guy one is on the ground gurgling behind me, while big guy two is on the ground whimpering in front of me.

With both of them down, I pull my gun and grab some zip ties from the car. I bind their wrists and relieve both of them of their guns, phones, and car keys. I also confirm by their tattoos that they are Southside goons. I do not understand the need to have identical markings—how do they ever sneak up on anybody?

"You guys might want to roll away from my car so I don't 'accidentally' run over some body part as I back out," I tell them.

As I drive away, my little angel says that I should call an ambulance to help the little tykes. My little devil suggests I use one of their phones and even suggests a script for the conversation.

"Operator assistance—what is your emergency?"

"Yes, I'm a concerned citizen. I witnessed a fight between some dapper gents and some thugs. The gents beat the crap out of the thugs and left them laid out in a parking lot." I give her the address. "The gents were headed east in a high-end, black BMW. What's my name? Sorry, losing reception." I end the call and throw the guns, phones, and car keys into a garbage can alongside of the road.

As my mind flashes through the last thirty minutes to try to make sense of them, one nagging thought lingers. What are the odds that De Cola walks out of my office mere seconds before Southside muscle walks in? Doesn't feel like a coincidence. The whole thing feels coordinated. Why is the federal government using criminals to bend a member of their constituency to their will? How do you fight an organization that doesn't care about rules and carries the force of law on its shoulders?

It takes me about fifteen minutes to drive to downtown Portland. Once there, I drive in circles, looking for a tail. Seeing none, I pick a parking garage that I know serves lots of nearby bars. As a result, there are often all-night parkers; one more isn't going to raise any suspicion. I take a ticket from a machine, drive to a relatively vacant portion of the structure, and park. I put my phone and cards under the driver's seat of the Jeep, lock it up, and head down to the street. I walk east for about a mile and do a couple of cute little moves to see if I have a tail, which I don't. I wave down a cab and tell him to head to Southeast Portland. No reason to let him know our destination any sooner than necessary.

The cab ride takes about fifteen minutes. I spend what feels like an hour of that fifteen minutes looking over my shoulder. I exit the cab ten blocks from the restaurant and pay the cabbie in cash. I wait for him to leave before I start hoofing it the rest of the way.

The restaurant is your average fantastic burger dive. They also have great potato skins and cold beers. Since it's become our designated rendezvous location, Sarah and I don't frequent it as much as we would like. Other than an occasional look-see to make sure it's still a good spot to meet in an emergency, we stay clear.

It's a one-story building with tinted windows all along the street. This time of the evening, the sun glints off of the windows, making it impossible for anyone to see inside. At night, the booths have blinds that can be individually closed. I stop a block short of the restaurant on the opposite side of the street and just watch the nearby activity for a few minutes. It bothers me that I can't see into the restaurant, but that just means it is a safe place.

I finish the walk to the restaurant. I enter and see Carl and Sarah at a table near the back of the place with a view of the room and street. The restaurant is about half full. From what I can tell, the staff is one cook and three waitresses. The space is long and narrow with booths along the window line to my right and a counter with stools to my left. Behind the counter, the cook is sweating into the customers' food. I won't need to add salt to anything. As I stroll toward Carl and Sarah, I ask a waitress for a cup of coffee.

Sarah is looking at me with concern. "Jake, you're limping—are you okay?"

"I'm fine. After De Cola left, a couple of Southside punks tried to jump me. One of them tried to head butt my knee. The other one probably won't ever play soccer again. Anyway, I'm fine, just a little stiff."

"Sarah told me about the feds visiting you at your office," Carl says. "What she couldn't explain is why you sounded the alarm before they even got there. What gives?"

"We got a case a few days ago from a woman who wanted us to find her missing boyfriend. We tried to track the boyfriend through a secret checking account. We didn't find the boyfriend, but we did find an IT guy named Finn Hankins. I interviewed Hankins a couple of times and have recruited him to our team. It's shocking what he can do with a computer. Anyway, the first time I visit Finn, I see surveillance outside his office as I'm leaving. I'm thinking they were law enforcement.

"During my first visit with him, he tells me my client is a prostitute who works for an escort service called Honey Bunnies. The second time I see Finn, he tells me the missing boyfriend was gathering info to blow the whistle on a nearly half-trillion-dollar money-laundering scheme. Now I'm thinking the surveillance might be mobsters. I tell him to go to ground.

"On another case, I'm tracking a Detective Smith, and I follow him and his 'girlfriend' to a company called HB & Associates. HB, sounds kind of familiar, right? The security guard at the building where the HB offices are located thinks it's a bunch of hookers—what a coincidence. Later I connect Smith to a guy named Simpton. Finn ties Simpton to the money-laundering scheme, and I tie them all to Southside.

"Now I'm thinking safe rather than sorry, so I warn Sarah. When I get to the office, the feds are waiting to grill me. When they finally leave, I try to exit right behind them, and two Southside thugs show up.

"Oh, and I recently met and started dating a complete stranger. She's a smoking-hot complete stranger who just happened to pop into my life as this all started, and she always wants to talk about the missing boyfriend. I think that's it in a nutshell; just your everyday world in the life of a PI."

After I take a breath, and Sarah and Carl remain uncharacteristically quiet, I start again and spend the next thirty minutes filling in the details. I know that the adrenaline is causing me to talk fast, and Carl has to feel like he's drinking from a fire hose. But he nods and knows the details will make more sense later.

"Needless to say," I finish, "we need a place to set up shop and figure this whole thing out. So I turned to the best espionage dude I know, but he was out of town. I was wondering if you had any suggestions."

"I want a pay increase," Sarah says. Her face says money isn't enough.

"You got it. I'm doubling your bonus this year."

"Doubling from what, smart-ass? I've never gotten a bonus before."

"I just happen to have what you're looking for," Carl says. "I have a safe house out toward Mount Hood with a confusin' title that can't be tracked to me. I set it up ten years ago for a situation just like this. Though I figured it would be me runnin' and hidin'. I have money, phones, weapons, and vehicles stashed out there."

"Perfect. I have another favor to ask—we need to pick up Finn. We're going to need his mad skills. And I'm guessing that someone is hot on his trail. We need to get to him before he's reduced to fertilizer."

"What about me? Should I go back to the office?" Sarah asks.

"No way; you'll be safer with us, and I need you to keep Finn focused. Sorry, Sarah, I've gotten you into another mess."

She smiles at me like it's no big deal, but we both know that it is.

"Let's roll," Carl says.

6:30 p.m.
"How did you know they were Southside..." Carl

I pay the waitress in cash and include an unmemorable 18 percent tip. We head out to Carl's nondescript SUV. It looks like a junker but sounds like a precision machine. It only takes us a few minutes to navigate to the address that Finn gave me. We park a block away from Finn's temporary housing in a spot that gives us a clear view of the entrance and the street in front of the building.

The three of us begin looking for trouble. The street is a wide two-way with ample room for parallel parking, and there are a dozen or so cars parked within a block, either way, of Finn's location. On each side of the street there are two-to-three-story buildings that look to be at least fifty years old. They look like they house local retail stores. The foot traffic seems light, which works to our advantage.

After about five minutes, Carl says, "At eleven o'clock in the red Pontiac are two tangos casin' the joint. They could be triangulating to Finn's location. I thought you said the boy understood electronics?"

"Actually, I said he was good with the internet and computer searches. I think he's a virgin when it comes to being tracked by humans yielding lethal weapons. I also think he's about to hit a steep learning curve," I reply.

"Well, son, how do we take these guys off point?"

"Sarah stays here and watches the goons, keeping us posted via phone. You and I stroll into the building just past Finn's. We'll lie in wait and hope the goons recognize us and come charging in after us instead of Finn. Once they enter, we neutralize them, grab Finn, and skedaddle."

"Roger that," Carl says.

Carl grabs a small bag from the back of his car while I put my phone in my pocket. I'll put in the earbud once we're in the building. Carl and I leave the car, circle back a block, cross the street, and casually walk toward the entrance we've chosen. Neither of us looks directly at the goons; instead, Carl pretends to speak to me, allowing him to look past me and watch their reflections in storefront windows. We make sure that they can't help but see us. We act suspicious and stupid, just the bait for the ignorant.

"They're makin' a call, probably for instructions," Carl whispers.

"Or backup," I say.

"Maybe; won't matter unless these guys wait for the backup to arrive."

We make it to the entrance, and the goons are still in their car. The entrance is a common entry for multiple businesses. As we walk through the doorway, we see that on the first floor there is a bookstore, a discount clothing store, a restroom, and a restaurant. We're lucky that the glass in the door leading to the street is frosted so the goons won't be able to see into the building until they've entered. More luck: the stores seem empty of customers. I go into the clothing store to the left of the street door, and Carl goes into the bookstore to the right. I hook up the earbud.

"Status," I say.

"Plan's working. They should reach the door in a few seconds," comes Sarah's voice over the phone. I give Carl a thumbs-up and pull out my gun. Carl follows suit. I hope a shopkeeper doesn't mistake us for bandits. But lady luck is still on our side; no innocents seem to notice us or threaten to wander into the likely line of fire. I hear the building door open. I wait a beat, raise three fingers for

Carl to see, and start a silent countdown. I want to allow the goons enough time to clear the doorway before we greet them.

As my last finger drops, Carl and I both peek around our respective corners, weapons pointed at the gents. "Freeze, bastards."

They both jump in surprise. Who trains these guys? At least they're quick to realize that they don't have a choice. The exit door is too far behind them for a run in that direction, and they haven't drawn their weapons. We have them covered, and we have them in a cross fire. They put their hands up, and Carl disarms them. We walk them into the restroom for a little privacy, and Carl pulls out some zip ties and secures them. While part of me thinks I can relax a bit, my training says these guys are massive and still dangerous. Where do the evildoers get all these guys? Do they have a giant-muscle factory somewhere?

While Carl gets their car keys and phones, I confirm with Sarah that no one is on the street at the moment. We quickly walk them across the street to their car. We put them in the backseat with Carl covering them, and I drive us all around to the back of the building across the street from the one Finn is hiding in.

"Why is Southside interested in us?" I ask them.

Dead silence greets us.

"Listen, punks, we can make this uncomfortable, or we can make it painful and uncomfortable, your choice. Why is Southside interested in us?" I ask.

"You're dead men."

Two minutes later, they haven't peeped. We decide they're worthless to us, and we're still concerned backup might be on its way. Carl opens the trunk and makes one of the goons lie down in it. He zip-ties his feet and duct-tapes his mouth. We make the second goon lie on the floor of the backseat and give him the same spa treatment. For added measure, Carl uses the duct tape to secure the second goon's feet to his hands.

I stomp on the cells and toss the pieces of plastic and electronics around the lot.

"How did you know they were Southside?" Carl asks.

"Neck tattoos—they're Southside muscle. We need to get Finn and get out. We don't want to be here when the other worker bees arrive."

I check in with Sarah. She tells me there are no new cars or threats out front. Carl's and my heads are on swivels as we head for Finn. As we walk through the building's front door, we almost smack right into him—he's right there at the door with a couple of bags.

"Where the hell are you headed?" I ask.

"Hey, buddy, good to see you. I watched part of your abduction routine. I saw those guys a while back and started packing and trying to figure out how I was going to get past them. You were plan A."

"What was plan B?" Carl asks.

"It started with me wetting my pants and only got worse from there."

"How did they find you?"

"I messed up and forgot to turn my phone off. But I left it upstairs. Let's split."

7:10 p.m.
"I'll post the video on the world wide web..." Carl

We load Finn's bags into the back of Carl's car, and we all jump into his lean, mean machine. Carl is driving, I'm riding shotgun, and Sarah is regularly scanning for tails. Finn blabbers on about being freaked out.

"You guys cut that awfully close," Finn says.

"Relax, cowboy, we got there, didn't we? Plus, this is just the beginnin'—there's a heck of a lot more to come," Carl says.

"More to come? What does that mean?"

"Jesus, Carl, give the guy a break. He's not going to be much help if he's freaking out on us," Sarah says.

"Don't worry, Finn, we have a safe house. Nobody's going to find you or hurt you," I say and try to believe it.

The ride takes a little over an hour as we head through town and out into the boonies of Mount Hood.

After we clear the city streets, the road meanders through open fields and past the occasional ski-themed restaurant. Eventually we are winding through tall firs, with an occasional vista of Mount Hood. The contrast between the lush, green forest and the mountain's stark, gray rock and bright-white snow momentarily clears my mind. A single cloud in an otherwise perfectly blue sky hovers atop the mountain, seemingly speared and held in place by the peak.

"What did you say to Jessica?" I ask Sarah.

"I told her to stay clear of the office for the next couple of weeks. That she still works for us and she'll be paid automatically. There's enough cash in the bank account for at least six weeks. I gave her Milt's name and number to call if she has questions but told her not to for at least two weeks."

As the highway begins to rise in elevation, Carl turns off onto an unmarked dirt road that pierces the green veil of the foreboding forest. We slow to a crawl as the uneven ground tosses us back and forth like kernels of corn being popped—thank goodness without the assistance of heat and grease. Tree limbs extend out into our path and scrape against the car. After about fifteen minutes of bumping and thumping, the ground smoothes out, our speed picks up, and we all begin to relax a little.

Twenty minutes deep into the woods, we enter a large, thick, green field spotted with fragrant purple and yellow wildflowers. An occasional sapling or bush squeezes out through the grass, trying to capture a piece of the sky. An old, dark-brown house sits in the middle of the field. According to Carl, the US Forest Service owns the land. He, through various confusing names, entities, etc., paid a ridiculously small fee for a fifty-year lease of the land and structure.

The single-story ranch is a manmade island in the midst of the colorful foliage. Its roof is covered with solar panels, and a porch wraps from the attached multicar garage on the left all the way along the front and around to the right.

Carl stops in front of the garage and asks us to unload ourselves and Finn's bags while he manually opens the garage door. He reenters the car and drives it into the garage, parking it beside a beaten-up, once-red pickup truck; a nondescript, dark-blue sedan; and a couple of dirt bikes. As I walk into the garage, I see all sorts of boxes along the walls. More are stored on planks that have been laid across the bare rafters.

"Wait here while I disarm the alarm system," Carl says, stepping through a door at the back of the garage. After a few seconds, he exits the house through the front door and invites us all in.

"So, Carl, I imagine the response rate to your alarm system must be about, what, a couple of days?" I joke.

"It isn't that kind of alarm system. When the sensors are triggered, they wake up cameras that I can view via my computer or phone. I have some...party favors for those who make the mistake of messin' with my space. Only had one incident so far—some lost hunters stumbled onto the place about four years ago. By the time I was done with them, I'm sure they were certain the place was haunted.

"Before we start plannin'," continues Carl, "let me give you a nickel tour of the setup. I have a thousand-gallon drum of propane buried in the back, and I'm sure you saw the solar panels as we drove up. I have enough dried food to feed us for months and an armory that is larger than that of some countries. I have blackout blinds for all of the windows so that at night no one outside will see any light from inside.

"I have prepaid burner and sat phones, wireless internet that bounces around various world hubs, plus cameras, trackers, etc. A little bit of everything. I also have multiple IDs for myself. I can get new ID for each of you as well, just in case. I have a provider who's reliable. He's not far away, and I'll make sure he knows I'm comin', so he's ready."

"What happens if we need to make a quick exit? Or do we just hunker down and fight?" I ask.

"In an emergency, there are three ways to escape. Option one is to jump into one of the vehicles in the garage and head back the way we came. Not a great idea since that's where a threat is probably coming from.

"Option two is to hike out. If you look out this back window straight at that tallest fir and move your eye line ten degrees to the right, there's a trail that'll take you into the back country. You can be in civilization in twenty-four hours.

"Option three is limited to two people. Take the dirt bikes out of the garage and head thirty degrees left of the same fir tree. There's a dirt road just beyond the trees. I've practiced the route at night, and I can be to the main road with no lights in fifteen minutes. The bikes make a lot of noise, but if you keep your lights off, no one is going to catch you. Any questions?"

"Yeah, should we know how to turn the alarm system off and on?" I ask.

"Probably not a bad idea. I'll work with each of you individually," Carl replies. "Nothing else? Good. There are five bedrooms, so grab whatever one you want except the first one to the right—it's mine. There are only two showers but plenty of hot water."

I pull Sarah aside and fight the urge to give her a hug. "I'm still so sorry to get you involved in this. I feel awful. I really didn't see it coming."

"Don't worry. We're fine. With Carl, we have a pretty good team. I'd bet on us."

"Me too."

9:10 p.m.
"You're a social media dweeb..." Finn

"Let's start with what we know," I say. "Someone has a large money laundering scheme in place, and it ties to Simpton. We can tie Simpton to Southside, and I think we can tie Southside to De Cola. We know that Tim Larson stumbled onto a scheme. And we know Jan Center brought us in."

"Don't forget about Abby," Sarah adds.

"I think the key is figurin' out the money launderin' scheme. Seems the money will tie it all together," Carl says.

"I think you're right, Carl. Finn, you and Sarah split the info needs up and start prepping profiles on everyone we know is involved. Carl, you and I need to visit your friend and get IDs in place, just in case. Then we need to go do some recognizance. Carl, I need to know more about those party favors you've got for uninvited guests."

"I have sensors all the way around the perimeter of the field. They're all tied into cameras that can be viewed on this monitor here. The cameras have multiple settings, includin' infrared and night vision."

"You guys need to slow down. I'm starving. I think the work needs to wait until we're nourished," Sarah says. "Carl, are you the master chef? I'm certainly able and willing to assist."

"Excellent. I have an apron that will fit you perfectly," Carl tells Sarah.

"I'll set up the equipment so we can start gathering data after dinner," Finn says.

"Okay, but be careful. Don't forget what you went through earlier today. There aren't any more white knights out there," I say.

"I'm a quick learner, buddy. I've got it covered."

Finn begins unpacking his bags. He picks out a section of the living room, rearranges the furniture, and starts assembling his equipment.

With Finn busy setting up his command center and Sarah and Carl playing chef, I decide that my best use is to start a fire and find the liquor. Carl directs me to a large, covered stack of firewood. While I'm outside, I look at the house from multiple angles and distances to better understand what Carl told us.

The only light I see is emanating from the moon and the stars. The moon is little more than a sliver, so the world is terribly dark. Above the trees to the east is the snow-crested peak of Mount Hood. Even in the dim light, the snow looks fluorescent. The only sounds are the wind whispering through the treetops and the distant splash of the river. The beautiful night brings Abby to mind. I try to figure out how she fits in to what's going on, if at all. "You'll find room for her," says my little devil. I load the wood carrier, haul it back into the house, and start the fire. Next, I ask Carl where the liquor is. I take orders and start pouring.

Sitting in a chair with my drink, I watch the team at work. Finn is in his element with gadgets and cords; Carl is the master of the kitchen, with Sarah laughing at his side. I can't believe I've done it again. I can't believe I've put Sarah in harm's way. I'm upset not because she lacks skills, because she doesn't. She's strong and smart and more than capable of taking care of herself. But I know I'll never forgive myself if she is hurt. I light a cigarette and place it in an ashtray on the arm of my chair. I wait anxiously for the wafts of smoke to soothe me.

After dinner we discuss search strategy.

Finn begins. "First off, no matter how good we are at bouncing signals, eventually we'll make a mistake, or somebody better than me will figure out where we are. Once we start searching, we should assume that we have three to five days before we need to leave here. When we leave, we'll need a plan to go mobile and move from place to place. I have an idea for that. I can search social media for people going on vacation within certain zip codes. I'll map one each day and give you the address so that if we have to sprint out of here, we'll have a rendezvous spot."

"Do people really leave that kind of information on the internet?" I ask.

"Come on, buddy, look at what I found out about you, and you're a social media dweeb. You're just an accidental user. Real people are looking for intimacy, and they think—they hope—everyone is their friend.

"Any questions? Good, next let's discuss internet searches. I've set these two computers up to search safely. Only Sarah and I—I repeat, only Sarah and I—will touch them or any other computer that's connected to the real world. The risk of error increases exponentially based upon the number of people connecting."

"Including smartphones, by the way," I say.

"Yeah, yeah, yeah, including smartphones. Take the batteries out and leave them disabled. Carl, is the machine that monitors the perimeter hooked up to the outside world?"

"Not now while we're here, but it automatically connects when the security system is triggered."

"Good. Leave it unconnected. Sarah, let's divide up these search needs."

"Let's plan on meeting after breakfast to review what you two have discovered. Do you need Carl or me for anything?"

"No, I think you're probably more of a distraction then an asset," Finn says.

"Well, then, you won't mind if Carl and I head off to bed."

"Looks like Carl beat you to the punch," Sarah says.

I turn to where I thought Carl was standing. He is already dozing in a chair. I turn back, and Finn and Sarah are so focused on their gizmos that I may as well not be here. I wander off to a bedroom, strip down, crawl in, and pass out.

Sunday, March 25

7:30 a.m.

"You two must be mocking someone. It better not be me..." Sarah

The next morning I awake to the smell of freshly cooked powdered eggs. Carl is working up a sweat, Sarah is in the shower, and Finn is sawing logs somewhere.

"How'd you sleep?" Carl asks.

"Like the dead. I have no idea whether or not my bed is comfortable—I didn't feel it. How about you?"

"Pretty much the same. I did wake up once. Finn went to the bathroom to take a leak and didn't close the bathroom door. So I was treated to a momentary water show. What a slob."

"What do you expect from a guy whose fingers have never touched living flesh, except his own?"

"You two must be mocking someone. It better not be me," Sarah says as she enters the room. She's dressed in relaxed casual clothes, easy to lounge or take flight in. "Carl, make sure you leave the dishes for Jake. If we're going to do all of the cooking, he can do all the maid work."

"Wait a minute—what about Finn? I started a fire and poured drinks last night. What has he done?" I whine.

"Let me correct somethin'," Carl starts. "After the pee part of Finn's water show, there wasn't a tap-water show."

"Ohhh," groans Sarah.

"Point taken," I reply. "I'll hop in the shower after I eat, and then my clean hands will do the dishes. What do we need for the new IDs?"

"Just your driver's license and cash, and I have lots of cash. You will repay me later," Carl says.

Breakfast is ready, so we wake Finn. He looks very elegant in his jam-jams and sleep hair. One side of his hair looks like it did last night; the other side looks like it got pancaked by an offensive tackle. None of us allow him to touch us or our utensils.

The food is pretty good, surprisingly good, in fact. I think it has more to do with Carl's doctoring than anything the manufacturer did. I shower and dress, then clean and dry the dishes. By the time I'm done, Carl has gathered our driver's licenses and is ready to go. Finn and Sarah tell us to take off; they're not far enough along to share much yet. Carl and I head out to the sedan. Sarah and Finn can barely manage a wave at us over their shoulders as we leave.

It's a sixty-minute drive to the ID artist's home. When we get to his neighborhood, we park on the opposite side of the street from his house and several doors down. We watch the street for problems and decide about fifteen minutes later to go up to the house. Carl has already sent some sort of coded message to the guy so that he isn't surprised when we show up on his front porch, armed.

The house is a basic split-level in a housing development of basic split-levels. There must be one builder for every neighborhood in this city. Just like in Tim and Jan's neighborhood, the only way to distinguish these boxes is by their paint color. This one is a god-awful avocado. Not a fresh avocado, a "several days in the sun" avocado. There must not be a lot of money in faking IDs.

We step up onto the porch, and before we can knock or ring, a stubby guy swings the door open. He's dressed in raggedy, but mercifully clean, sweats featuring the Portland Timbers soccer team logo. His hair is cut boot-camp short, and after a two-second look at us, his eyes shift to the street.

"Hi, Carl, glad to see you. Who's your friend?" the ID artist asks as his eyes continue to sweep the street.

"Jake, meet Ponch; Ponch, meet Jake."

"Ponch? Did your parents lose a bet?" I smirk.

"No, smart-ass, it's because of my athletic physique. Come in before the neighbors think I'm paying man-whores."

We enter the house, and he directs us downstairs. A female voice yells out from above, "Ponchy, I need you to take the garbage out. It stinks. That crappy breakfast you made is raunchy smelling. Ponchy? You need to do it now."

"Sorry, guys, I'll be down in a minute," he says to us. Then he turns and shouts, "Okay, Janey, on my way. Can you keep it down, though? I've got customers. And keep the kids upstairs while I'm working."

We enter a basement that wasn't meant to be a living space. The ceiling is low, and I feel the need to duck. And some of the walls don't have drywall, just old, dirty studs, tar paper, and siding. The place was built when insulation was considered a rich man's luxury. Off in one corner are bright lights with tables, photo equipment, and a background cloth hanging from the ceiling and several computers and printers. By the time we've taken it all in, Ponchy is back.

"Okay, Carl, how many people and how many sets?"

"Three people, two sets each. Full service. I've got cash and pictures." Carl hands an envelope to Ponch.

"Give me twenty-four hours. If I get them done sooner, I'll be in touch."

"Sounds good," Carl says, and we blow the joint.

As we step outside, my Spidey sense tingles. "Carl, someone's watching us," I warn.

"Okay, let's scan wide and walk slowly," he replies.

As we reach the car, I see it: the nose of a car parked on a side street off of Ponch's street. From this distance, it has a striking resemblance to the car I saw in front of Finn's office the first time I visited him.

"Seventy-five yards at eleven o'clock."

"I see it. We can't let them go or they'll take Ponch down and grab our IDs."

I agree with my eyes, and we both get into the car. Neither of us looks directly at the threatening car.

Carl starts the car and casually drives down the street. He takes a left on the corner before Ponch's house and a block short of the street where the mystery car is sitting. Once around the corner and out of sight, Carl quickly makes a U-turn and parks with the engine idling, facing the direction we just came from. We wait patiently for the other car to come around the corner.

It isn't but a couple of seconds before it does. Carl hits the gas and speeds right at him. I expect the other car to turn and run. Most of these surveillance types aren't looking for a confrontation. They just want information. But to my surprise, the driver of the other car doesn't turn and run—he signals and pulls over to the curb.

Sun glare makes it impossible to see who is in the car. It could be full of clowns or Special Forces, for all I can tell. We sit, guns drawn, anxiously trying to decide our next step. Before we can make a decision, the driver's side door of the opposing car opens. And my jaw hits the floor.

An armed Abby Dicer exits the vehicle. Her weapon is gripped in both hands but pointed down. She's looking very hot and very much like a fed.

10:45 a.m.
"I don't get romantic with targets—I shoot them..." Abby

I am dumbfounded. All I can do is stare and try to get my brain cells aligned and functioning again.

Carl looks over at me and asks, "Jake, what's wrong? Do you know her?"

I still can't respond verbally; all I can do is stare at her. Finally, Abby, who's just been standing and staring back at me, decides what the hell. She holsters her weapon and walks toward us like we've met for a date. She walks to the back door of our car on my side, opens it, and slides in. "Hi, Jake; hi, Carl," she says nonchalantly.

186

"What the hell?" is all I can blurt out.

"Good to see you too, Jake. I imagine you have a couple of questions."

"You think?"

"I'm a fed. And I've been tracking De Cola, whom you recently met. De Cola led me to Larson, who led me to Finn, who led me to you, Jake. Crazy-small world, isn't it?"

"I thought De Cola was a fed."

"He is, but he's a dirty fed."

"Oh really, he's a dirty fed. How are we to tell you apart?"

"Come on, Jake—I'm much prettier that De Cola, wouldn't you agree?" She smiles at me and Carl. I feel my face beginning to respond in kind, but stop at the last second.

"What do you mean De Cola's dirty?"

"Well, you see, there's a battle going on inside our government at the moment. The battle is all about money laundering. I'm sure you've at least figured out the money laundering part."

"Where are your manners Jake? Don't you think you should introduce me to the woman who just pointed a gun at me?" Carl asks.

They wait for me to respond, but I'm still on tilt.

"I've never seen you quite so shy, Jake. Hi, Carl. I'm Abby, Abby Dicer," she says as she and Carl shake hands over the seat back.

"How the hell does she know my name?" he asks me.

I just raise my hands and try to say I have no idea.

"Oh, I just did a little homework on Jake. I wanted to get to know him and his circle of friends, just in case we started getting serious."

"Serious. As in, 'relationship' serious?" Carl asks.

Finally my brain rebalances. "Can we get back to the war thing? What do you mean a war inside our government?" I ask.

"Battle, I think I said battle. Anyway, money laundering and the transfer of illegal funds has become the biggest business on the planet. Within a few years, there could be more illegal money in our banking system than legal money. The US has known about this trend for a long time, but we can't stop it."

"Why not? You stop everythin' else you don't like!" Carl exclaims.

"The primary problem is liquidity. If they chase the illegal money out of the banking system, the world won't be able to pay its bills. Plus, the IRS likes to collect the tax revenue that's generated by the fake businesses."

"Still don't get it. The government could freeze all financial accounts and go one by one to figure out which are legit and which aren't," Carl says.

"That would be impossible. First off, the bad guys would know about the freeze before it happened and would clear their money out. Second, freezing legitimate accounts is at best illegal and at worst political and economic suicide. It's not going to happen.

"Imagine hundreds of billions of dollars disappearing overnight. The US would be a credit risk. China, Russia, and all of our trading partners would pull their money out of our banks and flood the market with treasury bills. The US would cease to exist economically in a matter of hours, and maybe for forever."

"What you're saying is the US is in an alliance with gangsters and terrorists. That doesn't register," I say.

"Let me give you an example. By law, banks are obligated to watch for and report any money laundering they discover. Yet recently an international bank was caught actively engaged in money laundering. A snitch notified the feds, who shut down the scheme. But what is most interesting is that no one was criminally prosecuted. The bank paid a fine and promised not to be naughty again. They made, or probably still make, more in one day from handling illicit funds than the fine they paid."

"So, let's say everything you say is true. You're a fed, and De Cola's a fed. Why are two feds fighting seemingly on opposite sides of the battle?" I ask.

"I don't agree with what De Cola and his branch is doing, and I've been looking for a way to get the US out of the laundry business. But no one is going to take me seriously without proof. De Cola is the weak link. De Cola is a facilitator. His job is to eliminate threats to the status quo—or at least keep things from going public. On the surface, he's employed by the US government, but his true client is a loosely affiliated group of very wealthy and successful criminals. He caught wind of Tim Larson snooping around and decided to investigate. He wasn't sure how much Tim knew, so he hired Jan and brought her to Portland to get close to Tim. Tim fell hard for Jan but somehow got wind that he was in trouble and disappeared. I'm pretty sure that De Cola has him. That means we probably won't see Tim again. De Cola doesn't hold threats; he extinguishes them."

I look at Abby but don't see a smile. She's serious as a heart attack. "You're saying Tim's dead," I say.

"I think Tim is dead."

"What about Jan? Isn't she at risk?" Carl asks.

"She's gone too—I don't know where. I'm sure she has a new name and identity. She's an off-the-books agent De Cola uses to get close to men. By the way, Jake, did she get close to you?" Her face shows she has an intense interest in my response.

"She tried, but I shut her down." I smile at her.

She hesitates before she says, "Right." She watches me for an instant longer and seems to trust my answer. "Anyway, De Cola makes problems and people disappear. But what you need to know is that De Cola has decided that Jake knows too much. He wants you, Jake, and once he has you, it won't take long for him to focus his attention on Sarah and Carl. He's already after Finn."

"And you?" I ask. "Why do we trust you? You've been playing me like a violin. How nice are you?"

"I needed to know if you were involved with Tim and Finn. You're right—I got to know you to learn what you knew. But while you and Carl where staring at me a few minutes ago, I decided we could help each other. Jake, I don't get romantic with targets—I shoot them. I like you and want to protect you from De Cola."

"I find it hard to believe that a fed just up and joins the apparent target of an investigation. Where are all of your buddies in this battle? Why don't you have an entire army here?" Carl asks.

"De Cola's connected. Like I said, the government is caught in the middle between a need for cash and closing down illegal trade activities. The only way to change anything is to bring the public spotlight on the problem. There are people in the agency who agree with me, but just a few. And none of them are going to stretch their necks unless there's a high probability of success.

"But right now, right here, this is about us. De Cola wants us, all of us. He knows we're a threat. Our best play is to work together. You have mass, and I have inside knowledge. What do you say? Partners?"

My head is pounding as I listen to all of this. A missing boyfriend becomes money laundering becomes my close friends and me against the US government and a large criminal organization. She's right: we're in over our heads. And her partnership question is just a nicety—she has our ID artist dead to rights, and somehow she's tracking us. If she weren't armed and gorgeous, I'd tie her up and store her in the trunk. My little devil smiles at that last image.

I look at Carl, who, for the first time that I've known him, looks just a bit scared. He nods.

"All right," I say, "what do you suggest?"

"I'll follow you to an easy place to leave my car. Then I'll ride with you back to your mountain hideaway. I have a plan that has a reasonable possibility of success. I've learned enough about Finn and Sarah to feel confident that we can make it work. I can't do it on my own, and you guys don't know how to evade detection, believe me. What were you doing down the street?"

I look at Carl. He looks back and shrugs his shoulders.

"Getting new identities," I tell her.

"Not a bad idea. Do you think he can handle another customer?"

Carl tells her that with the right amount of money, Ponch could document me as the Pope. We head back to Ponch's house. He's none too happy when he sees Abby. While she's a stunning woman, right now she's all fed, and that offsets everything else. But Ponch accepts her info on Carl's assurance this isn't some sting—again. We leave in our separate cars, Abby telling us to follow her. For the second time in as many days, Carl is oddly silent, but I don't have time to worry about that. He'll start talking and asking me questions about Abby when he decides the time is right. Abby leads us into a cemetery parking lot. She gets out of her fedmobile, breaks up her cell phone and scatters the pieces. She opens the trunk and grabs what looks like an overnight bag. She hops into the backseat of our car, and we head back to our apparently not-so-secret hideaway.

"How do you know about the place in the mountains?" I ask her.

"I saw De Cola pay his social call on you back at your office. I even saw you take down the two tough-looking bad guys. By the way, that was very efficient the way you neutralized them. One will need a straw to eat, and the other will always walk with a limp."

"Did you hear that?" I ask Carl. "She digs my efficiency."

"It can be a very attractive trait," Abby says.

"Can you two stop with the datin' ritual? You saw him take down a couple of grannies, then what?" Carl asks.

"They were hardly grannies," I say.

"Then I trailed Jake from his office to the parking garage to the cab to the restaurant. While you were in the restaurant having snacks, I found Carl's car and put a tracer on it. The rest is just kismet."

I can feel my little devil laughing hysterically. Jake Brand, PI, BA: private investigator and badass. Tracked and monitored by a lovely fed. Even my little angel is snickering at my cluelessness.

1:00 p.m.
"I can see why you're both single..." Abby

The drive back to the ranch is painfully quiet until we get through the town of Sandy. Up until this point, I see Carl regularly rotating his eyes from his side mirror to the road ahead and then to the rearview mirror. I know that he's sweeping for tails, but I surmise he's also worried about Abby. He's confirming that she isn't positioning herself behind him with a garrote. I presume he's decided that I'm too whipped to stop her.

"Carl, you know I'd kill her before I'd let her kill you, don't you?" I try to break the ice.

"I believe you believe that, but I haven't heard little Jake's vote yet. So no, I'm not convinced," he replies.

"Come on, guys, if I wanted to kill you, you'd already be dead. I would've picked you off as you stared stupidly at me from your car over by Ponch's house. Plus, I've known your hideaway location ever since you got there. Which reminds me, Carl, when we get there, I should disable the tracer on your car just in case someone else tries to link to it. "

"Sure, we were sittin' ducks," begins Carl, "and you could have taken us out any number of times. But it's difficult for me to trust someone who is willing to date Jake, let alone ooh and ahh over his ability to disable goons."

"I understand completely and normally would agree with you. But I think Jake has potential. He's definitely a project, and rough around the edges, but a little spit, and some rubbing, and I think I could take him out in public."

"Kind of like community service?" Carl asks.

"I take it back—you're right to worry about her, Carl. You're on your own."

"Ahh, did I hit a nerve?" Carl asks.

"I can see why you're both single," Abby says.

"I don't see any man-anchor on your finger, sweetheart," I say.

"Now you're just bein' mean," Carl says. "A woman at her age, not married? It has to be painful to have that big of a hole in her life."

"Not really. I like me. So do you—you just won't admit it. Besides, while I may not be married, I'm definitely not lonely. Men just seem to be infatuated with me. Take Jake here. He was smitten the first five minutes of jujitsu. Gosh, I think he was hooked when he looked into my eyes the first time. Remember the first time, Jake? Looking at my reflection in my rearview mirror in front of Finn's? Admit it, Jake, you've been putty ever since," she says.

"Oh, I remember. I remember you tucking your tail and running away. Why's that? I wonder. Perchance a forbidden desire for a slice of Jake? Hmmm?"

"Sorry, Abby, Jake lives in an alternate reality that occasionally he voices out loud."

"Okay, enough. If you children can't say anything nice, maybe you should just be quiet. Carl, you watch the road so we don't get pulled over. Abby, you look out the back window for a tail." I pout.

Silence prevails for about two minutes until Carl says to Abby, "I think *you* hit a nerve."

"Shhh," I reply with all the intellectual skill I can muster.

"'Forbidden desire,' OMG," she says to no one in particular.

"Ahhh," I reply.

The rest of the drive is silent, in words, but not in looks and snickers. Every so often, Carl looks at Abby in the rearview mirror. I'm convinced she's making faces at me, but I'm too mature to take the bait and too defensive to turn and confirm.

After we pull up at the ranch, Abby and Carl destroy the tracer. When we walk into the house through the garage, Sarah and Finn immediately start calculating their best escape route. I calm them and recite our experience to them. They smile in a "she's here; can't change it; don't trust her" way.

"So, I guess we should go ahead and share our search results with you. We may as well start with what we've discovered about Abby Dicer. Sarah?" Finn motions for Sarah to proceed with their info.

"She's a fed," Sarah informs us, reading from her notes.

"Now let's shift our attention to De Cola. So far we are coming up with a zero. Maybe our new club member can help us out."

"De Cola was a fed at birth," Abby begins. "Be careful how you try to search for him—he has traps on the web to identify anyone trying to profile him. I can get you into the fed system through a back door. But after we use it, we have six hours to vacate this location. And by vacate, I mean we can't be on the road between here and Portland. We have to be able to disappear in a crowd. All you need to know for now is that he has the full force and strength of the US government backing him. Plus, every major city in the US has a criminal organization that he can leverage. In Portland, they've recruited Southside. So he can come at you with warrants or criminals, doesn't matter to him."

The room is deathly quiet for several long seconds, or short minutes, when Sarah asks, "And why do you want to be on our side?"

"I think Jake is cute," is all Abby says.

Everyone turns and looks at me. I feel my blush coming on.

"Well, duh." I grin.

"Oh brother," Sarah says.

"Simpton is next on our list," Finn says. "He doesn't have a criminal record, but there's a lot to connect him to the laundering business. I singled out his home wireless system and hacked into it. I searched everywhere I could for whatever info I could find and came up with zilch. Except for one thing: he has a black box. He has a machine that is occasionally connected to the network but is constantly changing its IP address. As a result, I can't get into it from the outside. The only way to look at it is to do so in person."

Then Sarah starts in again. "I've been charting the laundering scheme. I've identified thirteen banks and fifty-two businesses. An estimated $200 billion, with a *b*, is in the system at any one time, and probably a half trillion a year clears through the accounts. And it's growing."

"Actually, the total in the country is closer to a trillion. You're just looking at the western quarter of the country," Abby says.

Our faces all go blank as we try to imagine that many zeros dressed in green.

Carl looks at his phone. "Guys, I've got to run. Abby must have lit a fire under Ponch—he has our work done. I'll go pick it up."

We say goodbye as Carl leaves, and Sarah continues, "I don't have any info on any of the systems but what Tim had started to document. Maybe with time, lots of time, and some hints, I could track the rest. But I think we should plan on just dealing with the western US. Anyway, I've set up a matrix of how all the money moves, banks, account numbers and names, etc. But I can't access any of the money or tie it to anyone without passwords or electronic keys. Finn and I think those may be on Simpton's black box."

"Do we need the box itself, or can we just strip the info out of it?" I ask.

"Either way, if you can get me three to five minutes with it, I can download the content," Finn says.

"We can't take the machine," Abby says. "If we do and Simpton sees it's missing, he could reroute everything in an hour. All we'd have to show for our efforts is a brush with death and a high-end computer with old and cold information."

"So we need to go in, and we need a good guess about where the black box is located. Finn, does his security system have cameras?" I ask.

"Yes, and I can get house plans from the county."

"Next, we'll need a diversion. I've got an idea for that. Once Carl gets back, he, Abby, and I can plot that out. Finn, can you teach us how to get the info off of the machine, or do you need to be there?" I ask.

"I can do everything remotely using his cameras, a camera attached to your head, a cell plugged into your ear, and your hands."

"Good, you're too big and slow—you'd be a target no one could miss."

"If I didn't need you to stay alive, I'd be spreading all kinds of internet stories about you, buddy. You know that, right?" quips Finn.

I laugh, sort of, and let him and Sarah start preparing materials for moving in and out of Simpton's house.

Abby and I move off to the side, and I ask, "What are our odds?"

"If we have a really good diversion, and Simpton's security is undisciplined, and Finn is as good as he thinks he is, and we get really, really lucky? Fifty-fifty."

"That's what I was thinking. Piece of cake."

4:30 p.m.
"We're marking up a drawing of the house..." Finn

Carl's back in three hours. He picked up our IDs and then circled and backtracked as best he could to make sure he wasn't followed. He suggested to Ponch that he might be burned and it was time he reinvent himself. Ponch assured Carl that it was already in the works. Having Abby the Fed visit him was enough to freak him out. Ponch is a pro at relocation: new IDs for him and his wife and his kids and a new home. Unfortunately, his current house is going to have a serious fire tonight, but it's a rental.

Carl hands out our IDs, two sets each. One set to get us into either Canada or Mexico and one set to get us into a second country after that. At this point, we're all prepared to be new people, with new jobs, friends, and loved ones, maybe forever. I try to believe the prepared part.

I look over at Finn as he looks down at his at his envelope in his shaking hands. I look at his face, which has turned pasty white. I move to his side.

"You going to be sick?" I ask him.

He looks at me without seeing me. "I've never been anyone but me."

"I find that hard to believe. I'll bet you've been six feet five and two hundred pounds of rock-hard muscle on the internet."

He smiles weakly. "Well, I suppose I've played some parts in the past, but this is different. This is a new name, a new home, and looking over my shoulder. I don't think I can do it. I don't know how to do it."

"It's easier than you think, Finn. And we're not talking about forever," I say, while thinking, *I hope that's true.* "Carl and I have been through this before."

"This is hardly the same as a Special Forces assignment with the US government *on* your side."

"True, but we can help you through it. Some of it you'll have to figure out on your own. But you're smart. Cheer up—the alternative is lifetime imprisonment or death. You have so much to fight for."

He nods and opens his passport to learn his new name.

I open my ID and read my first new name. "Dirk Dagger?"

Everyone laughs. Sarah tells me it seems apropos, and Abby just smiles. Abby has become Christie Wind, Sarah has become Irene May, and Finn has become Kurtis Gillis. Carl already has ID as Kevin Ratchet. We all agree not to share our second identities with each other. It may save one of us the embarrassment and shame of ratting out our friends if we're caught and tortured. Or in Finn's case, caught and fed. I suspect that for a plate of nachos, he'd spill everything.

Abby tells us the work is very professional and will suffice for our purposes. She still thinks we'll end up back home in a few weeks after the dust clears, and if we follow the plan.

Time to put together the details of said plan. A plan that is going to bring down an evil empire within the US government; a plan that is going to set organized crime back decades; a plan that will save our lives and our identities and our way of living. Or maybe we just get crushed like bugs.

"Finn and Sarah, do you have any new info to share?" I ask. "I've caught Carl up on the material he missed earlier."

"Right now we're marking up a drawing of the house that we can use as part of both planning and execution. It should be ready for detailed planning tomorrow midday, buddy," says Finn.

"You guys keep smacking the keys; we'll work on the other phases," I say. Abby, Carl, and I move to the other end of the room so that we don't have to listen to Finn's heavy breathing. It's become very annoying, almost as much as his bathroom habits.

"Let's get some ideas on paper," I begin. "We tweak, edit, organize, critique, tear it up, and start over, whatever it takes to have the best plan possible by tomorrow. Tomorrow we begin to execute the plan; we don't have the luxury of waiting around."

Carl and Abby both nod.

"We have to get to the black box. Since we can tie Smith to Simpton and Southside, we can use a client of mine who is in direct conflict with both Smith and Southside. He can create a diversion in front of Simpton's house while Abby and I go into the house through the back. Carl, you'll provide cover, and we can all retreat together. That's the first piece.

"The second piece is taking down Smith. If he survives as a duly empowered law officer, we'll never be able to come home. He'll finger me to Southside or go cowboy and try to take me down by himself. I'll go to a second contact of mine who has a working relationship with Southside. This means they aren't at war yet but will be soon enough. I'll have him arrange to buy a big chunk of Southside blow. We'll have the blow planted in Smith's car and use pictures I have of him taking envelopes from Southside muscle to get his blue brothers interested in him. They already hate him. The rumors about his involvement in bad busts, the cocaine, and the pictures will get him killed, or jailed forever. Milt can trigger the investigation once we have everything in place."

"We'll need to do a bunch of reconnoiterin': where do we park cars, what equipment do we need, where are the guards, how disciplined are they?" Carl asks. "Abby and I can do that tomorrow while you meet with your guys. Then we meet back here and go over what Finn and Sarah have pulled together and decide what we do with the info on the black box to get rid of De Cola and Simpton."

"It works for me," Abby says.

"Good, let's get some dinner and get to bed. The next few days are going to be long and tense," I conclude.

Dinner is not amazing but surprisingly better than it looks. It's clear that Carl has spent a lot of time learning how to doctor freeze-dried food. He should write a cookbook, if he lives past the next couple of weeks.

After dinner, we all head to bed. I strip down and climb in between the sheets, but sleep doesn't come rushing at me like last night.

My mind is going a hundred different directions at a thousand miles an hour. I've got the lives of four good people in my hands. And just as scary, my life is in the hands of four good, but fallible, people. I don't know which thought chills me more. I can't help but go over and over each step of the plan. I review how the steps are connected and the many ways any one of those steps can fall out of alignment and put us in a world of hurt. What if Jankowitz won't agree to be the diversion? What if Chucky can't get the blow? What if Smith doesn't respond to the altercation? What if I wet my pants?

I've been in bed for about twenty minutes when I hear my door open and close very quietly. I sense but can't see someone in the room nearby. The darkness is complete with the blackout blinds in place. I slowly move my hand to my .38, located under my pillow, when I hear a soft whisper.

"Don't shoot me, Jake. I come unarmed," Abby whispers. "I can't sleep. I thought maybe you couldn't either, and we could talk about your plan. Or not talk at all."

"I think we go with option two. We wouldn't want the rest of the herd to feel left out."

I hear the soft rustling of clothes. I can tell she's as blind as me, so I hold the covers up for her as she fumbles forward. Finally touching the bed with her hand, she slides under the covers and up to me.

"I hope you don't mind. I never sleep with clothes on," she whispers. I feel her fingertips move across my chest. "I notice that you sleep the same way. We have much in common." We're on our sides, and our upper hands begin tracing each other's backs, shoulders, arms, and heads. When her hand moves to my face, she guides my lips to hers. I feel the brief flick of her tongue. All the while her free hand cradles my neck. I respond in kind, and we begin to settle into a relaxed rhythm. We're in no hurry.

I pull her closer still. Her breasts press against me. Our feet entwine and caress each other. I brush my hand against her cheek, tracing down along her neck to her shoulder and then to her breast. She smells fresh and clean. Our breathing quickens as we become greedy with our movements. We each work thoughtfully to satisfy and be satisfied.

We spend most of the rest of the night introducing our many and varied body parts to each other. We learn each other's pleasure points. We become connected down to the molecular level. I learned a long time ago that for me sex is less about the physical act and more about the intimacy. Don't get me wrong—the physical act can be lights out, as it is with Abby. But to be completely naked, physically, intellectually, and emotionally, is exciting. To be as vulnerable as is possible, to want the other to be pleased more than you do yourself. It's a connection that can't be described and isn't always experienced.

I'm not a halfway man. I've tried, and I hated it. I don't want to wake up and not know the person next to me. Sure, you know her name, but you don't know her. So many things have happened so fast that my relationship with Abby is being swept away by the tornado that spins around us. I don't want to end up in Oz. Oz wasn't real. I want to end up in Kansas. Normally I'd try to slow things down. But when you aren't sure how long you'll be alive, it doesn't make sense to hold back. The danger of the moment merely makes the experience more dynamic by a magnitude of ten.

Monday, March 26

7:00 a.m.
"You really know how to keep a secret..." Abby

I wake up by myself. No, I'm not by myself—Abby's smell and my memory of her linger in my senses. But physically, at some point in the early morning hours, she excused herself and left for her own quarters. We both needed a few hours of sleep to go with our lifetime memory. And sleep wasn't going to happen with us in the same bed.

I think about what it all means. Since my divorce, I haven't had much to do with women. Well, I did have that one moment with Sue's attorney, Sally, or Attila the Sal. And there was the relationship with Heather, which lasted for several months before she threw me off a cliff. But other than them, the past couple of years have been composed of a series of scattered dates with uninteresting women.

I know that I'll need my best poker face to not give us away to the others. I'm not a kiss-and-tell kind of guy. What will be even tougher is the morning-after conversation with her. I want to let her know that the evening was great and special, hoping she responds in kind. I want to be certain that she knows that I'm interested in continuing the relationship. But I want to do so in a way that isn't confusing or awkward.

I get out of bed, dress in sweats, and head to the kitchen, where someone is actively cooking. Carl and Sarah are the chefs, and Abby is nursing a cup of coffee. Finn is still asleep. Even after the magic of last night, the rest of the world keeps spinning per usual.

"Well, hello, young man, we have canned-grounds coffee, freeze-dried eggs, bacon-flavored bits, and stale-bread toast." Abby smiles. "How did you sleep?"

She had to ask that in front of everyone? I smile, look down at the counter and back up at Abby. Before I can say a single word, Carl and Sarah both look at me. Then, in unison, they swivel their gazes toward Abby and then back at me.

"Oh my God, you randy goats, you so totally did it last night," Sarah says.

"Whoa, what are you talking about?" I ask.

"It's in your lips, your tell. Always is when we play poker," Sarah says, and Carl nods his agreement.

"Way to go, Phil Ivey," Abby says. "You really know how to keep a secret."

"Oh, please, you're just as bad. Your tell is in your eyes. You should feel dirty," lectures Carl.

"Hey, buddies, what's up?" Finn asks as he drags his sorry ass into the room.

"Little Jake," says Sarah, "or at least he was last night."

"I am clearly behind the curve here. Why are you referring to Dirk's dagger?

"Because last night Agent Abby romanced it," Carl replies.

"Buddy, you know you're too old to be having sex, right?" Finn asks me with a look of disgust.

Before I can punch him, Abby replies, "Jake, the jig is up. We might as well embrace it." She moves over, and we share another one of those luscious kisses that last forever but not nearly long enough. The others erupt in disgust as we try to kiss our way through their and our own laughter.

9:00 a.m.
"I've got a fed crawling up my butt..." Milt

Everybody eats, showers and dresses, and prepares for the day. Finn and Sarah work away on the computers as Carl, Abby, and I pull together the items we'll need to complete our tasks. I gather some cash and ammo for my .38. Carl and Abby grab surveillance equipment and review a series of maps with Finn.

Finally, Carl, Abby, and I say goodbye to Finn and Sarah. I get into the pickup to follow Abby and Carl, who are in the sedan. We head down the dirt road toward the highway to set up tomorrow's all-in poker play. We leave Finn and Sarah to clean up the dishes—though I hope Sarah takes the lead on that—and finish plotting the strategy to be used inside of Simpton's home.

In town, we split up. I see Abby looking in my direction as we part company. I sense her warm smile even after we've both turned away. I light a cigarette and place it in the ashtray. As it smolders, I begin to relax a little. "What if Carl doesn't allow smoking in his vehicles?" asks my little angel. "Jake will blow smoke in his face," says my little devil. I tell them both to shush.

My first stop is a meeting with Chucky. I figure he's at his office, so I head through town to the Driftwood. I park on the street and casually check out the traffic and pedestrians. I decide it's clear of spies and assassins—though the ease at which Abby tracked me has really damaged my self-confidence—so I head in. Chucky is sitting at his table, facing the entrance, his back to the wall. I grab a coffee and nonchalantly sit on a chair facing him. It's late enough in the morning, and early enough before lunch, that we're the only customers in the place. There are two employees, a young man and woman, who seem to be in the early stages of a rutting ritual. The young man says something with a grin, causing the young woman to giggle. He touches her arm, and she giggles. He belches, and she giggles.

I turn my attention to Chucky, who has a mental middle finger pointed directly at me. "Hey, Chucks, do you remember being as young as those two? I imagine you were quite the mover and shaker with the ladies before your face was deformed."

"Jake, I must admit that you are a mystery to me. I've tried every way possible to make it clear to you that I don't want you to darken my door. But like a hungry mongrel, no matter how many times you get kicked, you keep coming back. My mistake was giving you a scrap of food years ago. Forget about reading between the lines. You couldn't take a hint if it thumped you on the head with a baseball bat. Leave me alone. Whatever it is, I'm not interested, and most of all, I don't care," he says with heart.

"As frightening as your bat sounds, I have an offer for you. I think it's one that may just bring a ray of sunlight into the dirty, smelly, grotesque world that you call home. But first I have a question for you. Are you good friends with Southside? Do you see them respecting your boundaries any better than I do?" I ask.

"First off, that's two questions. Second, you know I'm not naive. I know they're greedy bullies who won't be satisfied with anything less than everything. But if your question is am I at war with them? No, I'm not. And since you're so curious, let me be clear: I'm not interested in going to war with them. And don't think because I've answered your silly questions that I care about what you're about to say next. I'm lowering my Cone of Silence. You no longer exist."

"Before you shut me down, just listen a little bit more." I pause to make sure I have his attention. "Chucky, you just admitted what you and I both know: that Southside isn't going to stop consolidating until they control everything. That means that either you will eventually be forced to fall into line with them or you will be squished like a bug. But, Chucky, I sense you're not a follower. I see that you have always been and always will be a free soul. You're a hippie in a world of suits, if you will allow me. A hippie who will always need to control his own destiny." I pause again to see if I still have his attention. His silence is deafening.

"I have a plan, a plan with very little downside to you but immense upside. And I don't need much, Chucky. I just need you to make a buy. I want you to buy a big bag of blow. But it has to be Southside blow, and I need it today. I have lots of cash; I'm not asking you to front me on this. I'll pay you twice the street price; you'll keep the extra cash, and I'll get the blow. And maybe if I'm lucky, and at no risk to you, I can put a dent into the Southside juggernaut. You're never involved, never mentioned, and never in front of anything or anybody."

He looks at me and thinks about it. "That's easy to say. But you and I both know that the Southside guys that I buy the blow from could put two and two together. But even more important, you'll know and I'm not sure how much I can trust you." He hesitates for a second, looks around, and leans into me. "I hope you realize that if any of this does blow back on me, I'll come looking for you."

"Wouldn't have it any other way. So you're in?"

He nods and asks, "When today?"

"Within three hours, or the deal is off."

"Not only are you deaf, you're pushy. You got the money on you? I'm not a bank," he says.

I slide a thick envelope over to him.

He looks around the room. Once he's convinced no one is watching us, he picks up the envelope and begins flipping through the bills. I can tell he's quicker and probably more accurate than an electronic money counter. "Whoa, you got some change coming."

"It's all yours. I'll see you back here in three hours."

"Okay, but if this blows back at me, you better leave town and start using a new name," he says.

"Understood. Thanks, Chucky." I leave the restaurant knowing that there's a good chance I'm leaving town with a new name even if all goes well for Chucky.

It takes me about an hour to track down Jankowitz. We agree to meet at his Cadillac Escalade that's parked on a side street in Northwest Portland. He tells me that every so often he likes to scope out the trade, see who's working and what they're selling. He's always observing who the players are, making sure he's not being played. But never ever does he touch the cash or the product. He knows how to stay above the fray but still control it. I park behind him and walk up to the passenger side rear door.

"So, Jake, my man, I'm getting awfully nervous. Where's this thing headed?"

"I have a plan, Alvin. I have a bunch of pieces moving around, and there's one I need some help on. You're the only guy who can swing the weight."

"Lay it on me, brother."

"Southside and Smith are connected to a guy named Simpton, who has a home up on Council Crest. Simpton has something I need. In order to get what I need, I need a diversion." My eyes say, "That's you." His eyes reply, "Hell yeah."

"To make it all work, I'll make sure Smith is invited. While Smith is trying to avoid getting shot by either Simpton's muscle or yours, you're going to plant some Southside blow in his car. I'll provide the blow. The cops will discover that, plus some very incriminating pictures I already have of Smith, resulting in the humiliation and demise of our dear public servant. The DA won't have a choice but to dismiss the charges against you since the blow in Smith's car will also be chemically consistent with the blow found in your home. Any questions?"

"Just one: can I shoot the bastard? You know, kind of like make a citizen's arrest but with lethal force?"

"Sorry, Alvin, you're going to want to skedaddle once the blow is planted."

"You are a sweetheart. I love you and that creative thinking thing you got going. You sure you don't want to be on my payroll?" He smiles.

"Thanks for the offer, but I'm a free agent at heart. I'll need to know how you're going to set up the diversion; we don't want to stumble into each other. Your guys need to know not to shoot us."

Alvin starts to snicker. "Come on, Jake, I wouldn't shoot a pal like you." He slaps me on the shoulder with a bit too much gusto.

"I appreciate that." My little devil suggests that I should shoot Alvin right now. My little angel tells my devil and me to chill. "There will be three of us positioning behind the house. Two of us will go in, and one will stay out back providing cover. We'll all wear baseball hats. I'll be back in three hours to deliver the blow and finish working through the details with you."

"Perfect, catch you on the flip side."

I get back into the truck and head over to the meet with Chucky. I'm early, too early to be sitting in the lounge. I park a block away where I have a clear view of the entrance. It's closing in on two in the afternoon. The lunch crowd has cleared out, and there isn't much movement on the street.

I check my watch. Now Chucky's late, and he's got my cash. But more important, I don't have the blow. I start thinking about how to adapt the plan if Chucky can't or won't deliver. The current strategy doesn't work without the cocaine, and I don't have another way of getting enough on the sly quickly enough. The entire plan would have to be changed. All of a sudden someone taps on the passenger window. I jump like a nine-year-old at his first haunted house. I look over to see Chucky. I unlock the door, and he jumps in.

"I thought you were a high-end private dick. How did I sneak up on you? Hell, I wasn't even trying. If I were a bad guy, you'd be dead right now. Hmm, I think I missed a great opportunity."

"I got a lot on my mind, Chucky."

"Here you go. By the way, there's a fed out there trying to find you. Do you know a De Cola?"

"What's he saying?"

"That you're a fugitive. He says there's a warrant out for your arrest, and he's personally fronting a nice reward for your capture, dead or alive. He really doesn't like you. Too bad we're such close friends," he says with a smile, "at least for a while."

"I appreciate it. I'm going to owe you one."

"I don't know, Jake—if this plan doesn't work, you may be worth too much cash to ignore De Cola's offer. You know, if it's not me, someone else will flip on you. Wouldn't you prefer that a friend gets the reward?" He shows me his biggest Cheshire Cat grin as he gets out of the truck, and I take off with a sour feeling at the pit of my stomach.

I head over to the rendezvous point with Jankowitz. Normally I read a book or listen to music while I wait for a meet, but not today. Chucky scared the crap out of me. Everything is rattling around in my brain. After about forty minutes of mental Ping-Pong (I lose), Jankowitz shows up with a lieutenant.

"Jake, meet Gersh; Gersh, this is Jake. Gersh is my point on this and checked out the address. He has a sprinkler repair van that we can load with muscle and fire power. They'll try to talk their way in. But if they can't get in soft, they'll smash the gate and take up positions inside the compound. At the same time, two cars will pull up and drop shooters along the outside of the fence to provide cover. We'll be wired for sound. Here's a phone. When you're in position, you call us. When you're ready to leave, you call us. Gersh's crew will be wearing handkerchiefs over their faces."

"I like it." I pull out a map. I point to the street in front of a house behind Simpton's place. "We're going to park here and cut through this yard and scale the backside fence. We'll exit the same way. We'll call you when we've exited the property. Give us ninety seconds after the call to get to our car. You guys head out this way so that we're not dragging chasers into each other."

"When do you want to do this?"

"Tomorrow night at six."

"Jake, this is going to be fun."

I hand the blow to Jankowitz, and he and Gersh take off. It's time to set up phase three. I need to get to Milt and avoid De Cola while I'm doing it.

I pull out a burner phone and dial.

"Hello," Milt says.

"I need to meet, privately and quickly. Two blocks south of the last poker game. Watch for company," I say. Milt knows it's me by my voice, and he knows there's trouble because I've been out of touch. Plus, I'm guessing he's on Agent De Cola's dance card.

After a brief hesitation, he says, "Okay," and hangs up.

Twenty minutes later, we are speaking in person, and he confirms my suspicions.

"What's going on, Jake? I've got a fed crawling up my butt as if he's going to find you there. Have you been stalking some politician again?" he asks.

"You'd think it was something like that. I need your help." I hand him an envelope. "These are pictures of Detective Smith exiting his abode with a high-priced hooker. She works for a company called HB & Associates—the company address is in the envelope. There are also pictures of Smith taking an envelope from Southside muscle, along with a tape of one of their conversations. The tape and pictures tie him to a Mr. Simpton, who is behind a massive fraud. I have it on good authority that tomorrow around 6:20 p.m. Smith is going to be at Simpton's home. My source says that if someone were to search his car, he might find a big bag of blow. The blow will be chemically identical to the blow that Southside is selling. I need you to trigger the search."

After he looks at all of the pictures and finishes listening to the tape, he smiles. "This envelope will cost him his pension. The blow will put him away for life. The over/under on his lifespan in prison will be a year. Are you going to signal me when to start?"

"No. Make your call to the cops at 6:15 unless you hear otherwise from me. If the deal is a bust, I'll ping you on your cell, so keep it close and charged."

"Okay, but one question. How did you get into this mess?"

"A client with cash. Turns out she's one of the bad guys."

"Jake, if you were taking care of yourself financially, you wouldn't have to take on sketchy clients. Now look what's happened. Now everyone's scrambling to stay alive. No amount of money can be worth this."

"You're right, of course. But right now I just need to get my plan in place. You can lecture me later."

"He's such a granny," says my little devil.

"Oh no, you aren't getting off that easy. When this is over, you're sitting down with my financial planner. No ifs, ands, or buts."

"He's more a nagging mom," says my little angel.

"Got it. You'll make the call?"

"Of course. Be safe. I don't want to be confirming your identity down at the morgue."

"I imagine if things go sideways on this deal, I won't make it to the morgue. But seriously, thanks, Milt. In a few weeks, if all goes well, I'll have quite the yarn to spin. Oh, and by the way, I've hired a new receptionist. She has instructions to call you in two weeks to see if you've heard from us. If it's safe, she can go in to the office and keep things moving. If not, she gets paid to stay away. Don't let her take any risks."

"No problem. Jake, be safe," Milt says again and shakes my hand with the most serious and sincere expression I've ever seen on his face. He's making me think this plan might have a high degree of difficulty. He gets out of the truck and walks away.

9:00 p.m.
"Ahhh, I thought you'd never ask…" Abby

Carl and Abby are already at the ranch when I arrive. Abby gives me a big hug and kiss before I can say anything. I'm really enjoying not saying anything.

"How did it go?" I finally ask.

"Perfect," Carl says. "The plan we put together last night should work fine. Simpton's got cameras, which Finn will be controllin', leavin' only the guards as Simpton's eyes. The guards are heavily armed and may be well trained, but they seem bored, which means a high level of sloppiness. That should play right into our hands. In case they get a look at us, we bought two new cars. We parked them along our exit route. Tomorrow we'll drive the truck and sedan to the attack cars and then drive the attack cars to Simpton's house. Afterward, we'll reverse the process or just take off in the attack cars if we have to. They don't look like much, but they run great."

"Great idea," I say, and I proceed to fill them in on my day. "So we're down to the final pieces. First, we need to map out our plan for inside the compound. Second, we need to figure out what we're going to do once we have all of the codes from Simpton's black box. And third, we need to set up our routes out of the country. Finn, what information do you have about the inside of the home?"

"It's two stories with a basement. The upper story is bedrooms and bathrooms. The main floor has a large entry area, dining room, formal living room, family room, kitchen, and den. The basement has a bedroom, bathroom, and large common room.

"The plans show massive wiring going into the basement common room. If I were a betting man, I think that would be my first choice for the black box. Choice number two would be the main floor den. But the den has windows facing towards the street. It doesn't seem all that secure, but I don't think we can ignore it.

"There's no outside door to the basement. There are windows that seem big enough for a person to slip through, but I don't know for sure. There's one window into the basement common room. If the window won't work, you'll have to go through the back porch sliders into the eating area next to the kitchen. Then you'll go down this hallway to the right, over to these stairs, and down to the basement common room. As you can see, to get to the basement, you have to go past the den. I think you should check the computer in that room first.

"Once you're in front of a computer, Abby, you'll need to wrap this"—Finn hands her a headband, like an athlete wears, with a wireless camera connected in front—"around your head. Then flip this switch and point this camera toward the computer screen."

Abby puts on the headband and turns on the camera. She moves it around until she can see the captured image on the computer screen.

"You should test it again outside the compound before you start the madness. Here's a phone that has one number programmed, the number of this second phone that I'll keep. When you're ready, call me. Once we've identified the correct machine, you'll put this flash drive in a USB port. This icon should pop up on the desktop. Right-click on it and toggle to *Run*. At that point I'll be able to unlock his screen, if he has a password, and begin downloading everything we need. When the download is completed, I'll tell you, and you scram."

"How do I know if I have the correct computer?" Abby asks.

"My program will send a ping to my machine. If it's the correct machine, I'll let you know. I'll be able to tell by its IP address."

"We'll need to go through this again," I say, "so either one of us can do it in our sleep, just in case. Now, here's what I'm thinking we do after the raid," I continue. "If we get the right data from Simpton, we'll reroute all of the money out of the companies involved in the scheme. I'm thinking we find some federal government account and just dump it. The feds will investigate and use the money trail to catch the bad guys. Does anyone have a better idea?"

"That isn't going to work," says Abby. "It will take the feds months to figure out that they have $300 million extra in an account. The reality is they may never figure it out. I think we want to be home quicker than never. I suggest we send all of the money to someone detestable. My vote is for De Cola. We set up accounts all over the world. Then funnel the money from those into his personal accounts. Some of the money we split off to fund our get away. When Simpton realizes all his cash is gone, he traces it to De Cola. We also leak word to the IRS that De Cola has massive unreported income. He'll have the feds and the mob after him. He'll be forced to go into witness protection, or die. It blows everybody up and leaves us all out of it."

We all look at her in awe. Eventually, Carl stands and begins clapping, and we all join in.

"So here's the timing," I say. "Tonight we pack our getaway bags—travel light but don't forget the important things like IDs and phones—and make bank and travel arrangements. Carl, since you're the only one who knows our second aliases, you'll need to have Finn show you how to transfer money to our final destinations. You'll stay hidden until you get the all-clear email to the email account that we'll set up tonight.

"Tomorrow, Carl, Abby, and I go to the stashed cars and time our arrival at the target for 5:55 p.m. We're out by 6:20. If something goes wrong, we're on the run from there. If all goes well, we'll come back here, get a hot meal and a good night's sleep.

"Once you're at your final destination, send an email letting everyone know you made it. Then we lay low for at least two weeks before we begin contacting each other through these email accounts. Hopefully, within four weeks we're all home. Any questions? Good. Let's get our itineraries pulled together."

As Carl, Sarah, and Finn, huddle up and begin putting everything in place, I walk over to Abby and put my arm around her.

"If it's okay with you, I'd like to meet up at the same final destination," I tell her.

"Ahhh, I thought you'd never ask. Where should we go? Definitely someplace warm."

We all rehearse every step multiple times. We double- and triple-check our getaway bags and iron out the little details. We all know that something will go wrong. "Yeah, right, like Finn has a clue," says my little devil.

Everybody heads to bed. Tonight there's no pretense: Abby walks right into my room. She cuddles up, and we both drift off to sleep.

Tuesday, March 27

5:40 p.m.

"Ride 'em, cowboys..." Gersh

Carl scouts the yard from which we're going to breach Simpton's yard.

I should be concentrating on helping him scout, but I can't stop thinking about today. I woke with a numb left arm. It was pinned by my torso, the bed, and a sleeping Abby. Being with Abby last night was completely different than the first night. Instead of greedy hands and hot breath, we spooned each other and slept.

I don't remember the last time I slept so soundly. And as I think about it, I find that I'm truly at peace with the work plan too, in spite of the risk that we face. This morning, I even considered contacting De Cola and giving him everything he wants if he'd leave everyone else alone. He could have me if he didn't take action against the rest of the gang. But I knew that wouldn't work. He'd just smile as he cuffed us all, or worse.

No, I think, as I watch Carl work, this is the best option there is. Carl and Abby and I all have experience planning dangerous operations, and this is what we agreed upon. No second-guessing, no walking backward. Forward is the only direction open to us.

At 2:00 p.m., Carl, Abby, and I said goodbye to Finn and Sarah. Sarah and I embraced long and hard. I said, "Don't worry too much," with my eyes. Her eyes said she would try not to.

Finn was so busy playing with his keyboard that he barely acknowledged our departure. It's frightening to think that an entire generation of Americans is as skilled at the social graces as he is.

Traffic was light going in our direction, so we made it to the stashed cars much sooner than we expected. Rather than sit and wait in the cars, we found a diner a couple of miles away and grabbed a snack and Cokes. Carl drained his drink fast and started crunching ice between his teeth. I twiddled my straw and stared into the liquid. Abby looked out the window and occasionally at me; we smiled at each other and reassured ourselves with our eyes. Abby barely touched her sandwich, and Carl devoured his like he was afraid someone would snatch it from him.

Now, Carl gives us the thumbs-up, and we move into position. All three of us place our getaway bags in a bush a few steps away. We test all of our equipment: the head camera, the phones, and we make sure our guns are loaded and that we have extra ammo. I'm carrying my .38, Abby carries a Glock, and Carl has his own 9mm plus a M24 rifle with a Leupold scope, with which he can provide cover for us. None of us have suppressors; the diversion in front of the house should cover any noise we make. My angel and my devil are both scared silent

At exactly 6:00 p.m., I call Gersh. "We're a go."

"Ride 'em, cowboys."

I get my phone that connects me to Abby, Carl, and Finn, and I set up an earbud. We've worked out a protocol so we're not talking over each other on this party line. At 6:05, we hear a large crash. Finn is watching on the security cameras and tells us that Gersh crashed the gate, and his crew is setting up inside the compound. He can see other men are taking up flanking positions outside the fence. No shots have been fired yet—we all know that.

We don't see any guards in back. I look at Abby; she smiles and starts climbing over the fence. Once she's over, I toss our bags up and over to her. As I mount the fence, Carl says, "Break a leg."

Abby and I make a beeline for the window that opens into the lower-level common area. Abby checks to see if we can open it while I scan for bad guys. She gives me a thumbs-down; it can't be opened. So we move toward the back patio door.

We pause at the edge of the wall, out of sight of the glass patio doors. We hear the gun battle begin out in front. Finn confirms.

I move around the corner and almost smack into a bad guy. He and I freeze, staring at each other for an instant. Then I hear a bang, and red spray shoots out of the bad guy's chest. He's dead before he hits the ground. It looks like he's holding more lead than he can carry. I grab his upper body and drag him around the corner. He's left a blood trail, and his body isn't hidden especially well, but that's the best I can do under the circumstances.

Abby and I move quickly through the patio door and into the eating area. We both crouch low and observe. We see a table with seating for eight, a kitchen to our left, and a den directly in front of us. A bad guy is firing out of an open window that faces the front yard. He's kneeling near the first computer that we plan on checking. I look at Abby, and she nods.

Abby and I move across the room to either side of the doorway leading into the den. I signal to her to provide cover for me as I go in. I count down with my fingers from three and then move into the den in a low crouch. The bad guy is so intent on firing into the front yard that he doesn't sense my arrival from behind. I instantly get him in a choke hold. Once he's unconscious I lay him gently on the floor. Abby moves into the room and turns on the computer and inserts the flash drive. I move back to the doorway to watch the hallway and guard against interlopers. I divide my attention between the hallway and the open window to the front yard. Abby does a few keystrokes, and we hear Finn say, "Negative, that's not the correct computer. Hallway is clear. I don't have a camera on the stairs, but the basement is clear as far as I can see."

It's 6:12. We move into the hall and position ourselves on the near side of the doorway to the stairs. I look around the corner down the stairs and see that they are clear. I move down the stairs quickly while Abby covers my back. At the bottom of the stairs, we confirm there aren't any bad guys hidden or napping.

In the common room, there are three computers. Abby puts the headband on, turns on the camera, and inserts the flash drive into the first machine. While she works away, my recurring fears jump into my mind. What if Finn doesn't know what he's talking about? What if there isn't a black box?

I hear Finn say, "Negative, not our machine."

Abby moves to a second machine.

Or what if there is a black box, but there isn't any financial information we can use? What if this is all for nothing?

I hear Finn say, "Nope, not the right one."

Abby moves to the third and final machine, inserts the drive, and types. We wait, and we wait, and we wait, and then Finn says, "That's it! Good to go."

I feel relief that I can't enjoy since a gun could be unleashed on us at any moment. I try not to watch her work on the machine at Finn's direction. I patrol the room, watching the stairway closely, looking out through the windows occasionally. "Finn, don't forget to keep an eye on the hallway—we don't want to be ambushed down here."

"Buddy, you're such a little baby. You've seen me work, I'm a mega multitasker," he replies.

Abby punches a couple of keys.

We wait. And we wait.

"Finn, how much longer?" I ask.

"Same as I told you last night. The laws of physics haven't been suspended in that room. Three to five minutes to see if we can get in; two minutes to copy everything."

And we wait and wait. It's 6:17.

Outside, we hear lots of yelling. It sounds like the two sides are shooting less and talking more. I hope Gersh isn't selling us out for a pack of smokes.

"We're in," Finn says. "I'm in control of the machine." The next two minutes go on forever. We hear sirens approaching. The gunfire begins to pick up again.

Then Finn says the magical words: "Grab the flash drive and get out."

224

He doesn't have to ask twice. Abby pulls the drive free from the machine and stuffs it, plus the headband, into her bag. Once she's done with that, she picks up her gun and looks around, attempting to settle the objects around the computer in the same way they were arranged before we arrived. She moves a couple of items and says, "Let's go, stud."

"So, you've noticed?" I ask as I move to the base of the stairs with my gun pointed up toward the open door.

Before we can start moving up the stairs, we hear Finn: "Don't go up the stairs. Some guards have planted themselves in the hallway."

We freeze in position and wait a few seconds.

"Finn, are they still there?"

"Yes. They don't look like they're going anywhere. I think you should check that window to the yard. The stairs will be a video-game shootout."

6:21. I whisper to Carl, "Is the backyard clear?"

"Affirmative."

We move to the window, and I lift Abby up to check it out. In ten seconds, she scans the yard and has the window open; in three more seconds, she climbs out to the backyard. I hand up our bags and weapons.

"Get out of there, buddy! Dudes are moving down the stairs. Move, or they're going to shoot you in the butt," says Finn.

I'm up and out and softly close the window just as I see the first boot of the first bad guy landing on the last step of the stairs. Abby and I grab our stuff and sprint for the fence. I toss all of our gear to Carl as Abby scales the fence, and then I follow her. We grab our getaway bags and sprint toward the street. Over the phone, we hear Finn: "No one is following you; I think you're clear."

We pause at the last row of bushes and then casually walk to the cars. As we walk, I call Alvin and give him the all clear. As I drive away at 6:25 exactly, I'm careful to keep below the speed limit and obey all of the traffic signs. It must be the first time since my driving test at age sixteen that I've been such a law abiding driver. Abby sits quietly beside me, regularly looking for a tail. All of the way to Carl's cars, we listen to Finn. Finn tells us that Smith made it to the party and is in the midst of a confrontation with Simpton and the boys in blue. Gersh got out clean. Once we get to Carl's cars, I cut communications so I can concentrate on safe driving. We give each other big hugs, and I get an even bigger kiss from Abby.

"Where's mine?" Carl asks. Abby kisses him quickly on the cheek. He smiles. I turn him down.

Carl gets in the sedan, and Abby and I climb into the cab of the truck. We pull away from the curb at 6:30. I light up a cigarette and just hold it between my fingers, which I keep on the wheel. Abby finds a country radio station, and we listen to Dierks Bentley sing about a little white tank top and shotgun-toting dad. Abby sits in the middle of the seat with her arm draped across my lap and her head on my shoulder. Man, I could get used to this. We've just gone from near death to high school sweethearts in the blink of an eye. I feel my pulse settling down to something closer to normal. I watch the traffic move around with everyday folks attending to their everyday lives in peace. Not one of them is worried about a lunatic shooting at them, though they probably should. If the national stats are correct, 30 percent of them are armed, and 30 percent of them suffer from a personality disorder. It's the crossover group that scares me.

After two hours of roundabout driving, we pull up to the ranch. We're starved and drained now that we aren't still on adrenaline highs. Sarah and Finn are outside and excited, ready to celebrate.

"Damn, that was a smoking show," Finn says. "I taped it, and I've watched the whole thing three times. I'll bet there were several hundred rounds fired out front, but nobody was killed, just a few wounded. Buddy, you're going to love the last ten minutes." He invites us to sit around his computer while he moves the recording forward to 6:40 p.m.

From one of the cameras, we can see the front half of Smith's Caddy. There are several cops talking to him; he's arguing; they're trying to calm him down. This continues until one of the blue brothers starts jabbing a finger in Smith's chest. Smith does the only thing he knows how to do. He throws his hands up in the air in feigned surrender—and then throws a sucker punch at the finger jabber! Two police officers instantly grab and hold him while an additional two start searching his car. It takes all of thirty seconds for one of them to find the blow. Smith is livid up until he sees the blow. Then he shakes his head. He seems to plead, and then he loses it—screaming and battling as he's cuffed.

"Couldn't have happened to a nicer guy," I say. "Did you see what happened in the house when the cops cleared and things settled down? Did anyone hover over the black box?"

"Not that I could see. They acted pretty normal for a group of guys who had just been shot up. They didn't let the cops see the guy in back, who Carl shot. They moved him but didn't need to. The cops never even went into the house. Now, Abby, it's time for you and me to start the money march."

Wednesday, March 28

5:00 a.m.

"Get up, get dressed, get your bag—we have company..."
Abby

I'm still waiting for Abby to slip between the sheets and keep me company. She, Carl, and Finn have been busy moving money all night while the rest of us try to sleep, but I'm sure we're all reliving the action at Simpton's. Only after a mission is over can you assign a true level of risk to the whole shebang. I've decided that our recent experience deserves a rating of near death. We all gave up one of our nine lives last night. There are so many things that could have gone wrong that each time I began to drift off, another frightening possibility drifted into my cerebral cortex. What if a stray bullet had hit Abby while she was checking the computer in the den? Her back was turned toward the gunfight in the front yard—she would never have seen it coming. What if I had blocked Carl's shot of the bad guy who came out of the house as we were entering?

In many ways the evaluation process is healthy. The analysis supports a new level of confidence in yourself. You know that you can achieve a higher level of risk. You reinforce your good decisions and think of alternatives to the bad ones. Eventually you conclude that none of that matters. All that matters is that you're still thinking and breathing.

I must have finally drifted off again because the next thing I know I'm rattled out of sleep by a rude hand shaking me. "What the hell?"

"Get up, get dressed, get your bag—we have company," Abby says. She gives me a kiss, a caress of my hair, a look, and she's gone.

There's no way this is Grandma Mae with her famous beef noodles paying a social call. I'm dressed and out into the common area in about ten seconds.

Carl is at the dedicated security-camera computer looking intently at the screen. "Ten bogeys are movin' in from the highway, to the east of us. I don't see anyone tryin' to flank us from any other direction. My best guess is these are not trained government troops or cops; they're sloppy in their technique. But they're clearly armed and intent on moving in our direction. We have about ten minutes to execute a plan. I'm in control, no debate—there isn't enough time. Who can ride a dirt bike?"

Abby and I raise our hands.

"Okay, we're all goin' out through the back door of the garage. We're goin' to push the two bikes directly west toward the forest. The house will block the bogeys' view of our exit. When we get to the trees, Abby and Jake will fire up the bikes and head due south to the trail that I told you about earlier. You'll draw the attention of the bogeys, which means, of course, you'll also draw their fire. So keep your heads down and move fast.

"While the bogeys focus their attention on the two of you, the three of us"—Carl indicates Sarah and a rather frightened-looking Finn—"will run to the north for the other trail. I'll arm the house so that once a few of the goons are inside, they and the computers that we used to move the money and set up our escape disappear.

"Jake and Abby, your trail will start south, then turn east and end at the highway. Once you get to the highway, I think your only real option is to cross and head for the river.

"Once you reach the river, turn north. After about half a mile, you'll encounter a summer camp. You'll find a shed that stores canoes, oars, and life jackets. Dump the bikes in the river, grab what you need from the shed, and paddle down to the Chalet Inn. A car dealer I know will meet you there—his name is Stevie. He'll give you a clean car. Everybody understand? Does anybody have any questions?" We all look at each other, and we're all shaking our heads no. "Okay, from now on, nobody says anythin' unless it's to save a life. Damn, Jake, this is way fun."

"You've always been a sick bastard," I reply. Carl and I give each other a man-hug, right hands clasped between us and left hands patting backs hard, hard enough to draw tears. Sarah and I embrace. Here I go yet again, telling her everything will be okay but not sure if I believe it myself. "You'll be fine. Carl is the toughest son of a bitch I know."

"I'm fine, Jake. You be careful." She lowers her voice and puts her lips to my ear. "I still don't fully trust Abby. You barely know her, and you're acting like you've known each other for years. I don't like it."

"Thanks, kiddo, I'll be careful. Time to go." I look over at Finn and give him a "no hug, no way" look as we head to the garage with our packs.

Carl and I grab the bikes and start pushing them toward the forest. The others fall in behind us. We move in a silent single-file line at an easy jog. I hear Finn wheezing behind us, paying the price for years of sitting on his butt and working his fingers to the bone. The grass is knee-high, but the route that Carl is picking seems pretty level and easy to traverse. As quiet as we probably are, each step sounds deafening. Every so often, Carl looks over his shoulder to make sure the house is still between us and the goons and that Finn isn't too far behind.

Just before we reach the edge of the forest, we think we can hear voices. We all drop into a crouch and scan the dark void behind us. We've gotten lucky; the wind is blowing from east to west. It's pulling the sound of the gorillas toward us and pushing our sounds away from them. Clearly the goons don't understand how far sound can travel. But the best news of all is that we don't see any red laser beams lighting up our chests.

Carl signals us to resume our flight toward the trees. A few seconds later, we stop at the edge of the forest.

"I think your best option is to cut across the field to the loggin' road just behind that tree. It means time in the open, but if you try to travel through the trees from here, the bogeys could cut across the front of your path."

"Piece of cake." I say.

"Sarah and Finn, get to that second line of trees and lie flat, out of sight," Carl says. "We'll give Jake and Abby a few seconds to break for their trail before we start to move." He turns to me and says, "Okay, see you in about a month, with any luck."

"Thanks, Carl. You didn't have to get involved. But we'd be dead, or worse, without you. Keep an eye on Sarah for me."

"No worries, son; I've got 'er covered."

Abby and I board our bikes and simultaneously fire them up. Carl's a good man—both bikes start like they are brand-new, no second tries, no sputters, no warm-up, just instant, full-throated power. I look at Abby—she smiles at me in a wicked way for a brief moment, and she's gone, with me right behind her.

5:25 a.m.
"Ready to find a boat..." Abby

The racket produced by the bikes muffles all other sound, even my own breathing, which is working overtime. Abby and I must traverse sixty yards of open and rutted, rock-strewn grassland to reach the cover of the trees. We begin to see red lasers knifing through the dark around the field and on the trees. Half a football field of rough ground at a moderate speed with the risk of guns blazing at us—no biggie. We're tempted to drive at full throttle, but due to the limited light and uncertain terrain, we choose to maintain our modest clip. The worst thing to do is to spill to the ground and become stationary targets. Thirty yards to go.

I almost feel pity for the bad guys; with the amount of bounce we're experiencing along the uneven ground, we're impossible to target. Fifteen yards to go. My heart stops as I see a deadly laser spot land and somehow lock on Abby's head. I yell as loudly as I can, attempting to warn her to duck down, with no visible effect. I feel a sickening sensation in my stomach as I realize how helpless I am to avert impending disaster. Through my peripheral vision, I watch the bullet flash through the minimal light toward her head. A moment later, I hear the report of the rifle shot. But inches from her, the bullet strikes and lodges in a Doug fir, square in the trunk. I have no time for a joyous shout, but I feel relief now that she's protected by the trees. Just as I'm about to join Abby in the safety of the giant firs, I experience a burning sensation on my ass. It catches my attention for a mere moment as I remain focused on reaching the firs and surviving. Now's not the time to slow down for anything less than a final breath.

Abby is moving quickly along a trail that she can see. All I can see is her shapely derriere (damn little devil) bouncing up and down and to and fro in front of me. Off to our left, flashlight and laser beams swing into and around the trees. But none of them can penetrate deeply enough to spotlight us. The farther into the forest we move, the less visible the indications of our pursuers become. I hear cracks and hope the gorillas are shooting wildly in frustration into the trees at us and haven't pivoted and picked up Carl's trail.

Eventually the ground levels out, the trail widens, and the small amount of moonlight becomes adequate to guide us along our route. It's almost romantic, my little angel suggests, until we hear a huge roar and over our shoulders see a fireball several miles behind us and to our left. Sadly, it looks like the goons were in too much of a rush to get into Carl's house and triggered one of Carl's presents—sad for the house, at least.

We race until our path meets the highway. Abby stops and waits for me. It's a perfect place to cross the road—we can see for a mile in each direction, and we appear to be alone. We risk a brief breather.

"Ready to find a boat?" she asks.

"I've never canoed before—how about you?"

"I took a couple of lessons in grade school. With as much noise as these bikes make, do you think we should risk turning on the lights?"

"After we get a hundred yards back into the forest, if there isn't enough light and the undergrowth is thick, we may need to risk it. But let's wait as long as we can. Noise echoes and is more difficult to pinpoint than light."

"Roger, follow me."

We cross the highway and look for the trail. We're fortunate: the undergrowth is sparse, and we can hear the river over the roar of the bikes. It takes us about five minutes, moving slowly, to find the river and another two minutes to reach the shed.

The shed is locked but simple to break into. We glance inside, using the light of Abby's cell phone to guide us. We see several canoes, choose the darkest-colored one, and pull it out to the riverbank. While I roll the bikes into the river, my little angel tsk-tsks me for damaging the ecosystem. My little devil tells my angel to stop worrying about the fishes or we'll be swimming with them. Abby returns to the shed for oars and life jackets.

"I grabbed these too," she says, and she hands me one of two bags. "They're waterproof, and we can put our getaway bags into them, so even if we get wet, our stuff—"

She gets cut off as we hear voices moving toward us. We take cover behind a tree. We see light flashing, and I can identify two unique voices. I look at Abby and hold up two fingers with a questioning look. She nods.

I whisper to her, "We can't let them find the boats and walk away. They'll signal downstream, and we'll be toast. We have to disable them." She agrees. "You flank them to the left; I'll move to the right. If there's more than two, we circle around behind them and come back together to figure out what we're going to do. If there are only two, we'll have them in a cross fire. We'll disarm them and lock them in the shed. I saw lots of rope." She nods again.

Instantly and noiselessly, she's gone. I move off to the right, attempting to match her stealth.

A forest is never quiet. Even at night there are the sounds of the wind rustling the treetops, the splashing of a river, and the call of a bird. Our forest is particularly noisy. By the relaxed, raucous noise our pursuers are making, they must be convinced that they're on a wild goose chase. They carry on a conversation like a couple of grandpas in rockers arguing about which war was the toughest, World War I or their first marriages.

It's so easy to slink up behind them that I fear they're just the bait. That the real attack dogs are lurking behind, waiting for us to show ourselves. I look past the interlopers and observe that Abby is in position. I signal her, and we both set up behind tree trunks at point-blank range on opposite sides of the goons. In a calm voice, I say, "Hey, assholes, hands up." They jump and look around, but in the dark they can't be sure how many guns are pointed at them. Slowly, reluctantly, they raise their hands.

"On your knees, hands behind your heads. You'll both look forward. If one of you looks backward, both of you will catch a bullet." I signal Abby to search them. She begins to strip them of guns, phones, and keys.

As she pulls the second guy's gun, I hear a crunch behind me. I pivot and see another person silhouetted against the trees. I also see the glint of a gun pointed at my belly. As I begin to swing my hands up to fire at him, my mind is telling me it's over. He has me. I'll never get my gun up in time. Everything slows down. I don't think about death—I worry about Abby. If I'm down, how will she fare against three bad guys on her own? When my gun is halfway through its arc in the direction of the third bogey, I hear a shot. I jump at the sound but continue to swing around to target the third man. As my gun aligns with his chest, he freezes in position for a moment and then falls to the ground. I turn toward the source of the shot and can still see a faint whiff of smoke wafting up from the nose of Abby's gun.

I also see one of the first two goons trying to get up and take advantage of the shift in our focus. "Move another fraction of an inch, dummy, and you'll have a new sphincter in your brainpan," I shout at him.

He turns toward me and settles back down with a grimace that manages to convey both anger and resignation.

I keep my gun trained on the goons, but I risk brief glances at Abby. She's still facing the person she shot. "Abby, look at me," I say. Slowly, her gaze moves to meet mine. "I need you to keep these two in line while I check the guy behind me—can you do that?"

"Yes, yes, I'm fine," she says. She retargets the captives, and I sense she's completely refocused.

I walk over to the downed gunman. I keep my gun pointed at him while I kick his gun clear of his hand. His eyes are open, but he's not breathing. She's shot him square in the heart. To be certain, I check his wrist for a pulse, but it's not there.

"He's dead. We need to focus on these two. Are you with me?" I ask her.

"Yeah, I'm good," she replies with a solid tone.

I turn my attention to the kneeling thugs. "Now, I want both of you to strip to your underwear. You have ten seconds before I begin shooting. And not a sound, not even a sneeze."

They follow my instructions without any hesitation. These guys are not true believers in their cause. All they wanted was a payday, and now all they want is to survive. After they're undressed, we walk them to the shed. Abby grabs some rope and ties them to each other and a rack holding paddles. As I gag them, Abby grabs an ax and disables the remaining canoes. We exit and lock the shed door behind us. If the goons get free of the ropes, the door won't stop them, but if anyone wanders by, the shed will look normal and not like a holding tank. I gather their clothes, guns, phones, and keys and toss theirs plus the deceased's into the river. I drag the body into the brush, hiding it the best that I can.

"Why strip them down?" Abby finally asks.

"So you can see how truly fortunate you are to be with me." I smile.

"Oh brother."

"Actually, in my experience, it's harder to throw a punch or run in pursuit when in you're in your tightie whities. Are you sure you're okay?"

"I'm fine. I'm not happy, but we didn't have a choice."

I put my arms around her and hug and kiss her. "Of course you had a choice—we always have a choice. This time it was kill him or let him kill me. Thanks for saving my life."

"You're welcome. You owe me big time." She smiles up to me.

We quickly turn our attention to the canoe and our escape. We tie the straps from the water-tight bags to our life jackets. Together, we move the boat to the water's edge. The river is daunting, louder than our bikes and rushing by quickly.

"Looks like there's some snow melt coming down through the stream," Abby says. "The good news is that most of the rocks will be under water. The bad news is that any rocks or tree trunks that are above the surface are going to smash us to pieces at the speed we'll be going. If we do get dumped, turn so that your feet are going downstream first, to protect your head from the rocks. You get in front and just paddle like a son of a bitch. If you see a rock, point to it. Don't shout—I probably won't be able to hear you," she tells me as we push the canoe into the ice-cold water and shove off. I'm glad Abby's grade school apparently offered advanced canoeing lessons.

As we begin to move downstream, my whole body relaxes. There's something soothing about floating, even if there are invisible monsters lurking just below the surface, trying to snag us and break us in two. The river calms, and at least for the moment, I don't see or hear any white water. I take a quick look back at Abby. She gives me an equally quick smile but is otherwise completely locked into searching the water ahead for trouble.

Every now and then, we see homes along the river. They look dark and abandoned. Probably vacation homes occupied all of two weeks every year in the summer. As the sky lightens, we begin to hear the birds more, and occasionally we hear a vehicle off in the distance.

I'm torn from my comfortable place by an ugly sound in front of us. I hear the battle of water versus rock, the former slowly eroding the latter down into pebbles. If we were here in a thousand years, these rocks would be gravel. But today they're deadly obstacles that must be avoided.

Now I can see the effervescent white water; I can sense the water underneath the canoe accelerating and throwing us forward. I search for calm water off to the sides of the tumult. But the river in front of us drops in elevation, and I won't be able to see past the rocky drop-off until we're nearly on top of the first rock. I spot a calm avenue to the left of the roiling water. Before I can point, Abby pivots the canoe in the direction of the avenue of calm water. Instantly I see that we won't reach our desired point by heading to it in a direct manner, due to a craggy line of boulders that lies across our path.

Abby must see the same thing, so she spins us back to the right. I lose my balance and almost fall out of the canoe. But at the last moment, I grab the edge of the boat with my left hand. I end up bent over the edge of the canoe, which is way better than being overboard. Until I glance ahead and see a rock looming in line with my head. I manage to throw my right hand toward the rock. As my hand hits the rock, the force pushes me back into the canoe. I was almost a red wet spot on a gray wet rock. Instead, I'm back in the safety of the canoe.

I grab my paddle with both hands and commence paddling at a furious pace. At least in my mind, it's a furious pace. Abby spins the canoe to the left one more time, and we're clear of the rapids. We're in a smooth avenue of water that skirts the tumultuous battle in the center of the river off to our right.

The rest of the trip is calm and peaceful, if you ignore the fear of eminent discovery. We come upon the back of a restaurant. As we edge closer, we see a sign confirming that the structure is the Chalet Inn. We pull onto the shore and slowly, quietly land the canoe. The sun is nearly up, and we see a single car parked in the lot as close as possible to the water's edge. Sitting on the hood, facing away from us, is a man in a gray suit with a smoking cigar in his right hand. I point Abby to the shadowy edge of the building; her Glock is pulled and ready. I approach the man slowly, my .38 in my right hand, which I keep hidden behind my back.

Without turning toward us, he says, "You must be Jake and Abby. Carl said you'd probably shoot me if I wasn't careful. Do you mind if I turn and face you?"

"Not at all. Just keep your hands away from your body. I'm a trusting soul, but my friend hates, just hates, gray suits. Move over here to this side of the car."

The man moves away from the car and allows me to search him. I pull his ID, Steven Wysneski. I wave to Abby to come over.

"Here are the keys; Carl has already paid my fee. It looks like crap, but the motor is practically brand-new, and it's comfortable inside. It's registered to Dirk Dagger—is that you? No, don't answer. Don't care and don't want to know. Anyway, if you have any troubles, you can call me at this number, and I can try to coordinate assistance. I have connections up and down the coast. Best of luck."

"Can we give you a lift somewhere?'

"Thanks but no. Cheers." He smiles, turns, and walks over to the front steps of the restaurant and sits facing the rising sun. By the look on his face, he hasn't a care in the world. He seems at peace, capable of thrilling over the simple, everyday event of the rising sun, something most of us ignore in the rush of our daily grind. I decide to join him in his gaze toward the reddish-orange sky.

Abby steps up beside me, loops her arm in mine, and says, "Soon we'll be able to enjoy this every day."

We share a smile.

We load our stuff into the car, and Abby sends the unmanned canoe down the river. We hop into the car and agree that Dirk Dagger will take the first shift at the wheel. Christie Wind will catch some shut-eye. We head west on I-84 and then south on I-5.

The plan is to grab breakfast and change drivers in Eugene. From Eugene, we'll drive south on I-5, and then we'll cut off I-5 and head into San Francisco. From there we'll take 101 south to San Diego. It isn't the fastest route, but hopefully anybody searching for us will discount it. We'll dump the car and cross into Mexico as Dirk and Christie. Once across the border, we'll adopt our second identities.

I look over at Abby—damn, I mean, Christie. She's sound asleep, snoring like a logger, drool darkening the coat she's using as a pillow. "That is such a good look on her," says my little devil. It's been a long time since I've had these kinds of feelings. The last time was with Heather. But she wasn't looking for more than a few moments. I wanted more, and my vote didn't count. What if Abby's the same as Heather? I'm afraid that either she may not feel the same way about me or that my feelings have more to do with the fear, adrenaline, and stress of our situation than a mature connection. I know that if we live long enough, we'll find out. Can't worry about it yet—just drive, and don't get pulled over by an officer of the law.

Normally I'd be going ten miles over the speed limit, but today its sixty-five miles per hour in a seventy-five mph world. Everyone who passes us looks at me like I'm someone's elderly grandpa who was warned not to drive months ago. I hear a siren. I look into my rearview mirror, and I see a county sheriff moving rapidly down the highway toward me. Even though I know I haven't done anything wrong, I get juiced with adrenaline. My angel quickly reminds me, "Don't sweat it—he's not after you. Just pull to the side and let him pass." I do, and he does, nailing a speeder about a mile ahead of me. But the sound of the siren has awakened Christie.

"I'm practicing your new name, even in my thoughts, Christie."

"What a coincidence—I was dreaming of a dashing pirate named Dirk. You look amazing with an eye patch."

I laugh. "What do you want for breakfast, sweetheart? Don't forget that you'll be driving the next shift."

"I'm easy. Let's just hit a Denny's; eggs, bacon, toast, and coffee are sounding amazing right now. Nothing against Carl's cooking, but frozen and powdered food just isn't the same as the real thing. Hmm, never thought I'd say that about Denny's."

"You read my mind."

We see a Denny's, turn off, and luxuriate in our first real food in several days. Forty minutes later, we're ready to get back on the road. Now Christie is going to drive, and Dirk is going to drool.

10:30 a.m.
"I can't shake the look of shock…" Christie

Christie starts the car, but before she puts it in gear, she hesitates. I look over at her and realize that she's not happy. In fact, she seems anguished. It dawns on me that despite her excitement about the promise of food, she didn't eat much on her plate. Not so long ago she shot and killed one of the goons. Me, I'm elated, not that a man is dead but that I'm alive. If Christie hadn't shot him, he'd have shot me. Then he probably would have killed her. And she didn't have the luxury to shoot to wound. If she had aimed for an arm or leg in the dark forest as opposed to the center of his mass, she could have missed or at least not slowed him down enough. Plus, the two guys we had kneeling would have jumped up and added to our bad fortune.

But no matter how bad he might have been, he was still a human. She killed a human. A normal person doesn't just put that reality in a box on a shelf and walk away. A normal person is going to doubt her actions, and think about how she could have acted differently.

"Christie, I remember the first time I killed someone. It was overseas. Carl and I were on a mission. We were supposed to sneak into a compound, grab some files, and get the hell out without ever being seen. But it didn't work out that way. Either the target was tipped off or someone got unlucky and was in the wrong place at the wrong time. Anyway, Carl and I were in a room sifting through drawers when an early riser wandered by. Carl gave me a signal that he'd provide cover and I should take the guy out. Take the guy out silently—that meant with a knife.

"My training kicked in, and I managed to work my way out through the doorway and around behind the guy. He was just a kid, really, and…I did it. At the time I was high on adrenaline—it was just part of the job. But later, after we safely returned to our base camp, I lost it. The team's shrink spent some time with me. He said it is normal to be both happy that you survived and sad that a human lost his life in the process. Both feelings are fair and real.

"It took me a few weeks of talking it out, but I got better. I was able to balance what had to happen with what did happen. Do you get my drift? I'm not a shrink, Christie, but I'm a good listener. The shrink was right. The only way to move forward was to deal head-on with what I had done. It took me most of a year to stop seeing the blood and the body on the floor. I still think of it; the first is always the most impressionable. But I know that I had to do it. You need time, and I'm here for you."

I watch her as she listens to me. At first she seems angry. But slowly I see her change. It starts in her lips with a quiver and moves to her eyes as they moisten, and then her whole body begins to shake. I lean toward her and pull her into my arms. I hold her as she cries it out. I hurt. I want to bear this pain for her. After about ten minutes, the crying turns to sniffling. I hand her napkins from the restaurant, and she dries her cheeks.

"Thank you, Jake. I know it was the right move. But I can't shake the look of shock on his face as he realized he was dead. I've never ever shot anyone. I've had to pull my weapon and point it at people a few times. I've always believed I could pull the trigger; I just never thought I'd be so emotionally charged by the experience." She pulls gently away and turns the rearview mirror toward her face. "Oh my God, I'm not going to be out in public looking like this. Give me ten minutes in the restroom to clean up. Thank you so much, truly." I get a brief kiss and watch as she exits the car and walks back into the restaurant.

I roll my window down a bit and light a cigarette. I let the fumes drift across my mouth and nose while I close my eyes. I jump with a start, having almost fallen asleep with a lit cigarette between my fingers. I snub it out and close the window.

More like twenty minutes later, she returns, and we're back on I-5 headed south. The drive from Eugene through the Lake Shasta area of California is beautiful and green. Traffic is light, and for stretches the conversation is limited to my snoring, or so Christie tells me later. We drive down to Redding and cut across toward San Francisco.

We don't lose sight of the fact that someone might be following us. We exit here and there just to see who pulls off behind us. Christie even buys a pad of paper and starts writing license plate info down, double-checking each vehicle to her list. When we hit San Francisco, we decide we need true sleep. We look for a cheap motel that accepts cash. We find one, check in, and are so tired we both crash for a serious four hours.

At 1:00 a.m., I wake and hear Christie in the shower. The room is dark but for a sliver of light under the door to the bathroom. Our room is located in a back corner of the complex. It's as close as we can get to the equivalent of sitting with our backs to the wall. I turn on the TV and start searching the news programs. But there isn't anything on the shootout, the arrest of Smith, the mysterious deposits in De Cola's accounts, or Carl's blown-up ranch and, most important, our pictures aren't being displayed as America's most wanted.

Christie walks out of the bathroom in a towel, backlit by the bathroom light. She smiles at me. "I have a present for you once you take a shower. You're smelly right now. Be gone from my bed, or I shall have you cast down into the dungeon."

"Ah, my fair maiden, can I still call you that? I mean, I know that, well..."

"You better move fast, or this fair maiden might show a bit of her iron maiden side, buster."

I jump out of bed, just barely avoiding a slap on my still sore rump. My still sore rump? I turn and look at it just as Christie says, "Oh my God. You've been shot! Let me take a look at that."

We go into the bathroom, and I turn away from the sink so she can check out my wound. "It's just a scrape. Let me clean it up." She grabs a towel and starts scrubbing. It stings, and I straighten my back and gasp.

"Don't tell me that hurts—I barely touched you."

"With sandpaper; you barely touched me with sandpaper. You know, some of that skin might be worth saving."

"Oh, please. Men are such babies."

"Ouch! Why are you being so mean? I have a battle wound, and you're scouring me like I'm a rusted outdoor chair."

She stops and stares at me. There is no sympathy in those eyes. "Are you through?"

"Yes, ma'am."

She finishes and slaps my butt hard enough to leave a hand print. "See you in a few, you hunk-a-hunk of burning love."

I shower in record time, brush my teeth, and add a splash of aftershave. As I slide between the sheets, she sighs, "Ummm, you smell good. Come here. You've been a good little boy, and I have some candy for you."

"I don't know, lady, my mom told me to never take candy from a stranger, and I hardly know you."

"Can't you make an exception just this once?"

"I suppose," I say as our mouths meet. I don't think I'll ever get tired of this. Her soft skin is pressing on mine from the tips of our toes to our noses. Her smell is invigorating, and her hands are seeking. Our lips and tongues engage in an erotic dance. I caress her back, trying to memorize her shape and structure like a blind man learning to read. I open my eyes and watch her, her eyes closed, as she answers each of my caresses with an equally arousing one of her own. She moves from her side to her back and pulls me on top of her, inviting me with her eyes to be even closer.

It all ends too soon, and then we're driving through San Francisco to Highway 101. After a few hours on the road, the sun comes up, and the Pacific Ocean spreads out in 180 degrees. This time of the year, the coast road is spectacular, with the sun reflecting off of the massive, endless body of water. To our left, hundreds of acres of grasslands sway in a light breeze and are speckled with rainbow-colored flowers. But it's hard to enjoy—with the extra sleep, we've become more cautious and aware of our risk. The fear of being tracked is almost as bad as actually seeing your pursuers.

When you can see them, at least you can plan strategies to escape or disable them. When you fear them but don't see them, every car that passes you is a potential threat. Every stop for gas or food is a risk point. Every synapse in your brain is firing every second. The whole experience is exhausting but important. Fear focuses the mind. A focused mind survives longer.

Despite our concentrated attention on living another day, with the amount of time we have alone, we begin to share more about ourselves with each other. I hear about her prom night debacle; her date double-booked. When she discovered that she was number two on a one-girl date, she punched him out. Her mom was furious; her dad was proud.

I tell her about playing goalie for my college soccer team. The little success I had was a result of my desire to hurt members of the other team if they entered my eighteen-yard box with the ball. Occasionally I was able to block a shot, mostly with my face.

She was a serious student in college; I was a partier. She likes opera; I like football. She wants three kids; I want sex. I think we're a match made in heaven.

Thursday, March 30

6:00 a.m.
"Passport, please, señor..." Border Guard

Last night we drove to San Diego and found a hotel that would take cash. We got into bed and were too tired to do anything but sleep. This morning I let Christie sleep, enjoying her blissful calm. What will she look like when we wake up in a normal world? As I watch, her eyes open, and she begins to smile, but that changes to a grimace. "Oh dear God." She covers her head with her pillow as she rolls away from me.

"What's wrong?" I ask.

"Oh, I've made a really bad mistake. I didn't take my contacts out when we crashed last night."

"Oh no, are they hurting your eyes?"

"Well, in a way, but not the way you're thinking."

"I'm confused—what way are they hurting you?"

"Dirk, you know I'm falling for you, right?"

"I hope you are," I carefully reply.

"Well, honey, with my contacts in, I can see your morning face. Either you need to take a shower or I need to take my contacts out and blur you pretty. But right now I don't need to see the real you," she says from beneath the pillow.

"Blur you pretty?" My little devil is shouting, "Tell her what she looks like." And I listen. "I look bad?" I say aloud. "Have you looked in a mirror? You look—"

I hear my little angel screaming, "Mayday, Mayday! She's going to launch an Abby-to-Jake missile. You can't go there."

"—marvelous," I finish. "You look marvelous, and I would be happy to shower and wash away my distressful countenance."

"I can see there's hope for you yet, Dirk." She smiles at me.

Fifteen minutes later, I'm clean and back between the sheets. An hour later, she's in the shower, and forty-five minutes after that, we're packed and in the car. At the border, I say I'll go first and suggest she stay a few people behind me. "If I get pulled aside, make for the restroom until you see me clear of the crossing. If I don't come back out of wherever they take me, head back to the car and take off. You're on your own." I hand her the keys and smile at her.

I begin walking toward the border and don't look back. I come to a black, revolving metal gate and push through. There are very few people walking across the border today. I don't know if this is good or bad. Either way, I have my "it's great to be a tourist" expression on. After about two hundred feet, I walk through a second revolving gate. No one has said a word to me or even acted like they've noticed me. I grab a tourist declaration form and complete it.

I begin walking again and come to a structure that seems like a massive gas station, with an elevated roof and booths on a median. There are armed soldiers scattered about who casually glance at me. None of them level their guns and start shooting or shouting, which I take as a good sign. Just as I'm about to clear the structure, one of the soldiers calls me over.

"Passport, please, señor."

I fumble with my backpack, find my passport, and hand it to him. "Purpose and length of your visit?"

"I'm here on vacation, a couple of weeks. Can you tell me where I can catch a cab?"

"Very good." He hands my passport back to me. "Follow this walkway to the end. Take a right, and you'll see a line of cabs waiting. Bienvenido, señor, and enjoy your stay."

"Thank you." I move on without looking back. I arrive at the taxi line, and a young man pulls up in a beat-up Chevy.

"Where are you headed, señor?"

"The airport, but we need to wait for a friend of mine."

"Allow me to put your bag in the trunk."

"No, that's okay. I prefer to hold it."

It seems to take forever, but finally Christie comes around the corner. We climb into the back of the cab and sit silently as the driver takes control.

The drive to the airport is short, ten minutes. We pay him US $20, which makes the cabbie very happy.

While Christie waits for me at a table in a bar, I go into the men's room. I check to make sure I'm the only one there and pull out my second set of IDs from the compartment I'd sewn into my bag. I review it to make sure I'm ready to change my name. Once I feel comfortable with the new documents, I cut up my Dirk Dagger IDs and flush them down the toilet. Dirk and Jake are gone, and now I'm Gerald Jumper. Jerry Jumper? Ponch is sick, sick, sick.

I head back out to the bar and introduce my new self to Christie, who laughs. She grabs her bag and meanders over to the women's restroom to complete the same task. She returns and introduces herself as Mary Contra. We move to the departure display and study the outgoing flights.

"Gerald, I think this is where we split up. When we meet again, I intend to take a full inventory of you. Don't lose any parts, at least not any good ones."

"Be careful. We don't know who or what might be looking for us. If they see you lusting over me, they might think you're my secretary."

"Let them think wild thoughts—I'm not afraid of what the world thinks of us. Adios, amigo." She kisses me and embraces me. I see a tear form at the corner of her eye, and then she's turned and is walking over to the ticket counter. I try not to watch.

It's my turn. Mary is going to fly to Mexico City and board the first flight available to Belize. Once there, she'll check into a cheap motel. I'm to fly to Mexico City, check into a hotel overnight, and then fly on to Belize the next morning. That will give both of us a chance to see if anyone is following. If we have any doubts, we're to leave a message for the other at the Royal Palm that simply says, *Ciao*. If we're clear, we check in and relax for a couple of weeks and watch the news.

I can't believe how exhausted I feel. I just finished several hours of sleep not four hours ago. But the strain of navigating a foreign country, of splitting from Mary, and of examining every pedestrian for some misplaced look or movement is draining. I do my best to relax, but then all I can think about is Abby, Finn, Sarah, and Carl. They're all escaping from the US in fear of gangsters and our own government.

I check a newsstand for any mention of our merry band of bandits. Finally in one business section, I see an article that briefly mentions a discrepancy at some twenty banks on the West Coast. An accounting (damned accountants) error resulted in the shifting of several hundreds of millions of dollars. The article is vague about the details, and it doesn't mention us or De Cola.

My plane is boarding, so I toss the paper into a garbage can. I find my seat and fit my bag under the seat in front of me. I'm fortunate: I'm on the aisle, so I can spread my legs out a little bit. A young man listening to music through earbuds occupies the middle seat. The music is cranked up so high I can make out the lyrics: "Yaaaa, ya, I'm really cool and a bad guy. Yaaaa ya, have sex with me, baby, because you happen to be in the vicinity," or something like that. It's clear he doesn't have any more interest in talking to me than I do to him. The flight lasts about three and a half hours, and no one tries to shoot me or arrest me. We land in Mexico City and once off the plane, I ask directions to a cheap nearby hotel.

I'm directed to the Segovia Regency, which turns out to be clean as well as inexpensive and nearby. It also has a decent burger, icy beers, and prompt room service. I light up a cigarette as I try to watch TV, but all I can think about is getting to Belize and reuniting with Abby. What if she isn't there? Or what if all that's there is a note with the single word *ciao* on it? What if I walk up to the check-in desk, and De Cola is waiting for me in Bermuda shorts, a Panama hat, and a big goofy smile, and with an even bigger gun? I turn out the lights and stare at the ceiling while my thoughts run wild. Just when I think I can't fall asleep, I do.

Friday, March 31

8:00 a.m.
"Señor, you are American, no..." Customs Agent

I jump as the alarm sounds the next morning. I shower and shave and take an elevator down to the front desk. I get a breakfast recommendation from the desk clerk as I check out, and then I walk out into the sun. It's a beautiful day—the temperature is already in the midsixties. In Portland it won't reach the midsixties until July. I find the recommended restaurant and order up a breakfast fit for a prisoner on his last day on death row. I'm not worried about my waistline today. I'm carbo-loading in case I receive a multiyear sentence courtesy of customs, should they deduce that Jerry Jumper is a figment of my imagination.

I ask the waitress for a newspaper and soon have a copy of the *News*, an English-language Mexican paper. I find a new article about the banking mishap. It's now being reported that it wasn't an error but may have been an attempted theft. According to a source inside the government, it's believed that the amount of money involved makes it the largest single theft in the history of mankind. I'm not sure the former owners of Manhattan Island would agree with that. The article mentions that the FBI is interested in one Franklin De Cola, a former agent. There's no mention of anyone else.

After breakfast, I grab a cab and head back to the airport. As has become my life, I spend more time looking for unusual behavior and tails on our drive than I do enjoying the scenery of Mexico City. In the airport I find a seat in the back of a bar, facing the front, and order a club soda. For the next thirty minutes, I watch the terminal's activity.

When I'm convinced no one is paying any attention to me, I walk to the ticket counter and buy a ticket on the next flight to Belize City. Two hours later, as I go through security, an agent pulls me out of line and asks me if I have anything to declare. I tell him I don't, and he begins searching my bag. While agent one is busy sniffing my underwear, agent number two begins reading my passport.

I know this guy. To be more precise, I know his type. He's a bully, a punk. His eyes are his tell. I know that he would love to take me into the back room for a little four-on-one time. Worst case, I lose a couple of teeth and go to jail for the rest of my life. Best case, I lose a couple of teeth and suffer the indignity of a cavity search, with no secondhand smoke afterward. I'm not going to give him the satisfaction.

"Señor, you are American, no?" the second agent asks.

"I am, yes, I'm an American," I reply with a big American vacation smile.

"Punk," says my little devil.

"When did you arrive in Mexico?"

"About a week ago. Spent a few days with some friends in Cancún and headed up here."

"Punk," says my little angel.

"Ah, Cancún is very nice. Have you enjoyed your visit to our republic?"

"Very much so—you have so much to be proud of."

Punk, I think.

"I am happy to hear so. But I notice, excuse my curiosity, but you don't seem very tan for having spent most of a week in a very sunny place."

"Crazy, isn't it. I have a skin condition and have to use heavy sunscreen and stay covered. My doctor told me no smokes, no tans, young man. He does that, calls me young man. I think he's actually younger than me but wants to seem superior. Crazy world, don't you think?"

"Punk," we all say in unison.

The second agent smiles and hands back my passport as the first agent zips my bag. "Have a safe trip...young man." His suspicions aren't strong enough to act on. Or maybe I'm just not his type.

"Gracias...amigo." I smile and make my way to my gate.

The paperback I buy from a newsstand before we board is the tale of a forlorn love between two people forced apart by a meddling family. The characters in the story make me feel normal, even though I know that isn't so. We transfer in San José, and I notice a small child seated behind me on the next plane. Just as I'm about to switch from almost asleep to dead to the world, the child begins to cry. The mom works hard to calm him, I notice, as nearby passengers become anxious and impatient. All of a sudden I see a miniature face peering at me from between the seats. I look at the child, whose nose can't be six inches from mine. He smiles at me and covers his face and then quickly pulls his hands away and smiles at me gleefully. I see the exhausted mom behind him. I look at my fellow traveler sitting next to me, and I can feel the stares of several others nearby. It's clear that all of the passengers have voted and unanimously elected me to be the plaything of this mini human.

"The proper response is peekaboo, I believe," my seatmate says. His smile is strained and challenging.

I spend the next hour entertaining the munchkin, mostly variations on peekaboo, in Spanish, which I don't speak.

We finally land in Belize, and I make it through customs, no sweat. I grab a cab and head toward the Royal Palm Island Resort. I ask the cabbie to take a couple of detours along the way. I tell him it's for sightseeing.

We reach the coast, and I take a water taxi the rest of the way to the resort. The island is stunning: white sands, swaying trees, a beautiful blue-and-green ocean, clear sky, and just enough of a breeze to keep the humidity at bay. There are also friendly people,

I'm sure. I can smell the alcohol, thank God; and I anticipate that mystical thing we all need at times: the illusion of seclusion.

The cabbie drops me off at a dock near the front entrance. I pay him and grab my bag and enter the lobby. The entrance is beautifully decorated with lots of flowers and people who look odd to me. I think they're what some people call happy. I walk up to the registration desk.

"Hola, I'm meeting Mary Contra. Has she checked in?" I ask in my best "I don't speak Spanish" accent.

"Sorry, señor, but no, no Mary Contra is in our facility." I feel my heart skip a beat as I expect the man to hand me a one-word note. He continues speaking, giving no indication of a note. "Let me check, no, I don't see a reservation either. Are you sure it is here you are to meet?"

"Yes, actually neither of us has reservations. We were just hoping to meet up and grab a room. My name is Gerald Jumper." I swallow hard; one more chance for that note. "Do you have a room available?"

"Of course, Mr. Jumper, we've been expecting you."

Whoa, that is not what I expected to hear. I slowly survey the room. I'm convinced that I've entered a trap. "You've been expecting me?"

"Your wife, Mary Jumper, is already in your room. Mary! Is this the same as Mary Contra?" The man's eyes twinkle. "Are you newlyweds?"

I smack my head and shake it back and forth. "This is going to be harder than I thought. Yes, yes, Mary Jumper, my new bride. Can you believe I don't even know my own wife's name? This whole marriage thing is going to take some time to adjust to. You say she's already checked in?"

"That's correct. We have you in a beachfront bungalow. Mrs. Jumper has prepaid for two weeks, and you have an option for two more. I'm rooting for two more, señor," he whispers to me conspiratorially. "Here is your key. And there is a note for you." What? My brain and my heart are in a tug-of-war. I know Mary is here, but I still fear any kind of note. He goes to a drawer located in the back cabinets, searches, and finds what he's looking for. He hands me a simple white envelope with my current name on the outside. "This young man will show you to your room. *Bienvenido y disfrutar de su visita*. Welcome and enjoy your visit."

"Gracias." I grab my bag and follow the lad as he winds through the building and out toward our destination. As we walk, I open the envelope. I anxiously unfold the single sheet of paper, and on it is just one thing...a kiss. It seems a fan of mine has pressed her lipstick-coated lips to the paper. My day just went from anxious to boring to anxious to great to unbelievably great.

We arrive at the unit. It's a two-story building painted in bright orange-yellow custard with ocean-blue trim. I feel instantly relaxed and at home. The colors inside and out blend in tone but differ in texture and movement. It has a magnificent view of the massive ocean and sky. Sea birds flock together in the distance. My mind imagines porpoises and whales out there just below the surface. But mostly I look for Mary Jumper.

"My bride, my little sweet pineapple, where are you?"

Not a peep. There are two bedrooms and a luxurious bathroom, all of which are empty. I look out back and the view just gets better. Below me, laid out in the sun in a skimpy two-piece white bathing suit, is Mary quite contrary. I think it's time to do some gardening.

"Excuse me, ma'am, but I see a red spot that may need some attention. In fact, it may be time to move indoors. You don't want to overdo that whole sun-worshipping thing."

"Jake," she yells as she jumps up and throws her sweaty arms around me. "What took you so long? I was about to start looking for a replacement husband." And then those same lips that marked the paper move to mine. I lift her and carry her back into the bungalow. The two-piece is off faster than a twist top at a Chicago Bears tailgater. I hold her in front of me at arm's length and marvel at her tan lines.

"I love, just love, the tan lines. But I must admit that the true measure of the success of this vacation will be whether or not you keep them." I pull her tight against me. We move into a bedroom as I quickly and clumsily undress. We hop into the bed and embrace like two oppositely charged magnets. Her mouth and mine become one. Our hands move across bare skin as we attempt to become closer than is physically possible. Everything happens fast, and eventually we slumber in each other's embrace.

I wake and head to the shower. As I relax in a steady stream of hot water, I feel her enter the shower and hug me from behind. I turn and we kiss, long and soft. We're in no hurry, we have forever or two weeks, whichever comes first.

"Have you heard anything?" I ask.

"No, I've been waiting for you. There's wireless internet at the beachfront bar. We can do a search for news and check the email accounts when we're ready. Plus, we should let everyone know we've arrived safe and sound."

"I don't know about that, my dear wife. I think I'm feeling weak. Maybe I should lie down and rest a bit more. I'm sure my recovery would be expedited by your magical hands and other mysterious parts."

"Hmm."

5:00 p.m.
"I'll ping Milt to start phase three..." Abby

Eventually even newlyweds need to take a break for sustenance. We agree it's time to join the world of other people and venture out for food, grog, and internet access.

"I don't know what it is about hot climates, but coffee sounds good," I say. Abby smiles her agreement.

We both finish cleaning up and dress. Abby, aka my wife, Mary, is the center of the universe in a yellow sundress that flows like a sunlit cloud on an ocean breeze. As we walk along the beach, we talk about our trips from Mexico City to here. She tells me about a man who sat across the aisle from her on the plane. He was definitely interested in taking her for a jaunt on his magical pogo stick. His interest faded when she told him she had just been released from prison. She had been held on suspicion of having cut her husband up into little pieces. The prosecution couldn't prove the case, so she was free to roam.

The beach bar is probably a third full. Can there really be this many people in the world on vacation? Who's doing all of the work at home? How does civilization continue with all of these slackers away from their assigned seating? Abby finds an open table and pulls out a computer, at which she begins to peck. I'm already stressed—less than ten hours in paradise and I've gone from exhausted to exhilarated to asleep to relaxed to stressed. I'm not on island time quite yet. But at least the coffee is good.

The bar is open-air chic, with everyone lounging on palm chairs. I watch a motorboat scooting across the sea while lazy yachts bob, anchored and peaceful. That's me: speedboat one second, anchored yacht the next. The only difference is that my boat, whatever it is, is always being chased by a second boat bristling with gunners.

"Okay," Abby interrupts my thoughts, "I have emails from all three of them. They've all made it safely to phase two. I'm going to send each of them an email letting them know that we're in good shape and that I'll ping Milt to start phase three."

As part of our original plan, we arranged for Milt to be our point of contact on what is happening in the real world. He'll be contacting both Abby and Carl, and Abby and Carl are to contact the rest of us. Since we are all safely set up under our second set of IDs, we can begin the phase. Milt's the natural choice for this chore. Given his connections, he'll be able to tap into both the federal and state investigations of the events that we triggered. Hopefully, he will soon tell us that everything is safe enough for us to come back. After Abby sends the email, she begins searching the news sites for more info.

"Here's an article on Smith. It says that a longtime, decorated detective was arrested for possession of cocaine and trafficking. He's being held without bail. Oh my gosh, you won't believe it. Smith claims that he's been framed—can you believe his bad luck?" she asks with an evil smile.

"I'm sorry, I can't get past 'decorated.' They must be talking about a birthday cake or his bedroom. I'll bet he turns state's evidence against Southside and Simpton. If he doesn't, he's dead in six months in prison."

"He may be dead way before that if Simpton and Southside can get to him. Okay, here's an article on De Cola. Goes through his background, years of service, and says that he and Simpton were the masterminds of a major money laundering scheme. They can't find Simpton, but they have De Cola."

"De Cola is the one we need to worry about. He's the only one who can connect us to any of this," I say.

"Wait, there's more—it says that the scheme was uncovered when De Cola attempted to steal from the thieves. The government has frozen De Cola's assets, measured at just over $300 million. They say it's hard to imagine someone generating that much wealth on a salary of $185,000 per year. That's amazing. He obviously has a great CPA and financial adviser."

"I'd hire his CPA in a heartbeat and only expect half of that. Is there anything from Milt yet?"

"Let me check. Yes, he's responded. Everything is quiet; he's certain our names haven't come up yet, but they still could. Oh, wow, he says that it hasn't hit the news yet, but Smith has disappeared. Looks like you called it. Milt thinks Smith has gone into witness protection. He says we should keep an eye out in case Smith shows up here with a couple of US marshals and a margarita."

We continue to search for more info, but nothing pops up. We decide we're hungry and head to the on-site restaurant. The restaurant is that perfect island-style venue: on the beach, open air, and casually formal. The place is crowded, but the tables feel spaced for romance. Conversations are going on around us, but they're just white noise that blends with soft Spanish-language music over the sound system. We feel comfortable having an open conversation and not being overheard. But we've agreed that in public places we're Mary and Jerry and we're on our honeymoon. The honeymoon part has not been hard to fake. In fact I intend to throw myself into the role completely. I tell Mary I'm a method actor; we'll have to engage in significant practice sessions back at the bungalow for the guise to work.

She smiles. "Don't worry about me. I just hope that your little jumper can keep up the pace I intend to set."

"If I live another two weeks, I'm going to kill my parents for this name. I don't think I'll ever get used to being Jerry Jumper. As far as keeping up with you is concerned, no worries there. How about right now, right here? Yeah, thought so—all you want to do is eat, drink, and make merry, whereas I want to eat, drink, and make Mary merry again and again."

"At your age, I doubt you have more than two make-merrys in a twenty-four-hour period. After that, you'll need a three-day break. I might as well get a book for all that free time I'll have. I think I'll choose some romantic novel about a real hunk of man, taking bullets for his damsel in distress and saving the world from treachery."

"You don't need a novel—that's our life. Just look at my previously unblemished butt. I know you want to."

"A butt scratch only covers the bravery thing for a max of thirty-six hours. You have about twelve hours left before you need to engage in some new feat of valor."

"Fair enough—I'll start plotting."

"I actually have an idea for it. Are you interested in hearing what it is?"

"Sure."

"Tell me about your ex-wife, your first wife, the only other one I've heard about, at least. You've told me you were gone for a while, and that hurt the relationship. But you've been awfully quiet about the details. I think you still think about her. I think you still care for her."

I consider Abby's request for a long second. Looking at my glass of wine and remembering the pain of my biggest failure, I decide it's time to be vulnerable. "Sure, why not. But then I get to ask you an invasive and hopefully painful question."

"Given that we're newlyweds, we probably should be asking each other uncomfortable questions."

I pause and gather my thoughts.

"I met her about ten years ago. She was a cosmetics salesperson at Nordstrom's. I was wandering through the store looking for a gift for my secretary, given it was Secretary's Day."

"I don't think that's what it's called anymore; now it's Administrative Professionals' Day."

"See how out of synch I am with the world? Anyway, I was meandering through the store when this gorgeous woman waved me over. She asked if I wanted to smell the perfume she was selling, and she sprayed some on her wrist and held it out to me. I, like any puppy dog would, said yes. She smelled amazing, a soft citrus. I suggested that the test was incomplete, and I asked if she would apply some of the perfume to her neck. She asked if I often sniffed my secretary's neck. I replied, 'Only when she's not looking.' She did, and I moved in for one of the longest sniffs of my life. I was instantly besotted by her. I asked for her number, and I asked her out.

"We dated for about eight months, decided it was real, and got married four months later. Everything was great at first. But a couple of things happened at the same time. She wanted kids, and I was sent overseas. We didn't see each other for twelve months. I could barely make contact with her because of the secrecy surrounding the mission I was on. When I got back, she insisted I was not the same person. She said I was quiet and not as funny. I said she was different as well, that she seemed stressed and impatient with me.

"About that same time, the milkman wandered across her path, and she decided to head to a different pasture. I was stunned and hurt. But slowly I realized we were both better off for the split. Our real failure wasn't getting divorced. It was not getting to know each other better before we married. The later stresses just widened the existing canyon between us. She has a couple of kids now. I ran into her a year ago and she seems to be happy. It's funny how you can be that intimate with someone, and then all of a sudden, they're gone for good. I do still think of her, but not in a romantic way. It's more like muscle memory. It's hard to break the habit of thinking about her. What about you? Ever marry, or nearly marry?"

She smiles. "Not so quick. We haven't finished with you yet. Did you want kids?"

"At that time? No, not really. That was one of my mistakes, not being open and honest with her about my feelings. It probably wouldn't have changed much. Probably would've accelerated the timeline for the divorce. But now I feel differently about kids. I don't want them tomorrow, but eventually I'd like to toss a football with a little Jake or Jackie. But I'm not in a hurry. I don't hear a clock ticking. Now it's your turn."

"I was engaged once. He was my high school sweetheart, captain of the football team and, unbeknownst to me, an avid fan of his penis. His little wiener exposed itself, or at least tried to, to every woman he came in contact with. I was fortunate—I found out about his wayward muscle before we merged everything. But it hurt. I don't think any of us ever think we're in second, third, or worse place with our spouse or fiancé."

The meal arrives, and we dive into delicious fish and vegetable dishes. The food is so good and seemingly simply prepared that I start to believe that I could be a cook. Ha. The reason it seems simple and perfect is because a professional artist made it, not me.

The table talk lightens up, and our relief is evident. I think we're closer to each other, having shared some of our wounds and fears. Trust is so hard to build and so easy to tear down. I know that early in a relationship hormones can confuse me into thinking I have trust. But what I really have is lust, which has its place, don't get me wrong. Eventually, when the lust burns off, if you haven't built stronger ties, you find yourself with a stranger. I went so far as to marry one; Abby was engaged to one. Our pain was stark and deep. Neither of us will forget it, but neither of us will let it rule us.

Some Day, Some Month

Some Hour

"My little angel is in heaven, and my little devil is frustrated..." Jake

"This must be what relaxed and peaceful people do," Abby says.

"What's that?"

"They sleep in, shower, get some breakfast, and lie on the beach."

"Doesn't that make us relaxed and peaceful people?"

"We're just pretenders. As hard as I try, I can hear the hounds off to the north. It's just a matter of time until they're too close to ignore."

She's right—we're just pretenders. But now isn't the time to dwell on the possible. Now is the time for now, not a minute later. "I have a novel idea: for the rest of this morning we lie on the beach, go for walks, shower, snuggle, and eat. Then this evening we nap, snuggle, go for a swim, and snuggle. Then later tonight we have a cocktail, eat a multicourse dinner with fabulous wine, and sit outside under the stars with a scotch and a nearby smoke. We top it all off by going to the room and snuggling. And no more talk of hounds."

She stands and walks to me. "Agreed," she says as she bends down and kisses me.

My little angel is in heaven, and my little devil is frustrated by how completely relaxed I've become. He can't wedge in a dirty look, a sour comment, or a cut in a coffee line. If someone were to cut in line in front of me today, I wouldn't even notice. I'd assume that he had a good reason. Hell, I'd invite him to cut in. Two days ago I would have gunned him down, and the cops would've patted me on the back and thanked me. I would've been cheered by the fifteen other people standing in line and received a community service award on the local evening news.

I stand and join her in the surf. We hold hands and stare at the distant horizon.

"What do you think is really out there, past the edge of the earth?" I ask.

"Freedom."

"Do you feel imprisoned?"

She hesitates as she considers her response while looking at the expanse of ocean. She turns to me and says, "Sometimes, but not now, and not here; this is freedom too. I love being with you, Jake Brand. I've lost track of time. I've stopped thinking of time as numbers and names. I just think of sunrises and sunsets. You've done that for me."

"For me it's measured in waking and sleeping, but yes, I'm there with you."

"Have you noticed the people around us? All of them, even the resort staff and vendors in town, seem completely relaxed, not a care in the world. At first I thought they were odd. Then I realized, when I saw new vacationers arrive, that the new arrivals are the old me, trapped by the tick of a clock. But now, at least for a few days, I'm not one of them. I'm liberated," she says.

She's right—I've seen it too. We've gone through a 180-degree personality change in less than a handful of hours. I'm convinced there are cameras trained on us, just out of sight. We must be the new stars of *Extreme Personality Makeover*. I'm certain we're being portrayed by the director as a caricature of a real couple, only we're real. Maybe we need a few more hours to completely release the velocity of everyday life. But we're on the mend. At least we can recognize the sickness.

I think the clarity that comes from slowing down allows me to see Abby more clearly. I see that makeup does matter. I see that she doesn't always thank me for opening the door. I appreciate how practical a lowered toilet seat can be for her in the dark of the night. I see her morning face, I smell her morning breath, and I hear her critiques of me. And I love it all. I love the package, not just the skin, not just the legs, not just the brain, not just the way she walks. It's all of it or none of it.

We talk about the past, whom we've been, where we are, what our families are like. But it's not the past we're really exploring; we're creating an "us" for the future. In the real world at full speed, it's hard for people to catch the nuance of a conversation. This slowdown mode is speeding up our connections. We're becoming glued at the brain.

And just to cement it all together, we're experiencing life in a way that only the two of us will ever know. Nobody will ever know that we lay on the beach for three cocktails yesterday. Nobody can ever know unless we tell them. These are our secrets, our shared unique universe. It has its own secret handshake, calendar, smells, and insights into each other and is based on shared memories.

I want this to last forever. I'm not talking about marriage, not yet anyway. But I am talking the R word, *relationship*. I know that the recent threat to our lives has strengthened our resolve. But I keep thinking that it's everyday life that will be the true test of our mettle. I fear that everyday life, the grind of doing the dishes, folding laundry, raking leaves, shopping for groceries, and paying bills, will be a greater challenge than guns. It's the slow erosion of our souls that happens when we're not carefully watching and paying attention that scares me. I know that we can offset the erosion by building new romantic moments. Simple things like her giving me a flower or my telling her she's beautiful when she might not be to anybody but me. Romantic dinners and long conversations, each of us sincerely caring about what the other is thinking and feeling. We need to work on continuous validation that we each exist and are important to someone, each other.

I'm excited and daunted by the challenge at the same time. A relationship with a smart, beautiful woman is like that. If you completely understand the emotional risk that you are taking, you'll freeze with fear. I'm learning that if you aren't willing to take risk, you can't win the ultimate reward.

Some Later Day,
Same Month

Some Hour

"There may still be a part of you I haven't completely mapped..." Abby

Time marches on, and pretty soon we've been secluded together for more than a week and less than a month. Our schedule doesn't vary much, and I'm completely happy with it. I've been reading voraciously, getting lost in the struggles and challenges of characters springing from the brains of creative types. But just to make sure we don't relax completely, each day we check our email accounts. Looking to see if we've received the all-clear signal and fearing we've received the all-clear signal. One day we spy a new email from Milt.

"I say we don't open it, not yet. There may still be a part of you I haven't completely mapped." Abby smiles up to me.

"I could tell you exactly where that spot is located. But I'm not going to because I know how much you like a challenge that involves a compass and a sextant."

"Do you think they'll miss us if we just disappear?"

"Not at first, but maybe someday when they realize that they need a cosigner on some loan. If we don't respond to his email, they might think we're dead. Or worse, they might come looking for us." I grimace. "I don't need to see Milt's ugly paunch exposed on the same beach as us."

She sighs a soft, sad smile. "I suppose you're right." She clicks.

The coast is clear. According to Milt's buddies, there isn't and won't be anything that blows back on us. Southside has been devastated, based upon info from Smith. Simpton's body was discovered at a campsite in the Columbia Gorge. Based upon its condition, his final days of existence were distastefully uncomfortable. As for De Cola, he's dropped off of the planet. The best guess is that he's turned state's evidence and is unraveling the careers and freedom of multiple participants in the scheme.

Nobody has seen or heard any stories about money laundering except for a brief snippet in a single news article. There was a vague reference to the recovered cash having been returned to its rightful owners. This surprises me—I expected the feds to confiscate the money as illegally gained profits. The explosion at Carl's place was said to have been the result of a faulty water heater, with no injuries reported.

"There had to be at least one bad guy in that house when it went up. Could they be covering everything up?" I ask.

"They must be. How else can you explain all of this?" Abby asks.

"I can't. But I think your story that there is a group of government types that doesn't want to rock the boat is being proven."

We ping Carl, Sarah, and Finn and start planning our trip home. Dinner that night is quiet. The sunshine has been great, and Abby has been amazing. If this is the faux honeymoon, I try to imagine what the real thing might look, feel, and smell, like. The thought of spending time together without looking for a tail or a red laser dot is especially enticing. But I'm excited to get home, start paying bills, dodging traffic on I-5, and wearing raincoats.

"I think I can read your mind," she says.

"That's not all that hard, sugar. Just take the last few days and multiply it by a bunch more."

Abby leans forward, chin on her hands, elbows on the table. I should scold her about those elbows, but I'm afraid one might pay me a painful visit. "That's not what I mean. I mean, I know how much you love home. You complain about the rain, the boring work, and the same ol' same ol', but deep down you love it."

I look straight into her eyes. "I guess I do. It's hard to think like that here, with you. But I'm a pattern kind of guy. I need to catch bad guys and rescue stray kittens. I suppose it's in my blood. Plus, could you truly appreciate this paradise without the contrast of everyday life in a normal place?"

"I'm not talking about your job. You could do that anywhere. I'm talking about Portland, and Carl and Sarah and poker and even Sarge. They've become your family. Have you ever thought about changing things up? Real change, not just your underwear, although that would be nice once in a while. I mean this, I mean Europe, Asia, the world. Have you ever considered selling everything and starting over in Africa? Sitting on a porch somewhere in the wilderness, watching giraffes and elephants running from lions? Sitting around a fire under the stars with no humans or cities for miles? Or hobnobbing with the social elite in Monte Carlo? What I mean is, have you ever considered creating the biggest badass bucket list you can think of and completing it now while you're young enough to do that stuff?"

I light a cigarette and place it in an ashtray upwind from me. "Of course I have, usually when I'm nearing the bottom of a bottle of Glenmorangie. But I know the world is real. And I do like my home. Home is an anchor, a connection that defines me, and it helps me truly appreciate what we've had here. Plus, even if I sold everything, I couldn't afford this for a week, let alone pay for months of aimless traveling. What happens when I run out of cash? Do I become a bartender on a beach somewhere? I think that would get old and boring." I look at my drink.

"Say it," says my little angel. "Tell her you love her."

"Jesus, you moron, you want her to puke all over his shirt?' asks my little devil. "Not that anyone will notice on that ridiculous pattern."

"What about you?" I ask. "Have you thought about splitting the fashionably boring everyday club and seeking new planets, new civilizations, to boldly go where you haven't before?"

"Same as you, I've thought about it. But like you say, it takes money. More money than I've ever had." She gazes out at the ocean. I can't read her mind, but I can tell there is a new sadness in her eyes. It's subtle, but it rises off her like steam after a hot afternoon rainstorm. "I guess you're right. Living the grind makes this so much sweeter."

"How well do you like Portland? Do you think it could be a home for you?"

"For a while—I'd like to get to know you better. I plan to do my best at that over the next forty-eight hours. And if you can keep up the pace, maybe there will be a reason to stay in Portland for a while longer." Her eyes are clear; the sadness is gone, replaced by carnal desire and mischievous glee.

"You do know you're talking to the Energizer Bunny—I just keep on going. Speaking of which—"

"I thought you'd never ask." Abby's eyes are more colorful each time I gaze into them.

"You didn't give me a chance to. I like a woman who knows what she wants."

We walk arm in arm from the restaurant up the beach to our bungalow. We're the only people on the beach, but we believe we're the only people in the world. The stars are so thick that they seem to form one bright light shining down on us—begging us to stay while sadly waving goodbye.

At the bungalow we don't waste any time tearing off clothes and falling into bed. Even though we've been together for a couple of weeks, the energy and passion of this night is stronger than any before. We are both still dealing with demons. Abby seemingly holds on to me for dear life. I sense that she is afraid that she'll be cast adrift as we leave paradise and return to civilization. But I'm prepared to be her anchor.

I fear that these feelings I have for her, this time together, will be that moment. That one moment you always look back on and remember as the best moment of your relationship. Hell, maybe the best moment of your life. It's the moment when we are perfect.

It's the moment some people spend a lifetime trying to create and re-create. I'm not going to let it be that moment; I won't make the same mistakes I made with Sue. I know that this time I'm committed to creating better moments in the future with someone.

We eventually drift off to sleep in each other's arms and separate into our own dreams.

The next morning I wake up to a soft breeze, cool temperatures, and no Abby. I stretch my legs and arms and call her name, but she doesn't answer. I rub the sleep out of my eyes and stare at the ceiling while my brain wakes up, remembering the softness and completeness of the night before. It feels so good just to lie here, not worrying about what I'm going to do next. I don't want to get up. I decide at a minimum I need to get up and take a pee. So I roll off of the bed and start to head into the bathroom, maybe Abby's showering. I'm hoping she's showering; I'd like to join her. As I walk toward the bathroom door, I notice an envelope propped up on the dresser with *Jake* written on the outside. I walk over to it and pick it up. As my fingers make contact with the paper, I get a really bad feeling at the pit of my stomach. This doesn't feel like an "I hopped down to the convenience store for scones" kind of note.

I open the envelope, pull out the single sheet, and begin reading.

Jake, by the time you read this, I'll be off the island, headed to destinations unknown. I'm not who you think I am. I want you to hear this from me. I have secrets that I wanted to share with you, but couldn't. One of those secrets is that when you and the others weren't looking, Finn and I set aside money in accounts for the two of us. Lots of money, so much money that I can go anywhere, anytime I want.

I wanted you to come with me so badly, I almost invited you last night. But I thought about it. What happens when you get tired of me? I fear you would. And when you do, you'd discover that you couldn't go back home—this is a one-way trip. I can't do that to you. I feared that you'd say yes, and you'd hate me in a year. But even more, I feared that you'd say no, and I'd hate you now.

It's better this way. I'm not a housewife, but that's what you're searching for. I love your dream, the picket fence, three kids, and an ashtray in the garage. I do love you with all of my heart, and I know that you love me. We don't have to say it for it to be true. Maybe someday we'll pass by each other on a breeze. Maybe someday, a hand will touch your shoulder and beautiful woman will ask if you can spare a secondhand smoke. You never know, Jake, you just never know. Ciao.

I have to read the note three times before I can trust what my mind is saying. After the third read, I crumple the page and stare at the floor without seeing it. I realize with a dull, deep ache just how much I wanted a future with Abby. This one is going to leave a mark.

I decide I need some air; the room is closing in on me. I smell her, hear her, and see her in every space. I walk down to the beach and settle into a lounge chair. The world is still revolving, and it's still beautiful and peaceful, but now it's empty, devoid of depth, texture, and flavor. I look down at the crumpled note in my tight fist. I pull out my lighter. I hold the flame at the lowest corner of the page and say goodbye to Abby forever as the smoke drifts up toward the sky and dissipates.

Friday, July 5

"I don't need your charity—focus on the cards..." Milt

"I see your $3 and raise you $3," I say. This is the biggest pot of the evening. I'm down $50 and two hours of dignity. If I win this pot, I will get back all of my money and half my dignity. It's me against Milt, mano a mano. I know he's bluffing: he's nibbling his lip. I take a whiff off of my slowly diminishing cigarette and make my face blank. It's time for that famous Jake manipulation: calm him into thinking I'm weak, when I know he's weak. Lure him in for the kill shot.

"Raise," he says and throws in the maximum bet, $10.

"I call. What do you have, Mr. Rags?"

"Jacks full of sixes, Mr. Broke," he snorts back. "Prove to me you're a terrible card player—show me your hand."

I grimace. I look around the table, and everyone is staring at me with expectant smiles. I look down at the backs of my cards lying on the table and flip over a pair of aces.

Everybody starts laughing except Carl and me. I look at him and shrug my shoulders. Who could have known? He just stares at me like he would a confusing clown.

"I told you he'd go for the lip nibble," says Milt to Carl. "Cough up that $20."

Carl reaches into his back pocket, pulls out his wallet, grabs a twenty, and tosses it at Milt. The whole time he's doing this, he never takes his eyes off of me. He stares at me like I'm dumber than a stick. "Really! Really? All it takes is a lip nibble to separate you from your panties? I think I lost more than you."

"Well, that'll teach you," I say, embarrassed to the core.

"Are you sure you want to be a partner with this guy?" Milt asks Sarah.

"Junior partner," I say, "she's a junior partner."

"He's so helpless he brings out my nurturing side. I do find it tiresome that he continues to believe that I'm in any way junior to him."

That would have been true before, but it was even more so now. Instead of a cash bonus, when we got back to town, I gave Sarah 49 percent of the business. *Give* is the wrong word. She earned it. She earned a lot more with the risks that she took and the tremendous value she delivered in keeping us all alive.

"Don't worry, Sarah, we can do the math. Jake, do you need to ask Sarah permission to take time off?" Carl asks, and everyone laughs.

"Ha-ha. Ha. You guys think you're so funny. No, I don't have to ask her."

Sarah leans toward Milt, cups her hand in front of her mouth, and whispers loudly enough for all of us to hear, "Actually, he does—I handle the calendars."

Milt snickers at me. At least he's talking to me. As soon as I got back to town, he forced his financial guy onto my calendar. It was at best an embarrassing meeting. The guy looked at my financials, looked at me, and shook his head.

We've been back in Portland for a few months. Sarah and Carl came back a day before me, and true to Abby's word, there's been nary a peep from her or Finn. It turns out that neither the government nor Southside took much interest in our disappearance. Everyone was so focused on scooping up the cash and plugging the leaks that we were never on the radar. Of course, we didn't know that. We feared for our freedom, if not our lives. It kind of ticks me off that they ignored us.

I told the gang, including Milt, about Belize, at least parts of Belize. They were all stunned when I got to the punch line and described Abby's departure. Carl couldn't believe I was foolish enough to fall for her that quickly, and Milt blew cigar smoke at me.

Sarah and Carl secretly decided to buddy up after our escape from the confines of the good ol' U S of A. Carl says it's because

I asked him to keep an eye on Sarah. They both say their friendship remained and remains platonic. Their body language says it's true, but their relationship has changed. They're more relaxed and more deeply connected to each other. They headed down to Argentina and became members of a winery staff. The vineyard was owned by an older couple who treated everyone like family. Evenings were spent with the entire crew eating dinner and drinking wine in the family home. They loved it so much that they plan to head back for a week or two and have invited me to join them. I agreed to come drink the wine and observe their work ethic. I plan on sitting on an Adirondack chair perfectly positioned so that I can catch as much of the arc of the sun as possible. The only grape squishing I'm going to do is with my mouth.

It's great to be home. There's perfect weather, lots of flowers, a lush landscape, and blue skies decorating long sunny days. At first it was all a shade grayer: the colors were there, but they were harsh, lacking warmth. I connected to Abby, and the connection was deep enough that it took some time to let go. Maybe this is one of those things you never completely rid yourself of. You just eventually put it in a mental box, tie a mental ribbon around it, and place it on a mental shelf. It's always there to bring down off of the shelf and revisit. But at least you don't have to deal with it every moment of every day.

"She was just a dame," my little devil says.

"A perfectly formed, fun, lovely, intelligent, entertaining dame," my little angel says.

But Sarah has truly saved me. As soon as she heard about Abby, she wrapped me in her warmth and helped put Humpty Dumpty back together again. She told me it was okay to mourn a loss of that type. I don't know what I would have done without her shoulder to lean on. I feel closer to her than I ever have. We spend more time together than we did before everything got crazy. We share home-cooked dinners and casual conversations on the deck watching the city lights come on as the sun goes down. If I didn't know it before, I know it now. Sarah is the best friend I've ever had. She knows me better than Sue or Abby ever did, and she still likes me. There is a tremendous sense of safety in a full disclosure relationship. Well, almost full disclosure.

"Hellooo! Hey, sleepy head! Jake? Jake? It's your bet," Milt shouts.

I look up, and the whole table is staring at me. I must have lost track of time while I was locked in my brain. "I fold," is all I can say. They all look at me with a little glint of sadness in their eyes. "Who dealt that crap anyway?" I ask no one in particular. I wink at Sarah. She physically relaxes, and the rest of the table follows suit. I can see the wave wash over each of them in turn like the wave by a crowd in a football stadium.

"You did," Milt says. "You have a concentration span equal to the lifespan of a gnat. You're losing money faster than Uncle Sam can print it. I don't need your charity—focus on the cards. Make this a challenge. I want to enjoy emasculating you, so stop making me feel guilty."

The game goes on into the wee hours of the morning, and I manage to lose my entire wallet—two hundred sovereign USD down the drain. Pretty cheap entertainment, truth be told. We all pitch in and help Milt clean up his place. Then I grab Sarah, and we head out to my Jeep. I fire it up and point the nose in the direction of home while Sarah dozes in the passenger seat. The evening is clear and warm. I have my window open, and the rushing wind clears my senses, helping me reset.

I glance over at Sarah and am surprised at how beautiful she is. Has she always been this attractive? Or am I seeing her with different eyes? A few stray hairs hang over her closed eye. I want desperately to reach over and brush them back into place.

At the condo I notice a text message on my phone. It's a YouTube link from a blocked phone number. But the video address catches my attention. In the middle of it is *FHgeek*. It makes me think of Finn.

"Sarah, does this mean anything to you?" I turn my phone toward her so she can see the message.

"No, but the only geek I know is Finn. Want to check it out?"

"Might as well."

We head over to the computer. Sarah types in the address, and up pops a screen with a video. The shot is of a tropical area with a beautiful blue sky and ocean. In the middle of the shot is a single cloth chair holding a single stocky, tan male. The gent is wearing a straw hat and, according to Sarah, very expensive sunglasses. Several lovely young ladies surround the man. Each is shown from her ankles to her neck, with nothing on but bikini bottoms. The smile on the face of the man, who can be nobody but Finn, is bigger than a Montana sky.

"Hey, buddy, heard you were back in town," Finn begins. "I knew you'd be worried about me, so I thought I'd send you a little Christmas card in July. Kind of breaks up the year, don't you think? Anyways, I'm doing fine, started a couple of new businesses. This is my staff— they'd shake your hand, or little Jake, but, well, you're not here. I wish I could tell you where here is, but I have a sneaking hunch that Big Brother is watching over your shoulder.

"FYI, I wouldn't be committing any crimes for a while. At least not until the feds are convinced we aren't hooked up. Shouldn't take long—just look at that piece of crap Jeep you're driving. Ha-ha, I crack me up.

"I've been watching you on the internet. You still have the electronic grace of a drunk gorilla on a circus ball. Anyhoo, best wishes and kisses to all. Your friend and little buddy..." And the shot fades to black.

Sarah and I both start laughing.

"I think he's homesick," I say. "You know, I'm thinking we need a nightcap and some Roberta Flack. I'm feeling that she and Donny Hathaway would be great company. You get the music, and I'll get the scotch."

"Sounds like a plan."

We get things fired up and sit on the couch looking at the West Hills lights. Sarah snuggles up to me for warmth.

"Jake, what are you looking for in life? What is it that you dream of?"

I sip my scotch as I consider her question. For some reason it makes me uneasy, as if my answer will prove to be important. "A partner, kids, a home without a mortgage, and time to sit and gaze at the stars. How about you?"

I sense her smiling at me. I feel her cuddling closer still. "I want the same, Jake. I want the same with a man who's my best friend."

As Roberta croons, I hear Sarah's breathing change as she falls asleep. I listen to the end of the album, drink to the end of my scotch, and march Sarah and myself off to our separate bedrooms.

Friday, July 6

9:57 a.m.

"Oh, that's right—you don't know, do you..." Agent Frink

I wake thinking of Sarah. Last night we shared our dreams, dreams that seem to align with each other. This morning I find myself confused, as if I've missed the end of a movie.

"Oh, please, she's falling for you, bro. You just need to open your eyes," my little devil says.

"Falling for him? Nobody said anything about falling, am I right, Jake?" my little angel asks.

Oh brother, what if they're right? What if Sarah is thinking of me in *that way*? Or worse, what if Sarah is everything I've ever wanted in a woman and friend? I duct tape my little advisers' mouths shut and get ready for the day.

Sarah has made coffee, and I grab a cup. "See you at the office in a couple of hours. I'm meeting the new client."

"Yeah."

"Everything okay?"

"Sure, everything is fine." I watch her walk back into her bedroom.

I meet Jimmy Knapp at the most ubiquitous meeting place in the Northwest, a Starbucks.

"Hi, Jake, I'm Jimmy Knapp; pleasure to meet you." He stands to shake my hand.

"Pleasure to meet you as well. I see you have a coffee already. Let me grab one and join you."

"Perfect," he says as he returns to his overstuffed armchair.

I order a vente coffee with room. Not because I need room for cream—I just want to reduce the risk of spilling scalding hot coffee on my hand. I pay and sit in an overstuffed chair that matches Jimmy's.

"So, Jimmy, how can I help you?"

"My partner and I sell and install security alarm systems for residences and small businesses. I'm the outside guy: I market, quote, and manage. My partner is the inside guy. He handles bills, invoices, inventory, and staffing. For the first few years, we ramped up the business and made pretty good money. This past year, profits declined but sales volume increased. I keep asking my partner how that can be, and he gives me answers that don't make sense. Answers like the timing of invoice payments, or somebody hasn't paid their bills, or he'll look into it. I can't get any answers that make me feel comfortable."

"Why are you talking to me? Why not talk to an accountant?"

"I tried that, but the accountant said the books were a mess, and Robert, my partner, doesn't want to pay the fees to get them cleaned up. That made me suspicious. Maybe nothing illegal is going on, but I need to find out more. Maybe it's employees stealing and Robert isn't seeing it. I don't know, and I don't know where to turn. I don't even know where to start."

"I think the starting point is to go through the books. My partner, Sarah, is damn good at going through records and following the dollars. While Sarah's going through your financial records, I can do some background work on Robert and some surveillance on the business to see if product is walking out the back. Between Sarah and me, we should be able to get to a pretty quick answer, a starting one, at least. You might want to consider hiring a forensic accountant eventually. Do you have a listing of bank accounts, and can you get us the authority to view the activity online?"

"I have copies of the bank statements and prior years' tax returns on a flash drive. I'm hesitant to get online access for you just yet. My partner will see the change. Here's the flash drive," he says as he hands it to me.

"Okay, I'll also need as much background on the business and Robert as possible. Stuff like who your major vendors are, who works for you, how many sales you complete in an average week, what the average gross sales price is, what you think the gross margin should be. Anything that you think will help us. I charge by the hour against an up-front retainer. If you're interested, we could get started this afternoon. Just bring everything you've got, plus a cashier's check for $5,000, to my office.

He thanks me and promises he'll meet Sarah and me this afternoon at 2:00 p.m. I give Sarah a call at the office.

"Have Jessica start a workup on Jimmy Knapp, Robert Crenshaw, and Security Techniques, Inc. Jimmy is our client—he thinks something is wrong with the finances."

Jessica stuck with us through the craziness, and she's been amazing at the actual work too.

"Will do. Are you coming in soon?"

"On my way. I should be there in twenty minutes. Want anything from Starbucks?"

"Nah, we're good. See you soon."

I head out to my car and pull into traffic.

Close to lunch, Sarah brings me a status update on Jimmy. "Case solved. There are records of five-figure debts for Robert at two Oregon casinos and one in Vegas. We may not know how, but we know why. Do you want me to write this up for Jimmy for when he comes in today?"

"No, not yet, let's get the check and any other info Jimmy might have, and let me do some due diligence. It may just be a coincidence that the company is short on cash and Robert is a bad gambler. I don't want Jimmy any more freaked out than he is."

"Good idea. I'll keep looking."

"Oh, and Sarah, if I did something or said something last night…"

"We're good, Jake; I was just in a funk this morning. No worries." She smiles and leaves my office.

I am just about to head out for some lunch when a delivery boy enters and asks Sarah for a signature in exchange for a package.

He's one of those kids who rides a motor scooter delivering packages around town. They have no fear, the way they zip in and about traffic. They create their own lane, and all I can do is tip my hat to them. It's obvious they haven't met my little devil.

Sarah hands me the unmarked envelope, and I rip it open. Inside is a key to a Jeep with a note that says, *Look outside, buddy,* and a pink slip. The pink slip declares that I'm the owner of a brand-new car. I hand the pink slip and note to Sarah and look out the window at the parking lot. Sarah joins me at the window. I see a bright-red Jeep Rubicon sitting in the parking lot. Sarah and I look at each other and shake our heads. But before we have a chance to say a word, we hear Jessica:

"Excuse me, sir. Sir? Sir, you can't just walk in there..."

As we turn we see a middle-aged man, thinning brown hair, medium height, wearing a three-piece suit and a bow tie. The clothes are so well tailored that it's easy to see that he is well muscled and well armed.

"Wow, what a beautiful car. You have a very kind friend," he says.

"I don't think I know you, and I don't appreciate your blowing past our secretary," I blurt out.

"Of course, Jake. I apologize. I was just excited to see your new car. Here's my card." The card says his name is Ellis Frink and identifies him as a treasury agent. Oh boy, here we go again.

"You must have made quite the impression on Mr. Finn Hankins to earn such a respectable gift," he says with a smile on his lips and a threat in his eyes.

"Finn who?"

He laughs, not a dark "I'm taking you to the hangman" laugh but a real, entertained laugh.

"Don't worry, Jake—you and Sarah are clear. Like Finn told you last night, we've been monitoring your assets, communications, etc., etc. You have proven to me that you're clean. And don't worry about the Jeep—we both know that's peanuts. Plus, I hated De Cola—he was an arrogant bastard. And thanks to his incompetence, and your strokes of genius, I have his old job. Think of the Jeep as a reward from a grateful country.

"I just thought it was time that I introduce myself to you. I feel like we're family, given that I've been watching you so closely for the past several months. And you haven't even known that I exist. Sounds like a very dysfunctional family, upon reflection. Anyway, as De Cola's replacement, I'm most interested in money laundering, bank fraud, that sort of thing. I imagine that isn't much of a surprise to you."

"If you've cleared us and you aren't after the Jeep, why are you here?"

"Good question. Mind if I smoke?"

"Not if you blow a little bit my way."

He looks at me oddly and says, "I'm not sure what that means, and don't bother to elaborate. I'm here because I'm still after Katie Jackson and your friend Finn. I thought maybe you might have a lead or two."

"I'm afraid I don't know a Katie Jackson, and I'm not being a smart-ass this time."

"Oh, that's right, you don't know, do you? You knew Katie under one of her aliases, Abby Dicer. There is a real Abby Dicer who works for us out on the East Coast. She isn't nearly as pretty as Katie, but they look enough alike that not many people could tell them apart from a photo. No, Katie is her real name. Did you know that she's wanted in five states and a couple of countries for cons that she's pulled? She's never been caught, and I don't know that there's enough evidence on any of the cases to prove any of the charges against her even if she were caught. But we know she's dirty. I was thinking that maybe we don't know as much about her as you do, though. My gosh, the stories that are still spun down around Belize City about the Americano love birds. The Latinos are so touched by romance."

I'd poke him in the face if he weren't armed, empowered to imprison me, and completely blowing my mind. I look at Sarah, who can't stop staring at Frink. I turn and look out the window. The sky is still blue, and the trees are still green, but they're rocking back and forth as if a bomb is shaking the ground.

"In other words, you're just here to jerk our chains?" I look him straight in the eye. I'm convinced that he's an egomaniac who's upset that he can't incarcerate all of us so he's settling with inflicting pain. He isn't the kind of person who walks away from a job empty-handed.

"No, Jake, it's much more than that. I'm sure that you've both heard that we apprehended De Cola?" Sarah and I nod. "Good, what you may not have heard is that Agent De Cola—"

"Former Agent De Cola," Sarah chimes in.

"Ha-ha, yes that's very witty, Sarah. But a more precise description is the deceased former Agent De Cola," Frink shares. And then he stares at us with bluish-gray eyes that twinkle with malice and humor mixed together like the perfect dirty martini.

After a few seconds that feel like a month, Frink's eyes soften, and a smile meets his lips. "I thought maybe you hadn't heard. Apparently De Cola couldn't handle his fall from grace and the prospects of a lifetime hiding from hit men and government agents. Apparently he hung himself with his shoelaces in his prison cell."

I smile back and say, "I'm sorry, I would've thought in a modern-day detention facility shoelaces wouldn't be allowed." He's bluffing; he doesn't even have a plausible death story.

Frink smiles and says, "That must be why you're a private investigator. Please, I apologize, but I need to make a quick call. It'll just take a second." Frink pulls out his cell phone, punches in a number, and listens as it rings. He looks off at the wall while we hang on every word. "Hi, Paula, yes, yes, still with them. No, no decision yet. Uh-huh, okay. I'll have to get back to you on that. But I called you because Mr. Brand has made a very interesting point. He believes that the detention center where De Cola was held may not allow prisoners to have access to shoelaces. Yet I believe the official record shows De Cola's death as suicide from hanging from his own shoelaces. Could you pull up the file and confirm?" He pulls the phone away from his face and whispers to us, "This will just take a second, so…Oh yes, Paula. It doesn't? Well, we do have a problem, don't we; just a second." He pulls the phone away from his face again and looks me in the eye and asks, "So, Jake, if you had been De Cola, embarrassed, imprisoned, haunted by your fall from grace, and wanted to end it all, how would you go about it?"

I hesitate. I have no idea where this is heading. I consider not answering him but surmise that Frink won't let that happen. "Well, I'm not sure. Maybe I'd sharpen my toothbrush and stab myself in my temple," I say in a joking manner.

"Oh, I like that a lot. Paula, did you hear that? Are they allowed toothbrushes? Yes…yes….okay, perfect, change the record. Good, thanks." And he hangs up, smiles, and says, "Now, where were we? Oh yes, the untimely suicide of De Cola, by way of his toothbrush, thanks to Jake."

You got to respect a Fed who likes his job. With a simple phone call, he joyously changes the manner of expiration of a human. Well, a sort of human anyway. What kind of training must they go through to be this dismissive of peoples' lives?

"It seems that Frank was convinced that he had leverage with the players in this little game. And in a way he did, but he made a fatal error. He believed that his leverage was what he knew, but it was actually with who didn't already know what he knew. A very subtle distinction that Frank never understood, to his great grief and till his bitter end. His handlers knew everything he did. We emptied him of his useful knowledge. We made it clear to him that none of his knowledge would ever make it to the press or some moral politician. Not that there are many of those around to be concerned with any more." Frink's expression never changes from that of a relaxed sociopath enjoying a moment of playing with the lives of a couple of kittens.

I decide to move the conversation forward. "That's very sad for Frank. Not that I'm going to lose sleep over his passing, but we still don't understand why you're telling us all of this. Why are you here?"

"Well, Jake and Sarah, before he brushed his brain, De Cola spoke of the two of you, as well as Carl, Finn, and Katie/Abby. He knew that you were on to the scheme, and he was preparing to take you all out. And by take you all out, I don't mean on a date. He was plotting your deaths. We have it all in our files. And you must know that anything in our files must be pursued, can't be ignored. But just like Frank's cause of death can be changed with a few key strokes, so can all references to you and your entourage. What I need to know, Jake, and I want you to answer as if your life—no, better yet, answer as if Sarah's life—is on the line. Do you know where Finn, Katie, or the money is located?"

"You know I don't. You already said so."

"No, Jake, to be accurate, I said I don't believe you know. I need to know you don't know."

"Well, I don't."

Frink stares at me for several seconds, not showing any sign of his next move. Finally he begins to shake his head maybe, looks at the ceiling, and says, "Jake, that's good enough for me. See how easy that was? I believe you, Jake. I'm going to let Paula know that you and your friends should be deleted from the final file. Whew, that's a load off of my mind. Jake and Sarah, I'm afraid I need to head out. Thanks so much for your hospitality." And with that Agent Frink heads toward the door. Sarah and I just stare at him.

"Oh, and just to be clear, even though your names won't be in the agency's files, they will be in mine. I hope I never discover that you knew more about the things we've spoken about that you haven't shared. And I hope I don't hear that you are going to publish your memoirs or meet with the press to discuss anything that's happened. Because if I do hear even rumors of such goings on, I will open my file and unleash the full force of the federal government against all of you. You may well become casualties of the Patriot Act. Seems I have the power to permanently imprison anyone, anytime, for any reason, for as long as I want. I know what you're thinking: how much fun can one guy have? And if you ever do get a whiff of the highly acclaimed Katie, let her know she has a fan who would love to meet her in person." He turns and leaves our offices.

Sarah looks at me with a "whoa, what the..." look on her face. "Did you have any idea?"

"None," I say as I remember Abby's farewell letter. No, I guess I didn't really know her.

I watch Frink get into the backseat of a black SUV and drive off.

"Jessica, cancel all of our appointments for the rest of today. We're going four wheeling."

Friday, January, 3

8:25 a.m.

"Tomorrow night may be the right night..." Jake

The past few months have been so busy at the office that I have money to burn, but no one to set on fire. Sarah keeps telling me I need a break, that I'm cranky and impossible to be around. She warns me that if I don't financially and emotionally invest in a vacation, I should take a stay-away-forever-cation. So, with barely any input from me, she booked me into a four-star hotel in Cancún, Mexico. Seems only fitting since Jerry Jumper was supposed to have been there in a prior life.

I arrive at the Portland airport an hour and a half before departure. I park in the long-term parking lot; I refuse to park in economy. I'll feel like a cow being herded into the hamburger factory for most of the trip as it is, and I don't care to rush the inevitable. In the security line, I can feel the tension building inside of me. The people in front and eventually in back of me all seem very nice, much nicer than me. But I want to scatter them like dust bunnies. My little angel is whispering soothing thoughts into my brain: "Alcohol, scantily clad young women, no phones..."

At the front of the line, a TSA officer looks at my ticket, then my driver's license, and waves me through to the scanners. Every TA officer looks like a close relative of Agent Frink. I'm tired of feeling hunted.

Five hours and three martinis later, the plane lands in Cancún. Knowing my childish tendencies, Sarah prepped me for the experience. She told me to get my little devil good and liquored up and duct taped to a rib. I'm to listen only to my little angel. But I can feel my little devil moving around. He's managed to break loose of his bonds. My flight buddies and I make our way to the baggage claim and customs. It's clear that everyone around me is beginning a two-week oasis in the desert of their lives. I'm not one of them; I'm not vacationing. I'm like a football player trying to get out of the locker room into the stadium so I can hit somebody. I want to make somebody cry. If everyone would just recognize my angst and step aside and allow me to move through the required steps unimpeded, nobody would get hurt. I've been exiled from the office and work. They're the only things that have kept my mind from spinning in meaningless circles around seemingly unsolvable emotions.

I stop and look at my reflection in a window. That's not true, not even close to true. It's been Sarah who's kept me sane. The realization of just how big an impact she has had shocks me. Now that she's not next to me, I sense being alone, truly alone, for the first time since Abby left.

At my hotel, an energetic young man grabs my bags and begins to share his joy of living in such a magical place with me. "Smack him," says my devil. "Listen to him," says my angel. I stash my bags in my room, change into shorts and a T-shirt, and head to the bar. This may be the only view I'll have of this entire city. I'm planning on staying at this bar until it closes, going to my room for sleep, and waking up at the crack of noon. Then I'm coming back and sitting down on this damn stool at this damn bar until they kick my sorry damn ass out of the country.

"Perdón, señor, cerveza, por favor," I say in Portland-accented Spanish.

"Here you go, señor," says the bartender, who looks Mexican but sounds American.

"You sound like you're from the States," I say.

"I went to college at San Diego State. Where are you from?"

"Portland, just got here and need to acclimate. I hope to jump-start the process with alcohol. Can I trust you to keep my glass filled at all times?"

"That's my job."

It's not all that hot but feels hot to me in comparison to home. I don't have lotion on yet, so I'm careful to keep out of the full sun. The beach is white, and the sun is bright. Sounds like a recipe for lobster Jake served with a chilled pinot gris.

The bar itself is more like a hut without walls. The interior houses the booze, snacks and staff. The exterior contains the clientele, which is varied in age, gender, race, etc.

As the evening wears on, the crowd at the bar thickens and grows pretty lively. There are some lovely maidens moving about. Maybe one is single and interested in domesticating me, at least for a few hours. Dinner is bar food: quesadillas, chips, and salsa. I finish cerveza numero I-don't-know and feel like it's starting to work. I'm actually smiling as people walk by and say hello. I'm no longer looking for weapons under loose-fitting shirts or warrants for my arrest. I'm thinking that maybe I should do this more often.

As the sun sets, the bar lights flicker on. There aren't many, and they're not bright. They throw off just enough light to complement the candles, which have appeared out of nowhere. After a while, the crowd at the beach bar begins to thin as the sound of live music wafts out to us on a light breeze. The music is coming from a second bar located inside the hotel and is punctuated with laughter and joyous conversation. I begin to feel the last of the tension of home rolling off my back. It flows down into the sand where it is absorbed and hidden from my mind. I catch myself smiling about happy times and how fortunate I truly am. I decide that if I'm going to be here, I should do it right. If I get back to Portland still a grump, Sarah may empty her .45 into me.

I sign off on my beach bar tab and head into the hotel bar. I decide it's time to switch to dirty martinis. Let's get this show on the road. I feel my body begin to move with the music. Not much, not enough that anyone else probably even notices, but enough that I relax even more. I find that most of us, especially me, shouldn't dance in public. I look like an old guy trying to flip a walker around, though in my mind I'm Gene Kelly. As time passes and the martini settles, I care less and less about what I look like. The movement is soothing, and that's all that's important.

That and the very attractive young woman I catch looking at me. I smile at her, and she smiles back. I look behind me to make sure she's beaming at me. I'm sure my total lack of confidence is intensely appealing to her. When I turn back around, she's moved from afar and is standing directly in front of me.

She asks, "Would you like to dance with me?"

I reply in my most suave way, "Okay."

She takes my hand and leads me from the outskirts and onto the dance floor. All of a sudden, I'm bouncing to the sounds of Mexican music with a beautiful, very young nymph. At least my little devil says she's a nymph. My little angel says she could be my daughter; time to get the duct tape out again, buddy. It's good I've had the beers and martinis. I'd be bright red with embarrassment if I cared about how my '80s dance moves really looked. Come to think of it, they didn't look very good in the '80s.

"My name is Cindy. What's yours?" she asks.

"Jake. Pleasure to meet you, sweetheart."

"So, Jake, you must have gotten here today. I haven't noticed you around."

"You are correct," I say.

My little angel says, "You are correct, very, very young lady."

"I just flew in this afternoon. I've only explored the hotel's two bars, and I'm thinking tomorrow could be more of the same. How about you? You look awfully tan. You must have been here for a while."

"We've been here for a week and have a week to go. I'm already bummed that the trip is going by so fast, so I don't want to waste any time. I know this may sound forward, but are you interested in going someplace private? Maybe head up to my room? I'm sure

I can provide you with a very satisfying experience. Consider it a welcome-to-Mexico party favor."

My mind must be off-kilter: did I just get propositioned by a youth within the first five minutes of meeting her? "Wow, I was not expecting that question. How did you decide that I was worthy of what I can see would be nothing less than a spectacular evening?" I ask with no attempt to hide my shock.

"Well, it's like this. We could be out here for five hours, and we wouldn't truly know each other any better than we do right now. Plus, to be honest, my girlfriends and I are having a contest. And you are my game piece," she says with a big smile.

At this point I'm no longer bouncing to the music. I'm staring at this alien creature and trying to identify its species. "Game piece? Is that supposed to be foreplay?"

"I know, confusing, right? My girlfriends and I have a game going. The rules are that we find the oldest man we can, have sex with him, and report back to the group. The girl who finds the man with the best combination of age, endurance, and good looks wins the prize. You're good-looking enough, you're definitely old, and I sense that you may score high on the endurance scale as well. At least I hope so," she adds with a greedy smile.

I'm completely dumbfounded. I feel objectified and dirty. I've been praying for a moment like this for years! Still, I can't help but touch on her three points: first, I'm only good-looking "enough"; second, I'm "old"; and third, I only "may" be able to hold up. You know us old, average-looking men—you can't expect performance guarantees. As I shift to thinking about her offer, I begin dancing again, standing a bit taller, moving a bit quicker with my dance steps. I laugh and swing her around as the song ends.

"So, you're interested?" she asks.

"Cindy, you have already made my trip worth the cost. But I'm afraid I'll have to pass. This is my first day here, travel tires me, and if we were to do this, I would want to be at my highest endurance level. I would never want to let you down. Sorry, but not tonight."

"That's cool. We'll be here for another week. If you change your mind, let me know. I know we could win the contest."

"I will absolutely let you know. Tomorrow night may be the right night," I say as she kisses me on the cheek and wanders off into the crowd.

I feel like I've gone from riding a tricycle to a Harley. And I didn't bring my helmet. I decide to head out to the veranda. I find an empty lounge chair to sit in, surrounded by empty lounge chairs. When I left Portland, Sarah suggested that this might be a good time to think about a business plan, but not for the business, for my life. She thinks I'm hiding from the world, working to avoid people. She wants me to move on, thinks that I'm holding on too tightly to my loves lost. I think she and Cindy are right. Tonight is the first night of the new Jake. Tomorrow, look out, Cindy.

I watch the stars and the sliver of a moon as they sit and stare back at me. I wonder how many aliens are up there staring down at me, hoping I'll do my funky-chicken dance move again. I feel I'm finally on beach time, measured by changes in light and not by a clock. It's the first time I've felt like this in what seems like forever. I let my mind drift to whatever subject it feels the need to bring up. I don't resolve anything, don't even try. Mostly I think about how comfortable it is just to sit and do nothing, with nothing planned for tomorrow, the next day, or the day after that.

I know I'm happier than I've been in a long time. My muscles relax, and I slip deeper into the lounge chair. As I sip my beer and glory at the moon and stars, I feel a hand on my shoulder. I turn and my breath catches. I smile at the beautiful, familiar woman behind me, fumbling for something to say

Finally she says, "Hey, mister; can you spare a secondhand smoke?"

CPSIA information can be obtained at www.ICGtesting.com
Printed in the USA
BVOW06s1522051115

425652BV00008B/70/P